Unlike Any Other

Also by Edward Londergan

The Devil's Elbow

The Long Journey Home

Unlike Any Other

A NOVEL

Edward Londergan

White River Press
Amherst, Massachusetts

© Edward F. Londergan 2022
All Rights Reserved

First published 2022 by White River Press
Amherst, Massachusetts • whiteriverpress.com

ISBN: 978-1-935052-74-6

Book and cover design by Lufkin Graphic Designs
Norwich, Vermont • www.LufkinGraphics.com

This is a work of fiction based on real events. It contains fictionalized scenes, dialogue and representative characters. References to real people, events, establishments, organizations, or locales are intended to provide a sense of authenticity and are used fictitiously.

Library of Congress Cataloging-in-Publication Data

Names: Londergan, Edward, 1957- author.
Title: Unlike any other / Edward Londergan.
Description: Amherst, Massachusetts : White River Press, [2021]
Identifiers: LCCN 2021021918 | ISBN 9781935052746 (paperback)
Subjects: LCSH: Spooner, Bathsheba, 1746-1778--Fiction. | Spooner, Joshua--Fiction. | Murder--Massachusetts--Brookfield (Town)--Fiction. | Executions and executioners--Massachusetts--Worcester--Fiction. | GSAFD: Biographical fiction. | Historical fiction. | LCGFT: Biographical fiction. | Historical fiction. | Novels.
Classification: LCC PS3612.O47 U55 2021 | DDC 813/.6--dc23
LC record available at https://lccn.loc.gov/2021021918

TO MY FATHER:

The best man I have ever known or ever will know

PROLOGUE

When the prisoners, three men and a woman, arrived at the place of execution under the harsh summer sun of a July day, they stared at the gallows, knowing their mortal end would happen within minutes. Mounting the stairs, they stood on the scaffold.

The ropes were hauled up, thrown over the thick oak beam, and secured. As the sheriff adjusted the nooses around the prisoners' necks, towering black clouds built dark and fast in the western sky. Booming thunder rolled through and broke the silence of the solemn proceeding. One of the men, a young Continental soldier, stood with his head bowed and said a prayer, neither mumbled nor choked with emotion, but aloud with deep sincerity and conviction. He looked up and saw his parents near the scaffold. His mother gripped her husband's arm, overwhelmed with grief. They would soon claim the body of their youngest of six sons.

The two other men, British prisoners of war, did not look at the crowd. They were far from their homeland on the other side of an ocean; no one here would care about their death. The sheriff put his hand on the lever to drop the platform, then hesitated, staring at the blackening sky, a thunderstorm poised to unleash Nature's fury.

People shrieked and cowered as lightning splintered the sky. The thunder exploded again and again, louder and louder as the moment came for the platform to drop and the prisoners to die. The storm burst upon them with such a terrible and violent ferocity, it was as if God Himself was furious with the appalling act of vengeance that was about to take place.

CHAPTER 1

When I turned nineteen, my world began to fall apart. Though I loved him with all my heart, my father, one of the wealthiest and most powerful men in New England, destroyed any chance I had of a happy life. He forced me to do what I knew in my heart was not the right thing for me. It was the biggest decision of my life, and it wasn't mine to make. I became a different person because I was forced to marry a man I quickly came to despise.

I'd been raised for a life at the highest level of society. The expectation was that I would be the wife of a wealthy, handsome, sophisticated, well-educated man who would treat me as I had been treated my entire life, growing up in wealth and privilege. A man who had a fine mansion in Boston and would be the loving father of my children. Instead, I was pushed into marrying a plain-looking man, a common merchant from Brookfield. But I get ahead of myself.

When Joshua first came to our estate in Hardwick to court me, the sky was deep blue and the air crisp and clean with red, gold, and yellow leaves fluttering in the wind, a perfect New England fall day.

His visit started badly when he followed Father inside and, stepping into the parlor, he tripped on the edge of a beautiful blue Persian rug, nearly landing on his face. He staggered for a few steps as his arms windmilled through the air. He caught himself on the edge of a table, causing two large ceramic figurines, gifts to my mother from John and Abigail Adams, to wobble. I thought they would end up crashing to the floor, but at the last minute they righted. Joshua gave a loud sigh of relief. Father caught him by the arm and spun him around to face Mother. Joshua composed himself and formally bowed to her.

"Oh, for God's sake," I heard Father mumble under his breath. He motioned for me to come to him. "Bathsheba, this is Joshua Spooner. Joshua, my daughter Bathsheba."

Joshua was shorter than me. He had brown curly hair, a high forehead, pointed nose, wide-set dark brown eyes, narrow lips, and fair complexion. Plain-looking, yes. I guessed he was only a few years older than me, but he gave the impression of being much older.

He looked me up and down. Since I'd been a child, I was told I was beautiful, although I was often unsure of that. I was slim and slightly taller than most women. My long black hair set off my green eyes, light red lips, and smooth pink skin. I knew I had a fine figure. If those things made me beautiful, then I suppose I was.

While we waited to dine, my mother, my only younger sister, Liza, and two of my brothers—Tim Jr., who was named after my father, Timothy Ruggles, and John—and I questioned Joshua about his home, business interests, and family. He answered all of our questions in a friendly manner and was deferential to each of us as he should have been. Then, luckily for him, the cook called us to dinner.

The meal, like all of those we had, was an overabundance of food. Always wanting to be the best host, Father insisted that his guests enjoy a wide selection of everything. Turtle soup, venison, meat pies, yams, sliced herbed potatoes, sauces, pickles, and gingerbread and cheeses for dessert were served in three courses. I wasn't hungry but ate a little bit of everything. Joshua picked at his food, clearly anxious.

To make conversation, I told him of my weeklong trip to Boston the past year, how exciting I had found it, and that I would love to spend more time there.

"I went with Father and attended a ball at the governor's mansion. It was a sight to behold. The ladies wore imported fashionable dresses, and the men were arrayed in colorful velvet and silk suits. The musicians gathered in the corner as the servants passed crystal fluted glasses of wine and champagne. I danced with Sam Eliot, whose father owns several ships." I sighed. "It was magical. That's the only word I can think of to describe it."

"Perhaps we can go to Boston someday," he said. "I'm happy to show you around. Having been there many times, I know it quite well. I go there a few times a year and, after we wed, you can come with me when I go."

While I was always forthright and never hesitated to say what I thought, that trait having been ingrained in my siblings and me since we were children, I trembled a bit and swallowed hard this time, knowing it could ignite an argument.

"You are presuming," I said, "that we will be together, which is not definite by any means, at least not in my mind." I shot a glance at my father. His face grew red, and I knew he was angry with me, but I didn't care.

"Well, ah, I thought this was decided," Joshua said, looking at my father for support.

My father leaned in toward me. "We've had this discussion before, Bathsheba. It is settled, and I'll hear no more of it. You will marry Joshua, and sooner rather than later."

"No one cares what I want or think," I said. "Why can't I make the decision that will affect the rest of my life?"

That question should not have been unexpected. Father and Mother had taught us to think for ourselves, to be independent, and not follow others if we had a different opinion. Make your own judgments, we were told, come to your own conclusions after hearing all the facts, have a stiff backbone, say what you think, and don't worry what others say.

I was, and always had been, more outspoken than my siblings. More than once it had gotten me into trouble. I tried to be considerate of others, but sometimes the words were out of my mouth before I had time to consider the consequences of what I was saying. I was also profane like Father. He didn't care what words he used to make his point regardless of to whom he was talking, whether it be the governor or one of our farmhands.

After all, we were a prominent family and not like others. Father had been a general and second-in-command of the British forces during the French and Indian War, president of the Stamp Act Congress, Chief Justice of the Court of Common Pleas, a well-known legislator, and adviser and confidant to the governors and other leading officials in Boston and on occasion in London. Before she married Father, Mother was a wealthy widow of a leading merchant on Cape Cod. Her family founded the town of Bourne. She ran a highly successful tavern and three shops by herself for the few years after her husband's death. She bore fourteen children—seven in her prior marriage and seven in our family. Mother and Father were not people to be trifled with.

"With no offense to you, Joshua, she should be able to make her own decision," Mother said, glaring at Father who shook his head. They held contrary views and strong opinions on most subjects.

"Joshua, I apologize for my daughter's poor behavior, and my wife's inappropriate remark," Father said. "This is not the introduction I had planned."

"Maybe it's best if I go," Joshua said as he stood. "Should we continue this some other time?"

"No," Father told him. "I'll talk to her. Please sit down. We'll be right back."

I stood, gathered the sides of my dress, and swept out of the room.

I made it as far as the parlor before Father grabbed my arm and pulled me into his law office at the rear of the house. He closed the door and stood looming over me, his face flushed with anger.

"Goddamnit, how dare you act this way in front of our guest. That is not the way you were raised, and you know it."

I fumed at his words and could be just as stubborn as he.

"We've talked about this before," Father continued to bark. "All with the same conclusion: you will marry him."

"Absolutely not!" I shouted. "I will not marry a man like him. This is my life. I'll have to live with the man each and every day. You won't. It doesn't feel right. Doesn't that count for anything?"

"You have no idea what is best for you. You are only nineteen years old; I'm fifty-five. I know more about life than you do."

"I may not know exactly what I want, but I do know that I don't want my husband selected for me. I want to fall in love and be swept off my feet."

He waved his hand dismissively. "That's a fairy tale."

"I want a handsome, wealthy, well-connected man from Boston who can give me the type of life I want and deserve, not some dull merchant from Brookfield. I want to go to balls and parties and socialize with people like myself. I want a happy, carefree life. Instead, you have me being an everyday housewife to *him*," I said, nodding my head toward the dining room. He shook his head and sat down wearily in his chair.

"Changes are coming, Bathsheba, changes that will destroy people's lives. I want to protect you from as much of that as I can, don't you see that?" He leaned forward and rested his arms on the desk. "In the next few years, the people here in Massachusetts will goad the king to war. Please trust me. I never want any harm to come to you."

I didn't say anything, but I nodded.

"Now, let's get back to dinner," Father implored. "Be nice to him. He is trying to do the best he can by you also."

It was uncomfortable when we got back to the dining room. Joshua seemed embarrassed by my outburst. I sat next to him and put my hand on his arm.

"I'm sorry, Joshua. I didn't mean to offend you in any way. Please accept my apology." I apologized because it was expedient, though not sincere.

After dinner, Mother suggested Joshua and I walk so we could get to know each other better. I wasn't inclined to do that, so instead of walking, I went to the stable. He followed.

"I want to see my favorite horse, Invictus," I said.

"You have more than one horse?"

"Of course I do, but he is the best of the three of them." I grabbed a couple of apples out of a basket and fed them to Invictus, who ate them in a few bites. "Isn't he one of the most handsome horses you've ever seen?" I rubbed the horse's forehead and kissed him above his nose. I noticed that Joshua grimaced at that. "Do you have any favorite animals?"

He scoffed at the question. "No, I have no favorites. Animals serve a purpose, and that's all."

"I will bring Invictus with me wherever I go when I wed." He smiled, no doubt because this was the first time I had mentioned marriage. "Regardless of what my father or you want, my marrying you is by no means certain. At this point, I think it highly unlikely."

I rubbed Invictus's forehead and scratched under his ear.

"I have a large stable so you can bring him," he said, looking around. "Though it's not as large or as fine as this."

I turned to him. He'd moved closer to me when my back was turned and our faces were only a foot apart. He leaned in and kissed me. I slapped his face hard.

"How dare you touch me!"

He rubbed his face. "That hurt."

"Good." I spun on my heels and walked out of the barn. Then I stopped and turned around.

He was a few steps behind me, still rubbing his face.

"Understand something, Joshua," I said. "If we marry, which is now even less likely than it was a minute ago, you won't lay a hand on me unless I want you to."

He gaped at me. "No woman has ever spoken to me like that."

"Do you understand?" I asked.

He clenched his jaw and contracted his brow. "We'll see about that. If we wed, anytime I want to touch you, I will."

I ignored him and walked into the house, leaving him standing there.

On a cold and windy afternoon a week after Joshua's visit, I bundled myself in a heavy woolen cape and went for a walk toward the village center. A bite to the wind reminded me that winter was on its way. Fat white clouds with dark gray bellies sailed west to east, chasing their shadows. I would rather have sat reading by a warm, crackling fire, but I needed to think. After another fiery argument with Father the day before, I was tired of his reasoning, for it was wearing me down. He was immovable in his belief that marrying Joshua was the best thing for me.

I did not like being forced into anything and never had, whether it was the best for me or not. I could be as strong-willed as Father and as obstinate as Mother. Making my own decisions was important to me. When Father announced that I would marry Joshua, without any thought or consideration for my feelings or desires, I was both hurt and surprised. After everything he'd taught me about thinking for myself, I felt that he'd betrayed me.

However, as much as I didn't want to, I began to consider that perhaps he was right. I knew that, despite all the advantages my father's wealth and power provided for me, I couldn't marry the kind of man I wanted because I had little contact with those types of men. Boston was two days' travel from our estate, which was not something I could do on my own. Looking at my parents' marriage, I knew I didn't want to end up in that type of situation. They were constantly arguing when they were together and continued to find fault even when they were apart. My older sisters, Martha and Mary, were happily married, and there was not much to offer someone like myself in Hardwick. I knew I'd have to leave soon. Maybe this was best for me.

I reached the village center and walked around the common. The ground was covered in fallen leaves, but it was still a vibrant green where the grass showed through. As I turned for home, I knew my dream of falling madly in love was just that—a dream.

Joshua and I saw each other again two weeks later when he visited. We were alone in the parlor, and I questioned him thoroughly about everything from music, the arts, and politics to raising children. I made sure to keep my distance, offering no opportunity for him to try to kiss or touch me again.

"How much education have you had?" I asked.

"I can read, write, and do numbers, if that's what you want to know."

"Do you have a library?" I asked.

He sneered at my question. "No, I don't," he said. "Why? Do you require one?"

"Yes, I do. I have many books. For several years I had a tutor, Mr. Wilson, whom my father brought out from Boston, and he instilled a love of reading in me. I can read Latin and also some French, though not as well as I'd like. I can't read Greek, but I'd like to learn."

After talking for a while more, Joshua left in a hurry, apparently having had enough of my interrogation and me.

"He is not a strong or well-educated man," I told Father when he returned from Worcester the next day. "He has no fixed opinions or principles. He is fine with whatever happens, no matter how large or small, important or unimportant."

"That may be," Father said, "but what of it? He has the wealth and social status that you can't get with many other men around here. If he were as opinionated as you, it would doom the marriage from the start." He looked at me for a long moment. "Look at your mother and me."

I walked to the other side of the room and stood behind a chair. "Yes, I know what you mean."

"So it may be a good thing for you to be the fixed compass, and he to maintain the wealth and business interests. He can provide well enough for you and any children you may have. He's from a good Boston family, a successful businessman, well thought of by many people, and has a fine house. Who else do you know that can offer you all of that?"

"I suppose he is against these traitorous revolutionaries. Is that why you chose him? Because of his politics?" I asked, walking to the window to stare out at the horses in the pasture.

"We didn't discuss his political beliefs, but that is one of many things I considered about the man. Some of his family are loyal to the Crown. If he does agree that we mustn't allow the ideas of the common man to overrule what we know is best for the colonies, then yes, I do take that into account."

I sat in the chair.

He came and stood next to me. "For the last time, you need to understand that Joshua is the best man for you. You need to accept that." He turned and went to the door on the other side of the room that led to his law office. "And," he added, "you are marrying Joshua as soon as possible." He went into the office and left me.

I turned toward the window, staring out at my future as somber gray clouds scudded along to the east on a strong, mournful wind. A shiver rippled down my spine.

CHAPTER 2

On the cold and snowy day of my wedding, January 15, 1766, over one hundred guests who had traveled from all over New England packed the church in Brookfield.

I stepped from our finest carriage pulled by four matching dappled gray horses. I wore a heavy, scarlet wool cloak that was fastened at my neck with a thick gold chain. My gown was a multi-colored, floral pattern silk, made from fabric imported from London. It was very expensive, and I ordered it without telling Father how much it cost. I had the gown made before I knew of my "arranged marriage." It was the most beautiful gown I ever owned.

All of the guests—family, friends, and associates of my mother and father's and Joshua's—were in the church waiting for me.

As I walked up the aisle, I saw Joshua's mother, Sarah Bridges Spooner. I'd never met her, but from the descriptions I heard, she couldn't be anyone else. Joshua said that shortly after his father died the previous year, she had married John Avery, an attorney. I later learned that the man with her was Joshua's stepbrother, John Avery Jr.

I admit that I was caught up in the emotions of the day. Still, a nagging feeling tugged at me, a foreboding sadness I couldn't shake. It felt like a mistake was about to be made, a sense of melancholy hanging over the day. Was the marriage to Joshua a well-intentioned blunder I was being pushed into by my father? I hoped with all my heart that I could find purpose and happiness in my new life.

Reverend Nathan Fiske, a slim man with a large head and hooked nose, officiated. He stood at the altar, waiting for Joshua and me to come to him. When we reached the altar, he began.

"Dearly beloved, we have come together in the presence of God to witness and bless the joining together of this man and this woman in Holy Matrimony. It signifies unto us the mystery of the union betwixt Christ and his Church, and Holy Scripture commanded it to be honored among all people. God intends the union of husband and wife in heart, body, and mind for their mutual joy; for the help and comfort given one another in prosperity and adversity; and, when it is God's will, for the procreation of children and their nurture in the knowledge and love of the Lord. Therefore marriage is not to be entered into unadvisedly or lightly, but reverently, deliberately, and in accordance with the purposes for which God instituted it. Into this holy union, Joshua Spooner and Bathsheba Ruggles now come to be joined. If any of you can show just cause why they may not lawfully be married, speak now, or else forever hold your peace."

No one responded.

Reverend Fiske looked at Joshua and me.

"I require and charge you both, here in the presence of God, as you will answer at the dreadful day of judgment, when the secrets of all hearts shall be revealed, that if either of you knows of any impediment why you may not be lawfully joined together in matrimony, and accordance with God's Word, you do now confess it. For be well assured, that so many as be coupled together, otherwise than God's word does allow, are not joined of God, neither is their marriage lawful."

Neither of us spoke.

"Joshua," Reverend Fiske continued, "wilt you have this woman to be your wife; to live together in the covenant of marriage? Will you love her, comfort her, honor and keep her, in sickness and in health and, forsaking all others, be faithful unto her as long as you both shall live?"

"I will."

"Bathsheba, will you have this man to be your husband; to live together in the covenant of marriage? Will you obey him, and serve him, love, honor, and keep him in sickness and in health and, forsaking all others, keep you only to him so long as you both shall live?"

I hesitated several seconds before answering. "I will."

"Will all of you witnessing these promises do all in your power to uphold these persons in their marriage?"

"We will," the congregation replied in unison.

"A reading from Ephesians, chapter 5, verses 22 to 27. Wives, submit yourselves unto your husbands, as unto the Lord. For the husband is the head of the wife, even as Christ is the head of the church and he is the savior of the body. Therefore as the church is subject unto Christ, so let the wives be to their husbands in everything. Husbands, love your wives, even as Christ also loved the church, and gave himself for it; that He might sanctify and cleanse it with the washing of water by the word, that He might present it to Himself a glorious church, not having spot, or wrinkle, or any such thing; but that it should be holy and without blemish."

He looked up at the congregation before turning his gaze upon Joshua and me.

"O gracious and ever-living God, who has created us male and female in your image: Look mercifully upon this man and this woman who come unto you seeking your blessing, and so assist them with your grace, that with true fidelity and steadfast love they may honor and keep the promises and vows they make; through Jesus Christ our Savior, who lives and reigns with you in the unity of the Holy Ghost, one God, forever and ever. Amen.

"Now that Joshua and Bathsheba have given themselves to each other by solemn vows, with the joining of hands, I pronounce that they are man and wife, in the Name of the Father, and the Son, and of the Holy Spirit. Those whom God has joined together let no man put asunder."

Joshua took my hand before we walked down the aisle to the door, followed by my parents and siblings and his mother and stepbrother. We mounted Joshua's carriage, which was pulled by two midnight black mares, for the short ride to Cooley's tavern.

Our wedding feast was splendid, with the most exceptional food and drink available. My father instructed Cooley, with his wife, son, and daughter, to pour cups of sack-posset, the creamy, thick concoction of boiled ale, eggs, and spices—a typical drink at New England weddings that everyone enjoyed. Madeira, spiced hard cider, small beer, and a punch made with hard cider combined with sugar, lemons, and limes were enjoyed as well.

I made sure that the most expensive foods in the most considerable quantity were served—salted fish chowder, stewed oysters, roasted pig and venison from Father's estate, duck, potatoes, several baked breads, Indian cornbread pudding, and pumpkin casserole. Trays of nutmeats and candy were also passed.

My cake was a thick, rich, spiced cake made with rum, dried fruit, and nuts, baked with a nutmeg inside and was served with coffee and tankards of spiced hard cider. The person who received the slice with the nutmeg was supposed to be the next to marry.

I saw pretty and amiable Abigail Foster, the twelve-year-old daughter of Jedediah Foster, a well-known lawyer who lived less than a mile from Joshua, looking around the room before seeing me chatting with a couple of other women. She ran over to us, a large piece of cake in her hand and the remnants of the first bite on her lips.

"This is the most delicious cake I've ever eaten. Bathsheba," she said before catching herself, "Mrs. Spooner, I mean. This cake is wonderful. I've never tasted anything as good."

I smiled at her as she put another small bite in her mouth.

"I'm delighted you like it," I told her. "If your mother will let you, you can have another piece."

She went off to plead with her mother to have another piece, explaining that she had my permission. Her mother looked at me for confirmation; I nodded, smiled, and gave her and Abigail a wave of my hand.

I busied myself with giving the guests the traditional gift of wedding gloves that were gold-laced and fringed, and featured rich gauntlets, and were far from an inexpensive gift, something my father reminded me of several times. Although it was not a custom, several of the guests gave me gifts.

Jedediah Foster approached me, smiling at my happiness. "You are a beautiful bride, Bathsheba. Joshua is a lucky man," he said, glancing over her shoulder at Joshua, who sat at a table in the corner drinking a large mug of rum and talking boisterously with several men. "You look happy," he said, handing me a small package wrapped in gold linen and tied with a scarlet ribbon.

"Well, it is my wedding day, after all," I said as I looked at the package.

"You may open it."

I untied the ribbon and unfolded the linen to see a gold-engraved, leather-covered Bay Psalm Book, in perfect condition, beautiful and exquisite, though it was quite old.

"You can use it on the Sabbath," he said. "Many of the Psalms are still sung, but you know that."

"Thank you so much, Mr. Foster. It's beautiful. I love it." I took a quick step forward and kissed him lightly on the cheek.

He blushed a bit and squeezed my hand. "You are most welcome, my dear."

At my right, my father was standing with Silas Epworth, an affluent Boston merchant and friend whom I'd met before. "Timothy, you've outdone yourself," I heard Epworth say. "The food and drink are up to, and possibly above, your usual high standards."

Father reached out and tapped on Epworth's protruding belly. "Coming from someone who has certainly tasted too much of the finest foods and drinks, thank you."

I smiled at his jest and realized I would miss hearing him make his little jokes.

"Bathsheba," I heard Joshua say. "I want you to meet my mother and stepbrother."

I nodded at both of them. "How do you do?"

"I've often wondered," Mrs. Avery said, "whom Joshua would marry." She looked at me like I was her social unequal. "And it's you." She gave me a condescending smile. She was short and plump with a double chin and beady eyes. The ugly dress she wore, dark brown with blue flowers, was appropriate for afternoon tea, but not my wedding. I thought of telling her so but decided to hold my tongue.

The stepbrother, John, on the other hand, stepped forward and took both of my hands in his. He was tall and thin with a pinched face and dark eyes in which there was a bright cruelty. He reminded me of a ferret.

"I want you to promise me something," he said.

"Of course. What is it?" I asked.

"I want you to promise me that you'll be the wife Joshua deserves. He's a good man and needs a good wife. We have high expectations of you, my dear."

"I will do my best. That's all I can promise." I smiled, nodded, and turned back to my more interesting guests.

After everyone had dined and drunk to their contentment, the women, as tradition dictated, asked me to throw my stocking for them to scramble after as a luck-bearing trophy. If the same woman caught the stocking that found the nutmeg, it was believed she would be married within a month.

"No," I told them. "I will not allow one of my garments to be used in that fashion." It was a ridiculous custom that had outlived its time.

"But Bathsheba," my sister Mary said, "it is an old custom and does not hurt anyone. It is just for fun."

"No."

"But . . ."

"I said no, and that's an end of it." The other women looked at me, unable to understand my unwillingness to enjoy what they viewed as a simple tradition. But I thought it stupid and belittling for the women and for me, too. So I would not do it.

To get away from their pestering me, I went into a small back room and sat alone near the fire, my dress covering the wooden chair. A short time later, Joshua came in, holding a tankard of sack-posset. He stood looking at me.

"You won't throw your stocking?" he asked, putting the tankard on the mantle.

"No, I will not."

"I am your husband. You will do as I tell you. Throw the stocking."

"I will not. Neither you nor any other man will tell me what to do, not on our wedding day or any other day."

He stood glaring at me and clenched his fists.

"You took a vow to obey me."

I did not answer for a moment. "I would like you to leave now," I said, dismissing him with a wave of my hand.

He glared at me for a moment before taking his tankard and leaving.

I learned later that he quickly downed two more mugs, no doubt to quell his anger, and then he became drunk and quarrelsome with some of the guests.

After the feast, a dozen or so people made their way to my new home. It was a short distance down the road, no more than a half mile. The house was the finest in town and beautiful in all aspects.

The big fan window over the front door flooded the entry with light, illuminating the stairs to the second floor. The banister, painted a cream color, set off the brown-gold-and-green-striped carpet on the stairs.

In each room, Persian rugs covered the honey-colored wide pine floors, and the walls featured wallpaper of different types and large windows. The east parlor, used for sitting and dining, had cream wallpaper with green figures throughout. The doors, trim, and wainscoting were painted a light green color, and a large mirror edged in gold hung over the marble fireplace. The west parlor, the best room in the house used for guests and entertaining, was similarly appointed, as were the bedrooms, each room reflecting the wealth of the owner.

One of the servants, Sarah Stratton, a widow, who did the majority of Joshua's cooking, had prepared many small dishes for the guests to savor while visiting.

"After I put everything out," she told me, "I'll leave, but I'll be back early tomorrow morning to clean up. But first, I wanted to give the two of you some privacy," she said with a twinkle in her eyes.

Joshua had a few more drinks and tolerated the guests. I could tell he hoped they would leave as soon as possible. He looked at me several times, a knowing smile on his lips and a lustful look in his eye. I considered the house a mess after the guests left and was tempted to take the dishes to the kitchen, but decided to leave it for Sarah. This was not a time for domestic duties.

When everyone had gone, Joshua led me to the bedroom. I'd thought about this time for weeks. Anticipating a sweet and tender moment, I was nervous. The previous week, my mother took me aside and told me it would be painful but only for a moment, and that it could be one of the most wonderful moments a couple shared. Now, as Joshua and I went up the stairs, my hands shook slightly, my anxiety increasing with every step.

He led me into the bedroom.

The large four-poster bed, with heavy velvet curtains to keep the chill out, was on the wall opposite the fireplace. He threw two more logs onto the fire, adding more light. The warmth of the room, from an earlier fire that Sarah must have built, was comforting to me.

Joshua took my hands, pulled me to him, and embraced me.

"I've waited for this moment," he said in a low voice as he ran his hands over my back. "Have you?"

"I've thought about it," I stammered, incredibly nervous.

"There's no need to be afraid," he said, as if reading my thoughts.

"I know," I said, my voice quavering.

He looked into my eyes, smiled, and kissed my hand.

"Let me help you get out of your things," he said.

"I want to do this by myself," I said. "I'll call you when I am done."

Cocking his head, he put a finger under my chin, moving it back and forth gently. "No," he said taking his finger away. "We are husband and wife."

He began to undress me. After untying the lacing, he turned me around.

"Wait!" I yelled.

Ignoring my plea, he yanked the sleeves, causing the left sleeve to rip at the shoulder.

"Damn it!" I shouted, stepping away from him. "My beautiful gown."

"Never mind the gown," he said, lust flaring in his eyes.

"Leave me alone," I cried, although there was no one left in the house to hear my protests.

"Take your clothes off," he commanded.

While he watched, I removed my clothing. I lay on the bed naked, one arm across my breasts and a hand covering my crotch. Joshua stood leering, taking my nudity in, before beginning to pull his clothes off, throwing them onto the floor. The lustful look in his eyes made me afraid. This was nothing like I'd thought it would be.

He pulled my hands away from my body and knelt on top of me.

Realizing there was nothing I could do, I lay there, submitting to my new husband, acting the part of a dutiful wife. I was shocked, hurting and injured in body and soul.

When it was over, he lay next to me, gently rubbing my tear-stained cheek with the back of his hand.

"I know that was difficult for you, but it will be better next time. I'm sure of it."

I rolled onto my side. He left a few moments later. I got up, put on my thick flannel sleeping gown and cap, got back into bed, drew the down quilt up to my shoulders, and pulled the heavy bed curtains closed. Exhausted, I fell into a heavy sleep, awakening only when he came back a short time later.

I heard him throw a few more logs onto the fire. Then he pulled back the curtains and got into bed.

I raised myself on one arm and watched him, afraid he'd want more.

"I am so sorry, Bathsheba. I didn't mean for it to be like that. Please forgive me." He stroked my hair. "I had too much to drink, and I wanted you so badly." He sighed, a look of contrition on his face. "You're a beautiful woman, and I could not help myself. Please, please forgive me."

I lay back down and ignored him.

Joshua left me alone much of the time, his days occupied with business matters and his nights with friends at the tavern. Managing the household did not take much of my time. For the next two months, I spent hours with my needlepoint and knitting. I was bored, lonely, and longing for the happy, active days of when I'd been home, safe and protected, having fun with my siblings, being immersed in my books, riding my beautiful Invictus. Dreaming dreams of a future that was not at all like the one I'd ended up with. Every day I yearned for my father's loving arms and even my mother's scolding. Deciding to speak with my father about the situation, I waited until Joshua went to his farm in Princeton. He would be gone for two nights. Harnessing the sleigh myself, I set out shortly after he left.

I found my father in his office.

"What is wrong, child?"

I shook my head.

"You can tell me."

"It's Joshua."

"What about him?"

I began crying, unable to hold my feelings in any longer. "He's a horrible husband, and it's all your fault."

"My fault?"

"If you hadn't forced me to marry him, I'd be happy." I was angry and leaned toward him. "Why did you do this to me?"

He seemed flabbergasted, but only for a moment. "I thought it would be the best thing for you. Joshua is a fine upstanding man in Brookfield . . . "

"No, he's not!" I said. "He treats me poorly. He hardly pays attention to me, and he doesn't seem to care for me."

Father's face hardened at the thought of me, his favorite child, being treated poorly.

"I'll talk to him."

"You will?"

"Yes. Is he away on business?"

I nodded. "He's in Princeton until Thursday and is going to Boston on Monday."

"I will be in Boston next week, too. I'll give you a letter telling him I want to meet with him."

Sitting at the wide desk, dipping a quill in ink, he took but a moment to write the letter, folded it into quarters, heated some sealing wax, and dripped it onto the letter before pressing it with a stamp bearing his seal.

"Give this to him. If he asks, you know nothing of the contents." He got up and wrapped his arms around me. We stood that way for a long moment. I missed feeling the comfort of his embrace. "Look at me. It doesn't matter how old you are; you will always be my daughter, my little girl. Never forget that."

"What is this?" Joshua asked when I handed him the letter shortly after he arrived home.

"I don't know. My father asked that I give it to you."

He eyed me suspiciously. "When did you see your father?"

I just smiled, took my hat off, and went up the stairs to the bedroom.

I was in Worcester, visiting Mary, several days later when I received word that Father had arrived at Brown's tavern on his way home from Boston. I made my way to the tavern and found him sitting near the fire.

"Daddy," I said. "I'm glad you're here."

"I thought you would be," he said stretching his legs toward the warm hearth.

I motioned for a cup of cider. Taking a drink, I leaned over the table.

"Tell me all about it."

He smiled, a look of amusement in his eyes. But he didn't say a word.

I poked his arm with my finger. "What happened?"

He drained his cup and sat back in the chair.

"I took him into a private room. He was smug with an irritating smirk. I told him you'd come to see me and told me some troubling things," he said. "He asked what they were." I never took my eyes off of Father's face as I drank. "I said that he'd mistreated you. Joshua choked on his rum when I said that and spat it all over his breeches. I told him that you said he misuses you."

"What was he like?" I asked. "Was he afraid of you?"

"I don't know if he was afraid of me, but his mug clattered when he put it down because his hand shook." He smiled. "He said that he wasn't sure why you would've said that."

"That bastard," I muttered.

Father looked around the room and lifted his cup. Another was soon placed before him. "I told him that I wasn't going to go into details, but that I wanted him to know that I take this seriously."

"What did he say to that?"

"Nothing. He looked at the floor."

"Figures," I said.

Father absentmindedly fingered the chain for his pocket watch. "I stood over him and told him to look at me."

Father has one of the most powerful and commanding voices I've ever heard, so I imagined Joshua sitting up straight, afraid of Father towering above him. I hoped Joshua's eyes had widened, and that he'd had a frightened look on his face.

"He admitted that you'd had some difficulties, and asked what husband and wife don't." Father let out a long sigh. "That made me think of your mother."

He sat momentarily lost in thought staring at the flames jumping off the crackling logs.

"I told him to listen to me," he resumed. "I said that you're my favorite child, and I won't have him or any other man mistreating you. When I asked if he understood me; he said he did. I said that he must treat you well with the respect you deserve, and that if I hear that he's not then we'll have another talk, but it won't be as pleasant."

I realized my fists were clenched. "What happened then?"

He took another swig and put the empty cup down.

"He smirked at me, a look that I found quite condescending. I grabbed him by the back of his coat and hauled him out of the chair. It was like picking up a kitten. I held him off the floor and put my face a few inches from his. I asked him again if he understood. He nodded his head, bouncing as if he were a puppet. He said that he did understand, but he smirked again, so I threw him into a chair and left."

I wasn't convinced that my marital situation would improve, but at least now I had some reason to hope.

We stood, and I kissed his cheek.

"Thank you, Daddy."

When Joshua returned from Boston, he found me in the east parlor at my needlepoint. "I met with your father," he said with a note of anger in his voice. "You complained to your father about how I am treating you? He does not seem to understand that you took a vow to obey me."

The next morning we went to church as we did every Sunday, sitting in the pew to which Joshua subscribed each year, as the most important people each had their own pew. Reverend Fiske spoke for over two hours on everyday aspects of being a good Christian to which Joshua and, I hate to admit, I also paid little attention. Joshua helped me get in the chaise for the short ride home and, after dinner, he went to the tavern, leaving me alone. Again.

"I want to bring Invictus here," I told him one morning a month later over breakfast. Sipping a cup of tea, I watched him. "The weather is better, and there is hardly any snow on the roads. I can get him tomorrow." I was excited at the thought of having Invictus here. To be able to ride him again whenever I wanted to would be wonderful. I missed him so much. I was sure that having him there would make me happy.

"No," Joshua said.

I was so lost in my reverie, I barely heard him.

"What?"

"No."

I was confused. "What did you say?"

"I said no, you cannot bring the horse here."

I was stunned to the point that I couldn't talk. I shook my head to clear it. I stared at him, loathing that he had lied to me.

"You told me that I could bring Invictus here after we were married," I said, slamming my cup down. "That is the one thing I asked of you, and you agreed."

"I've changed my mind," he said, continuing to eat, never once looking at me. "I don't want to incur the expense of boarding it. It costs too much," he said, then took a bite of egg.

"I don't care if you changed your mind, he is my horse, and I want him here. I'm going to get him tomorrow." I stood up.

Joshua looked at me, his demeanor calm and unruffled. "If you bring the horse here, I will sell it."

"You son of a bitch. You'll do nothing of the kind. You won't touch him," I said, seething.

"I will sell it. And if you persist in this, and if I can't sell it, I will have it shot."

"How dare you? What gives you the right to say such things about my property, my things?"

"You are married to me. You have no legal rights. You do not own any property. I own everything. If you bring the horse here, I will claim it as mine, and sell it or have it shot. It is no longer yours, nor ever will be again."

Dumbfounded, I walked into the east parlor. I paced back and forth, angry and confused. It was true that, whether I liked it or not, married women had no legal rights. I decided that perhaps for now it would be best to leave Invictus at the farm where I could visit him whenever possible.

I heard the front door close and realized Joshua had left. Suddenly tired from my emotional breakfast, I sat down and slumped forward, missing my most favorite thing in the whole world—Invictus. After a few minutes, I steeled myself and changed into a riding outfit. I told Sarah's son, Jesse, to saddle a horse for me. I rode off to Hardwick to see my father again.

As with my most recent visit, Father was home, although this time he was entertaining visitors. Excusing himself, he took me to his office.

"He said I could bring Invictus to Brookfield, then he changed his mind and said if I brought him, he would sell him or have him shot."

"Alright, alright. I see my earlier talk didn't impress him. Has he treated you better?"

"A bit, but he is still not a good husband." I thought of Joshua's rough, inept way of intimacy, but I couldn't tell Father because it was embarrassing. Instead I told him that I felt abandoned and useless day after day, and left it at that.

He dropped his head and sighed deeply. "I will be there tomorrow to speak to him again." He nodded, kissed me on the forehead, and went to the door. "I have to get back to my guests."

I spent some time with my mother, then went to the stable and fed Invictus apples before taking him for a gallop down the road. Then I returned to what now was my home.

The next day, my father arrived at mid-morning. I thought about visiting my sister Martha and her family, but I decided to stay to see what would happen. I anticipated that Father would give Joshua a beating that would bring him to his senses.

Joshua came jauntily down the back stairs and stopped in his tracks upon seeing my father. I stood in the doorway between the kitchen and the parlor and watched. They faced each other for a long moment before Father grabbed Joshua by the arm and shoved him out the back door. Putting his hand on Joshua's back, Father pushed him into the barn. I hurried after them.

Without a word, my father backhanded Joshua, dropping him to the straw scattered on the floor. He looked up at his father-in-law, clutching his cheek, fear in his eyes, afraid of what the man would do to him.

"How dare you not listen to me," Father bellowed. "She will bring Invictus here, and you will not give her any difficulty about it."

Joshua struggled to his feet, holding on to a stall wall to help him stand. He left out a deep breath and faced my father. He no longer looked afraid.

"She is my wife, and this is my home. I will do as I please."

Father picked Joshua up and threw him into the back of the stall. My husband hit the wall with a loud thump and slid to the floor groaning, landing in a pile of manure. I laughed and clapped my hands.

"Get up," Father commanded.

Joshua stood, his anger growing despite the beating. "You may be an important man," he said, "but you cannot tell me how to run my household. I will handle my private affairs as I see fit."

Father stepped toward Joshua until their faces were only inches apart.

"If you do not treat her well, I will ruin you."

Then my father came to me, kissed me on the forehead, mounted his horse, and left.

Joshua continued with his threats to harm Invictus if I ever brought him to Brookfield, so I kept him in Hardwick, which proved, at a later date, to have been a horrible mistake.

CHAPTER 3

AFTER HIS LAST MEETING WITH MY FATHER, Joshua treated me better, at least for a while. After the birth of our first child, Elizabeth, a little more than a year after our marriage, he showed little interest in the baby, and even less interest in me. It's true that he was increasingly busy with his business interests and traveled quite a bit to Boston, his properties in Middleborough and Worcester, and to his other interests in the general area. But I continued to feel abandoned—something I hadn't anticipated. I knew that relationships were complicated and did not always work well. All I had to do was look at my parents' marriage. They were married in name only; for all other intents, they were separated, each having a strong personality and fixed views that rarely, if ever, coincided.

One day while changing three-month-old Elizabeth's diaper, I finally accepted that I did not love my husband; I had no affection for him. I knew that, while Joshua wanted more in a wife than I was willing to give him, he had decided somewhere along the line that I would be the mother of his children, social hostess, and, most importantly, the source of satisfaction of his carnal desires.

I picked the baby up and cradled her in the crook of my arm. I lifted her onto my shoulder and kissed her head, smelling her special baby smell. As I walked around the room softly humming a lullaby, I realized I needed something for myself. I decided to have a summer party, to demonstrate to the town of Brookfield my skills as a hostess.

To my complete surprise, a few days later when I told Joshua about the party, he thought it was an excellent idea. He agreed to it without hesitation. Now that I was his wife, I could take care of all the social engagements. He was determined that I would make an admirable impression, even though the guests would be people only he knew.

Early August was hot and humid; some days were almost unbearable. Then the heat and humidity dissipated as quickly as they had arrived. The weather in the third week of the month was perfect; the party was to be held Saturday afternoon. I wanted the leading townspeople to see me as a refined and socially superior woman, the hostess who gave the best summer party. I wanted to be well thought of and respected, not because I was the daughter of Timothy Ruggles or the wife of Joshua Spooner, but for myself.

Sarah, with my limited help, had cooked for two days. We prepared Indian meal, molasses and butter pudding, curds, creams and custards, apple and pumpkin pies, tarts, and sweetmeats. We prepared veal and bacon, roasted chickens, and ham and beef that we cooked over a small fire for a long time. All of this—and more—was served accompanied by different nuts and cheeses, beer, porter, wine, punch, cider, and rum. I spared no expense.

Sarah and I saw to it that the house was thoroughly cleaned; to everyone's surprise, even Joshua assisted. Everything was washed, scrubbed, and polished from top to bottom—the floors gleamed, the windows sparkled, and everything was in its place. Some months before, I'd ordered from London a yellow gown of brocaded silk taffeta with light green flowers, and a linen bodice and sleeve linings. It had a matching petticoat. I had pale green, high-heeled leather shoes that matched the gown and were tied with a red scarlet ribbon. I spent an hour making my hair lustrous and my skin look soft and radiant. I glowed with pride, thinking it might be possible to be happy, at least for a little while.

Joshua came down the stairs, entering the parlor with a light step. I heard him and turned. He was dressed in matching soft green linen breeches and coat, an intricately woven white linen shirt and pale yellow neckcloth, blue cotton socks, and black shoes with engraved silver buckles.

"You're beautiful," he said.

I looked him over from head to foot. "Thank you," I said with a bright smile. "You look very nice, too." I placed my hand on his chest, touching the soft linen with my fingers. "Let's make this a perfect afternoon."

He nodded. "Yes, let's," he said, taking my hand. "Seeing you has already made it a good day." He kissed my hand.

I sighed.

The big walnut grandfather clock in the hallway, admired by everyone who entered the house, chimed the hour of two o'clock as guests began to arrive. In late May, I had planted a flower garden of roses, pink peonies, purple and white foxglove, evening primrose, sweet-smelling box, stock, phlox, and marigolds in the yard between the house and barn. I had a curving stone walkway built by local men, and the garden was formed around its twists and turns. The men also had planted three flowering honeysuckle shrubs.

The intermingling of plants offered a sense of beauty, simplicity, and usefulness. On that afternoon of the party, the perfume of the flowers wafted across the yard and into the house.

"Everything's so lovely," Dr. Foxcroft's wife said as she came in through the open doorway and into the hall.

"Thank you," I beamed.

"Joshua," Dr. Foxcroft said, "wonderful idea, this party. We've always said that we should do something of the sort but never have. There's never been a party like this in town."

"And now we won't, since it is obvious, Bathsheba, that you can do a much better job than I could," Mrs. Foxcroft said smiling.

"Thank you again," I said. "Please have some punch."

At that moment, one of the young village boys, dressed in his finest clothes, entered. He carried a tray with several glasses of punch, offering it to the doctor and his wife. I'd engaged a violinist who strolled about, the pleasant notes of his instrument reaching to every corner of the house and yard. It reminded me of the ball in Boston; I smiled at the memory.

The guests streamed in for the next half hour, spilling into every room and the garden. Four benches had been placed around the garden and provided welcome seating. The people laughed as they mingled, clearly enjoying themselves immensely. Two young ladies from town served food while Sarah bustled around watching for needed things, making sure everything was just so. Jedediah Foster, John Wolcott, Abijah Cutler, Thomas Banister, John Cutler, James Ross, and their wives, joined other townsfolk for an afternoon that I hoped would be a pleasant remembrance for years to come.

That evening, after the guests and the help had left and Elizabeth was sleeping soundly in her cradle, Joshua and I sat side-by-side on the divan.

"I've never had as fine a day as today," I told him.

"Really?" he asked.

"Yes. It was perfect. Everything was perfect."

"As were you."

I smiled at the compliment. "Thank you for making it a good day."

He leaned over and kissed me. I gave myself to him willingly that night.

A month later, it was as if the party never happened. One evening around midnight, I heard my husband lurch into the kitchen. I went down the stairs; Joshua stood holding onto the wall, looking haggard and drunk. When I went up to him, the odor of rum wafted toward me.

"You said you'd be home . . ."

"So what?" he said, cutting me off. "I'll come and go as I please. I was away on business to Oakham."

"That took four days? It's only a three-hour ride from here. Are you sure you didn't stay at the tavern there?"

"Shut your mouth. I will do as I want."

"You are a miserable man and a drunk." I turned and went back upstairs, hoping he was too drunk to make it to bed and would sleep on the floor in the kitchen. I lay in bed, softly crying, thinking of the mess my life had become. The afternoon of the party glittered like a diamond among the brown and tattered memories of the rest of my married life.

On the following morning, I realized I was expecting another child.

CHAPTER 4

I LONGED FOR A DIFFERENT LIFE. I was burdened with aspects of motherhood I never considered when my second child, a son, was born in January 1770. He was named Joshua, of course, after his father. But taking care of two children was taxing. Even though Sarah helped me when she could, I went to bed each night exhausted. I loved my children with all my heart, but I hate to admit that at times they were a terrible responsibility I did not care to have.

On a cold, clear late March night three years later, I gave birth to another son. I screamed at the intense pain racking my body and was certain the agony would never leave me, that I was destined to be in this pain forever. The sweat rolled off me in streams, and the midwives rubbed my face with a cool cloth. It was the most difficult birth I'd had. I heard myself screaming again; the pain was unceasing.

"Rest for a minute," the old midwife, Julia Bannister, told me. She had been delivering babies for more than four decades and was the most experienced midwife in the area.

I heard the door open and saw Dr. Foxcroft come into the room and watch Julia work. He must have believed he was supervising the entire proceeding, but I could tell that Mrs. Bannister knew better, letting him think whatever he liked as long as he stayed out of her way.

"Have you given her the mixture I brought?" he asked her with a note of condescension.

She shot him a piercing look. "No, and I won't, either." She bent between my legs to see if the baby was coming. "I see the very crown of its head." She reached up and patted my hand. "The baby will be born very soon."

"She should have delivered by now," he said. "I think it best if you leave."

"Oh, you do, do you?" Mrs. Bannister said. "I think it best if you leave. I've brought four times as many children into this world as you have. My forty years of doing this are better than your fancy title and studies. I know more about this than you ever will."

His mouth opened and closed as if he were going to say something and his brow contracted as he pursed his lips.

"If you won't go home," she said, "at least go away."

He left the room.

"Oh my God, will this ever end?" I yelled, pleading for the pain to stop, clenching my teeth so hard it hurt worse than the labor pain that then rocketed through me.

With a calmness she must have acquired during the many years she had done this, Mrs. Bannister smiled at me and stroked my cheek gently. "It will be over soon. The baby is on its way now. Breathe deep and push hard."

My breath came in short bursts. A moment later, I felt the baby leave my body. Mrs. Bannister wiped the blood from the baby, turned it upside down and gave it a smack on the bum, causing the baby to squall. She cut the umbilical cord and tied it. It was all done in less than a minute.

"You have another son," she said, putting the tiny baby to my breast. He was so small, half the size of a normal baby; his skin was nut brown. I offered a nipple and he began to suck. But he took the nipple for only a minute then spit it out and started crying. My other two had fed hungrily right from the moment they were born.

"Almost done," Mrs. Bannister said as if she was about to take one of her pies from the fireplace oven. I felt the placenta come out in a rush and heard it drop into the pan the assistant midwife held under me. Placing the pan on the floor, she began to clean me with warm water and a soft flannel cloth. It felt wonderful.

Three days later, it became apparent that the baby, whom Joshua insisted be named John for his father, was sick.

"He will hardly nurse," I told Mrs. Bannister when she came to check on us. "He cries most of the time." I held him in my arms and rocked back and forth, trying to soothe him, but it didn't work. He continued to wail.

Mrs. Bannister looked at him for a moment. "He's not sleeping much either is he?"

I shook my head. "No," I said softly, "just a few hours a day." I rocked back and forth again, but he continued to cry.

"What did Dr. Foxcroft say?"

"He gave me a mixture to give to him but, with the little bit I've been able to get him to swallow, it's not doing any good." I started to cry and my tears spilled onto his face. I held him against me, feeling his warmth, and cradled his fragile head in my hand. I kissed his forehead, and he fell asleep.

As a warm rain fell on an early April night, my baby died. He didn't cry but lay in his cradle listless and not moving. Around midnight, he stopped breathing. It took everything out of me. I felt hollow; no emotion surfaced in my heart. I was too numb to even feel sad.

He was buried the next morning in the Brookfield cemetery, in a spot near the road under a large elm tree.

"I think he would have liked this," I said to those around me. The poor children didn't know what to do. They watched as his small coffin was placed in the ground. Joshua stood next to me and put his arm around my shoulders. After a moment, he pulled me close. I folded myself into his arms. He held me for a moment before taking my hand. Even with the widening gap between us, we silently acknowledged that we had created this poor baby and felt, in our sorrow, some tenderness for one another. Reverend

Fiske spoke briefly, a few words meant to comfort us, although they didn't.

We returned to the house, which was unnaturally quiet without the baby's fretful cry.

Everyone was subdued. I can admit that there was some relief, too, that the almost constant crying was no more. The children, distraught, ate their meal in silence. I thought of the baby shoes and the clothes that would never be worn, and I hurried out of the room to cry.

Two days after John had been buried, Joshua left for Boston for a meeting with two London merchants. It had been arranged months before, and he could not change it.

Before leaving, he sat with me in the parlor, our legs almost close enough to touch.

"I'm sorry," he said. "I've never known heartache like this before."

I turned to look at him, surprised by his words.

He rarely spoke about his feelings for the children or me. "I know it happens all the time," he continued. "I mean, children die, but it never happened in my family." His look searched my eyes. "Did you have any brothers or sisters who died in childhood?"

I shook my head. "No."

"Just the fact that it happens does not make it any easier, though, does it?"

"No, it doesn't," I replied, staring at my hands in my lap.

"I have to go," he said.

"Yes. Of course. It's an important meeting, isn't it?"

"Yes. Harper and Parker is a significant trading firm. They've been in business for over one hundred years. It's taken more than a year to arrange this meeting. The firm and the partners are very wealthy, too. If all goes well, they can increase my fortune substantially."

I nodded, no longer listening.

He took his hat and coat from the rack by the doorway and walked through the kitchen into the yard by the barn. He'd hired Mr. Weldon's Negro to drive him, not only because it was better than riding a horse, but also it gave the impression that he was wealthy enough to have a Negro coachman. Joshua also had bought a new suit of fine clothes in an effort to add to the image.

I stood in the doorway, watching him. He climbed into the carriage and was off in a moment. I waved a sorrowful good-bye but he didn't return the gesture. He never even looked back.

The baby's death sent me into a state of despair. I believed it was my fault that he hadn't lived. I walked through the house day after day, alone in sorrowful thought of the baby I had lost. I felt dragged down by a heavy weight that never left me.

"Mrs. Spooner, come take a seat, and I'll get you a cup of tea with some of the chamomile I dried last fall," Sarah told me. "It will make you feel better, I promise."

Wandering around the kitchen before dropping wearily into a chair near the fireplace, I looked in the mirror and saw that my eyes were circled with dark rings, and my skin had lost its vitality. My hair wasn't brushed, and I must have had a vacant look about me. That was how I felt. I didn't spend time with the children because it was too painful. Better not to see them than to be continuously reminded of little John.

"I feel so listless," I told Sarah. "I have no interest in anything."

She puttered around the stove. After putting in two teaspoons of black tea to which she'd added a large pinch of dried chamomile, she grabbed a thick cloth to use on the hot teakettle handle. She poured the boiling water into the ceramic teapot that had purple and yellow violets painted on it. Then she set the pot on the table in front of me and brought a cup and saucer that matched the teapot.

"It was the same when I lost my two," Sarah said. "I cried for weeks with the first. It's a tough thing, but it does get better over time. Not that it hurts any less."

I turned and looked at her as if seeing her for the first time. "What happened?" I asked, pouring the tea into the cup.

"Well, I'm older than you, of course. The first was, oh, let's see, twelve years ago. A little girl. Jane. Lived only three months. Sick from the start." She shook her head. She looked out the window at the rolling hills to the west, as if lost in thought.

I didn't think she would say anymore, but she turned from the window and moved to the other side of the table. "The other one was Will. That was eight years ago. A fine boy, healthy and feisty." She smiled just a bit at the memory. "Oh, he was a good boy. Smiled and laughed all the time. He was almost two years old when he got sick." She wiped her eyes with the sleeve of her dress.

I took another sip of tea, raising the cup slowly to my lips, watching her.

"One day, he got the fever and broke out in a rash from head to foot," she went on. "He began coughing, hacking up gobs of phlegm. I did what I could, but it wasn't enough. I didn't have any money to pay a doctor, and my husband had died four months before. He had gone to sea and his ship sank in a storm. It was just me, Jesse, and poor Will." She choked down a sob. "Will died two days later. At least, he didn't suffer long." She grabbed a handkerchief from the pocket of her apron and blew her nose. "I buried him myself in the little cemetery down the road from our house." She nodded once. "I did that." She took the teapot and poured more tea. "Drink it up now. It will make you feel better." She put the teapot on the table, grabbed the milk bucket from the corner, and went to the barn to milk the cow.

Joshua came back after his two-week absence and seemed in a different state of mind. He had been elected a town selectman the previous month and also had taken on the responsibility of the treasurer's position at the church. People viewed him in a slightly different light than previously, and I thought that perhaps, after the past few years, he had finally realized his responsibility as a husband and father, and that he was turning over a new leaf.

I was in the kitchen when he came in. He was dressed in new red breeches and matching coat, and he held a black tricorn hat laced with gold trim that matched the color of his stockings. His hair was tied into a queue behind his head, dropping to slightly below his collar. He had not been drinking and seemed surer of himself, more thoughtful and considerate. I followed him into the parlor.

He sat in the chair to the right of the fire and gestured for to me take the other opposite him. I sat, smoothed my dress, and considered my husband. He leaned forward, his elbows on his knees and looked at the floor.

"I have done a great deal of thinking while I have been away, mostly about you and the children." He looked at the paintings on the walls. "The baby's death made me think."

This surprised me, for I'd thought he rarely considered us at all.

"I realize," he continued, "that I am not a good husband or father. I am away too much on business. I know I drink too much and spend more time at the taverns than I should."

"What do you intend to do about it?" I asked. "Suddenly, because my baby dies, you become the husband and father you should have been all along?" I knew I should have held my tongue—after all, Joshua had shown that he cared—but still, my temper rose. "And now that you have a change of heart, we all go along as if you are a wonderful person?" I straightened my back and stared at him. "You should have considered this some time ago. The children need a strong father, and I need a good husband."

"Well, no, I mean yes, I know," he said, evidently as startled as I was by my unexpected strong words. He looked at the floor, unable to meet my gaze. "All I meant was that I know I have to be a better man, that's all."

I stared at him. "While you are a successful and wealthy businessman, you don't seem to know how to be a good father or husband. Until this tragedy, you haven't even tried. I'm afraid you are a weak man, Joshua, and always will be. No amount of wishing you are something else will ever change the way you are." My voice was not raised, my words were of resignation.

"Yes," he mumbled. "I suppose you're right."

"Will you spend your day at the tavern again?"

"I don't know," he said sadly. Standing up, he put on his hat and shuffled out the door, a man seemingly defeated by life. I pulled the drape aside and watched him as he went down the road in the opposite direction of the tavern.

I felt poorly about how I had treated him. Perhaps he was genuinely trying to be a better man, and I had just thrown cold water on his attempt. I sat pondering, flattening my green silk dress over my knees. I put my hands in my lap, looked out the window, and wondered where my husband had gone.

Joshua didn't return until the evening of the next day. He straggled home looking worn, which he was, for I later learned he'd spent most of the time at a tavern in a neighboring town.

When he came in, we'd just finished dinner. He sat at the head of the table and looked at the children and me from red-rimmed eyes.

"Get me something to eat," he yelled towards the kitchen.

A moment later, Sarah came in with pieces of chicken on a plate and vegetables in a side dish.

He grabbed the chicken with his fingers and chewed noisily, swallowing the chunks as soon as he got them into his mouth. "Madeira. Bring me some Madeira," he commanded Sarah.

She hesitated, looking at me, unsure whether or not to get the wine.

"Now!" he shouted.

She moved quickly and returned with a bottle of wine and a glass, which he quickly filled, the wine slopping over the rim. He drank it down. He took a piece of carrot out of the side dish, tasted it, and spit it onto the carpet before grabbing the plate and throwing it against the wall.

"Joshua, stop this!" I demanded.

The children stood up from the table, most likely afraid of another fight between us.

"Shut up," he slurred.

"Sarah!" I hollered. She was in the room like a shot. "Take the children to their rooms." She hustled the children up the stairs.

"Joshua, your behavior is unacceptable. What do you think you're doing? What happened to your intentions to be a better man? A better husband? A better father?"

"I'm eating . . . leave me alone." He slurped more wine and chewed the last piece of chicken, leaving grease on his fingers. He wiped them on the edge of the fine linen tablecloth. Taking more wine, he looked over the rim of the glass. "I'm going to have you tonight," he said with a lascivious grin on his face.

"You're disgusting. And you are not going to have me, tonight or any other time."

"I can and will! You are my wife and will do as I tell you! You submit to my will," he said before laughing, thinking it the funniest thing he'd heard in days.

That night, I lay in bed, Joshua fast asleep and snoring beside me after I grudgingly submitted to his demand. The window was open, letting in the warm night air carried on a soft southerly breeze. I stared at the ceiling, thinking of the baby who'd left me too soon. Then I smiled just a bit, a sad smile but a smile, nonetheless. I thought of my father and was once again angry with him for forcing me into a marriage I didn't want to a man I did not even like. "If you'd only listened to me, listened to what I wanted, not what you needed," I whispered, "both of us would be much happier." I rolled onto my side, curled my legs towards my stomach, and put my right hand under the pillow. I looked at the wall until I fell asleep. It was not a good night, for I was haunted with unhappy dreams.

CHAPTER 5

I WAS IN WORCESTER during the third week of December when word reached us that over three hundred chests of tea from the East India Company had been dumped into Boston Harbor the previous week.

When I got to Brookfield, Cooley's, Reed's, and Waite's taverns were all abuzz with the excitement. Those damned patriots, as they styled themselves, were standing up to Britain. It was a daring act and made it clear to everyone that they wouldn't submit to rightful taxation or to the authority of the king. I was surprised at the level of enthusiastic support for the rebellious acts and the loathing for Britain in Brookfield. Conversely, Father had passionately defended the Tea Act in 1773 and former Governor Hutchinson's handling of the state of affairs.

I was concerned that the war was on its way and could erupt soon.

Three months later, my breasts were swollen and sore, and I was sick in the morning at the smell of food, sure signs of pregnancy that I knew all too well. In the interest of an uneasy peace, I had resigned myself to accept Joshua's tiresome sexual demands. It was, as my mother had informed me, my wifely duty.

In late May 1774, I'd had my fill of Joshua, and I went to Hardwick for a visit. To my surprise, our new governor, Thomas Gage, was there, visiting my father.

After dinner, they retired to the parlor. I followed them and took a chair by the fire. While Gage sipped at a glass of port, my father drank from a silver mug filled with cider. A platter of nuts and cheeses rested on the table between them. I got up, took some cheese and a handful of nuts, and sat down again, the governor watching me the whole time.

"And why, Bathsheba, are you here? We have important matters to discuss," the governor said.

"My presence won't prevent you from discussing them," I said. "I don't like these damned rebels any more than you do. I want to know what is going on."

He took a sip and looked at my father. "Tim?"

Father glanced at me and smiled. "It's fine for her to be here, governor. She's very bright and very stubborn. To get her to leave now would take all the horses in the stable," he said with a laugh.

Father put down his cup and leaned forward, placing his elbows on his knees. "I am increasingly concerned about the number of acts of rebellion that are taking place against those of us who support the Crown. I, and many others, have been harassed and assaulted. A crowd attacked me as I rode through Plymouth last week. I kicked one man in the head and rode off, leaving them yelling for my blood. I am not sure my townspeople will stand behind me much longer."

"You think I am not concerned?" Gage asked. "Why do you think I am here?"

"Of course, I understand why you are here," my father said, getting to his feet. "I'm thinking of forming an association of men like myself that are loyal and who pledge undying allegiance to the Crown."

Governor Gage cocked his head to one side, intrigued by the idea. "And what would be the purpose of this group?"

My father took a drink and began pacing next to his chair. "Essentially, it would be to right the wrongs committed against us by any means necessary."

"What do you mean?"

"Well, if one of us were attacked, or our houses, property, or families harmed, we would respond in kind."

"So it would be a group of men who would seek revenge?"

After a moment's consideration, Father nodded. "Yes, I suppose you can look at it that way."

"And what's wrong with that?" I asked. "Revenge can be a good thing if used properly."

"Bathsheba, please," Father said, sitting down.

"Have you lost your senses?" Gage asked Father, while ignoring me. "That would only further inflame the rebels and further complicate an already delicate situation."

Father glared at the governor across the table.

"I forbid you from forming it. Do you understand me?"

Father didn't respond. He pursed his lips and stared at his clenched hands, the frustration building.

"Do you understand me?" Gage repeated.

"Yes!" he said, standing up quickly, pushing the chair out so hard it fell over.

The two men looked at one another for a moment, both ready to argue their point. As Gage was the military commander, Father did not press the issue.

"There is something else we need to discuss, Tim," Gage said.

"And what might that be?"

"I am dissolving the Massachusetts Council and replacing it with a Mandamus Council. It's time that we exert influence on the colonists, and that is the only way I see it working."

"That sounds like a splendid idea," I said. "I wish I were a man so I could help exert some influence. There are a few I'd like to influence with my fists." Both of them laughed at me.

"I have no doubt you do and you would," the governor said smiling.

My father stopped pacing and sat down. "The House of Representatives will be furious at you for taking their power," he said. "The outgoing councilors will not look kindly on it, either. They have always selected the upper legislative body."

"Well, that will be gone effective August first."

"They will harass every man you name, to the point where they will not accept the appointment. Even if they do, I doubt all of them will serve. There will be serious threats and intimidation."

"I am naming new men. Only two of the current twenty-eight councilors will remain. I will announce that, and the dissolution of the Legislative Council, on July first."

"How many will you appoint?" I asked.

"Thirty-six. I am sure the rebels will hang each of us in effigy."

"As long as they don't get their filthy hands on us. If they do, any hanging will not be in effigy," Father said.

"Yes, you're right," Gage said. "They'd like nothing better."

Father contemplated this for a moment. "I expect that no more than twenty-four councilors will serve, perhaps less."

"We shall see," replied Gage.

Father frowned. "I have no doubt that I will be unwelcome here after your announcement."

"Who will not welcome you? Your wife or the townspeople?" Gage asked, rising from the chair.

"Oh, God, both." Father looked down at the floor and shook his head. "My wife is as much a rebel as I am a loyalist. It is a difficult situation, but I will endure it. She's wrong and very stubborn, but she will not get the better of me."

The governor looked at me. "And we know where you stand," he said.

"Damn right," I said. "No one ever misunderstood what my views are, except, of course, for my husband."

They shook hands. "Remember," Gage said, not letting go of Father's hand. "I need you to be with me on this. Don't get any ideas about starting that loyalist association. You're a good man, Tim, but I will not stand for it."

"Of course, governor."

Father and I followed the governor out, saying our goodbyes as he got into his carriage and rode away.

"I might just put together the association whether Gage wants it or not," Father told me. "Things will come to a head soon, this year or next, so I'd have it for that time. Once the war starts, I can do as I like."

Governor Gage's announcement of the Mandamus Council—and that my father was the first member selected—made Father the most hated man in the province.

It was a warm summer day when I left Brookfield at midday and went to Hardwick to visit Invictus and see my mother, although since our views of the coming war were in sharp disagreement, we found ourselves at odds. Still, she was my mother, and being with her was far better than spending time with Joshua, who happened to be home.

Word about the council spread fast, and when it reached Hardwick an hour before sunset, I'd just arrived and was having a bite to eat in the kitchen. Father was in his office when a large, rowdy crowd gathered in front of our home, yelling for him to come out, taunting him with curses and threats of harm with torches and clubs. Violence quivered under the tension of the crowd. It would not take much to set them off.

As the crowd assembled, Father appeared at the parlor window and stood watching the men. He knew all of them; many were our relatives.

"What are you going to do?" Mother asked, standing behind him. She surprised him, and he jumped a bit before turning around.

"I may tell them all to bugger off," he thundered. "How dare they come here and make demands of me? I brought many of them here. My farms have provided them work. They've earned a living because of my efforts, and they are here calling for my blood? How dare they! How dare those dirty bastards!"

"They want us out," she said. Her voice and body were tense. "You can go to Boston, but where will I go?"

He ran his fingers through his hair. "Damn it woman, they know you are with them, not me. They will not harm you. It's me they want."

"Then go," she said. "Leave now and be gone with you!"

He advanced on her quickly, towering over her, his eyes blazing and teeth clenched. "Don't you tell me what to do." He stared at her for a moment and went back to the window. "If it wouldn't make the situation worse, I'd throw you out tonight."

"You son of a bitch!" she yelled.

He ignored her and headed to the front door.

I ran up the stairs to look at the crowd from my old bedroom. When Father opened the door, the crowd surged forward and began yelling louder.

"Goddamnit!" he thundered. "Be quiet!" His angry voice resounded across the yard and beyond. The crowd slowly quieted. He stood on the front step and drew himself up to his full height, squared his shoulders, and looked at each of them.

"You're here tonight to harass me. I brought many of you here, gave all of you employment, helped you and your families when you needed it. Every one of you has prospered because of me, and you stand here now making demands of me." He glared at them. "Go home. Leave me be." The men looked at each other, unsure of what to do. Some started to turn away while others looked sullen. "Go home now," Father said to those closest to him. "There's no need for this. Go home, men." As he started to close the door, some men at the back of the crowd rushed forward.

"You're a traitor!" someone yelled.

My father marched into the midst of them, his angry eyes locked upon the man who had yelled.

"My nephew calling me a traitor. Well, I can believe it," he said in a loud voice. "You're much like your father, Ephraim." He stomped back to the house and turned around before entering. "All of you. Leave now." He slammed the door shut.

I continued to watch and, after a few minutes of sporadic grumbling, the men dispersed, heading to either the tavern or their homes.

My mother came up to my room. "You'd better leave in the morning," she told me. "They know you side with your father. It might be dangerous for you here."

"It could be just as dangerous in Brookfield."

"Do what you want then," she said banging the door closed as she left.

CHAPTER 6

THE MONTH OF AUGUST was hot and dry. Temperatures reached well into the nineties for a week, and it had not rained in over three. Dust from wagon wheels and horses' hooves lifted into the air; it was a long time before it settled back onto the ground.

Tensions continued to flare between Father and the townspeople. The earlier scene was repeated three times and didn't progress beyond a loud and ferocious argument. Then one day, four of Father's prized cattle were poisoned. That same night someone threw a rock through the parlor window. Two more rocks smashed through the upper story windows.

My brother John was traveling to Worcester and stopped to see me. He told me all that had happened.

"Within a minute of the last rock breaking the window, Father yanked the door open and walked outside, two pistols in his waistband and a rifle in his hands. He was something to see," John said. "'I'll shoot the next bastard who throws anything at my home,' Father told them. The tone of his voice had left no doubt in the minds of the crowd that he would do precisely that. The air was still, and no one moved. Something thumped against the side of the house, and Father fired the rifle at the back of the crowd. Men scattered at the shot. When they realized no one had been hit, they converged on the house again. Father reached into the doorway and grabbed two more loaded rifles and leaned them against the house next to where he stood. 'I won't miss the next time,' he hollered. He stood before them until they began to leave. I thought they'd burn the house down," John said.

Father was banished from Hardwick a month later. When he made it to Brookfield, he stopped at my home.

He was dressed in the full military regalia of his general's rank and had ridden his black charger, a massive warhorse. His uniform was a brilliant scarlet red cutaway coat, with dark blue lapels, gold buttons, and yellow braid epaulets; it covered a light tan waistcoat. A dark red sash across his broad chest and a dark blue tricorn hat edged with gold braid on his head completed his splendid appearance. He must have been an awe-inspiring sight to the people of Hardwick whose daily dress was dull brown and gray colored clothes.

He was furious at what they'd done, especially at his brother Benjamin. I sent Sarah's son, Jesse, to tell Martha that our father was here. Luckily, Joshua was away.

When Martha arrived, we sat in the parlor. I was six months pregnant and had trouble getting around. My back hurt, my feet were swollen almost all the time, and my stomach was often upset. The entire summer had been hot, and even just sitting there, I was bathed in sweat.

Father paced back and forth, punching his fist into his palm.

"The mob, led by your uncle Benjamin, may he rot in hell, has taken all my properties. Everything . . . the farms and houses, barns, cattle, horses, all my possessions. They banished me, tried to arrest me. Do you believe that? Trying to arrest *me*?" He rose and walked to the window. "Stay away from that kind of people; they are wrong in their refusal to submit to the lawful authority of the king. Goddamn every last one of them." He stopped pacing and looked at us. "It's all about my appointment to the Mandamus Council."

"Invictus!" I gasped. "What happened to him?" Fear clutched my heart.

Father let out a deep breath and dropped his head for a moment before looking up and taking my hand.

"They took him," he said.

My hand flew to my chest.

"I can't believe it. Invictus . . . gone?"

"The last I saw of him, your cousin Joe was leading him through the back pasture. I'm sorry, Bathsheba. I wish there were something I could do, but there isn't."

I got up and walked to the window, silent tears running down my cheeks. I could feel Father and Martha looking at me. I vowed I would try to get Invictus back somehow. I wiped my tears with the heel of my hand and went back to join them. My anger at Joshua flared to a burning point because he had not let me bring Invictus to Brookfield.

"When I reached the bridge over a small river, the town militia, captained by your uncle Benjamin, accosted me and wouldn't let me pass. You know what he said? He said that they came to arrest me and that I was their enemy."

"What did you tell them?" Martha asked as he went to the window.

"I told them that they will not arrest me, and that I am certainly not an enemy," he said in his commanding voice, one we'd heard many times before. "I told Ben that if they let me pass, I'd be gone but would come back with my men, my association, and fight them." He turned quickly and came to sit in a chair next to us but only for a moment before he sprang up and started pacing again. "They are a mob! A common rabble resisting the rightful rule of the king!" He stopped pacing and glared at us. "Do you know what my brother told me? He said that if I came back and tried to cross that bridge, I wouldn't reach the other side alive." He finally sat, moving his sword out of the way. "These people are a mob of the lowest sort. They will bring ruin upon us."

Martha and I looked at each other. "But we can't stay away from them," Martha said. "They are the people who live with us. Many in this town believe strongly in the patriot cause and are ready to march at a moment's notice to protect us."

Father looked at her. "Yes, yes, the men are all set to march against the world's most powerful army. If fighting breaks out, they don't stand a chance."

"If Gage sends three thousand troops to Worcester to look for the powder and muskets as he promised, there will be a fight, and these men will do whatever necessary against any opponent—including the British Army," Martha said with a determination I'd never seen in her before.

"My daughter," he said as he shook his head. "You are a fool." He turned to me. "Did you know that these men have threatened to block the courts from opening? How dare they!"

"What do you mean how dare they?" Martha asked. "The courts will not open. British authority does not exist anywhere but in Boston."

His jaw clenched and a spark of anger flamed in his eyes. He and Martha stared at each other for a long moment before Martha stood. "Goodbye, Father," she said.

He stood and watched her walk out of the door. He sat down and sighed.

"Where is Mother?" I asked, shifting position to make the load I was carrying more bearable.

"With your brother Tim," was his short reply.

The thought occurred to me that I could take the children and go with him. With Joshua away again, I could pack up the children's belongings and mine. And we could leave. It was so simple. I'd leave behind the troubles with my useless husband and rebellious neighbors. The prospect of getting out of my marriage was so exciting I could barely contain myself. I'd be with Father in Boston.

"I want to go with you," I said.

"No," he said without a moment's thought.

"I don't want to stay here. It's not good for the children or me. It's the perfect time for me to leave. And I have this little one to think of," I told him, putting a hand on my belly. He looked at me, considering the suggestion.

"I don't know what it will be like in Boston in the coming months. I'm sure it will be difficult and not the best place for young children, especially a newborn. We'll not be able to stay there for long, as the rebels will somehow force us out. I am sure of that. And I have no idea where we may end up. I'll write to you if I can, but I think, even with Joshua's shortcomings, that you're better off staying here."

Those words were a great blow. I realized that it was my last best hope of getting away from my terrible husband.

"I may never see you again," I said as tears began to slide down my cheeks.

"That may be true."

I didn't know what else to say. While I didn't see him often, I knew that I always could if I needed or wanted to, but now that possibility might be gone for good. The prospect of staying with Joshua made my stomach turn and my head ache. The likelihood of not seeing my father ever again made my heart sink. He came, sat on the divan, and held me. When I realized it was most likely the last time he ever would do that, I sobbed. He held me for a few more minutes and then stood up. He gazed at me with the love and affection he rarely showed.

"I have to go," he said, putting on his hat.

I stood up and walked outside with him.

A dozen men stood in front of the house, waiting for him. They yelled when they saw him. I noticed that the men, all of whom I knew, were looking for trouble. Three of them held rocks in their hands, while two others held rough wooden clubs.

"So, Ruggles, hightailing it to Boston?" one man taunted. "Need to find someplace where you are liked? Being banished from your town serves you right."

Father's face flushed, the hot anger rising inside him.

"You damn Tory!" yelled another, taking a step closer. "Go to hell!"

I put a hand on Father's arm. "No, please. I don't want them to hurt you," I said.

His head snapped around, and he looked at me. "Me? Get hurt?" he said, shaking his head. "They won't hurt me."

We ignored the men and stood on the steps in the sunlight. I hugged him again and began to cry. The men were silent as they watched us. Father touched my face with his fingers and kissed me on the cheek, then mounted his horse. He looked at the men but did not say anything as his horse pranced from side-to-side, anxious to be off. He looked at me one last time, gave me a sad smile, and kicked his horse into a trot.

All I could think of was when he had left for the French and Indian War and how much I had missed him. I felt like that same sad and lonely little girl again, and I began sobbing, knowing in my heart that he was gone for good. My last memory of him was watching him ride away. He looked magnificent, dressed in his full uniform, on his large, black stallion.

Four days later, Sarah was in the kitchen cooking, sweating profusely in the heat. The air was hot and humid, and the fire had been blazing most of the morning. When I came down the backstairs, the heat hit me like a hammer.

"Open all the doors and windows," I told her. "It's horrible in here. At least some breeze can come in." I went around opening the kitchen and parlor windows, feeling the limp, damp breeze against my hands. Sarah stirred something in the kettle and went out the door and stood with her back against the house, fanning herself.

"Oh Lord, it is hot," she said.

I followed her out, wiping my brow with the sleeve of my dress. I went to the water bucket and handed her a dried gourd full of water. She drank it in one gulp. I stood in the shade as she wiped her face and neck with a kitchen cloth.

"What do you hear about the courts?" I asked. "Both the Court of Common Pleas and Court of General Sessions are to convene tomorrow."

Sarah shook her head as she got another dipper of water.

"You don't know, do you? The courts will not open tomorrow, ma'am. Men are coming from all of Worcester County to stop them. I've heard that five thousand men will be there." She took another drink. "All the men from here are marching out early to be there for ten o'clock." She took another sip and looked at me. I think she felt sorry for me. "While I haven't been here often this week, I thought you'd have heard. No one tells you anything because you're his daughter. It must be difficult."

I dropped my head and stared at the ground. "It is," I whispered.

The next morning, well before dawn, the entire town, except my children and me, had assembled on the town green. I stood in the window of my bedroom, fearful of what might happen, watching hundreds of men, armed with muskets, begin to march. They passed the house in formation, led by two young boys who were playing the fife and drum. Some townspeople streamed after the men; they were clearly determined to see the last vestige of British authority in the county crushed.

That night around nine o'clock, the men returned, some jubilant, some somber. Most of them marched together in a loose formation while others lagged behind. I had been curious all day about what was going on, so I went out to the front yard. As the men came by, I spotted Ephraim Cooley.

"Ephraim!" I yelled hoping to get his attention.

He looked around for a moment, confused about who was calling his name.

"What happened?" I asked.

Several men stopped and leaned on their muskets.

"I'll tell you what happened," one of them said. "We prevented them from opening the courthouse. All the justices and magistrates, except your father, of course, scurried off to Heyward's tavern, where they wrote a letter announcing that they'd close the courts for today only. We didn't accept it. We lined the road from the tavern to the courthouse, thousands of us on each side. To get to the courthouse, they had to pass by us, hat in hand, and read a statement." He cleared his throat and spat into the dust. "Then we sent them home. The courts are closed until we decide to re-open them."

Another man, a tall farmer from the western part of town, took a step toward me.

"Your father would have marched the gauntlet, too, if he wasn't hiding in Boston."

I winced at the thought of Father being subjected to such humiliation. Better that he was in Boston. I watched them go, and only after the last one went by did I go inside.

Over the crisp fall, and snowy, cold winter, life went on for us. Farmers burned the fields, as was the custom, preparing them for new plantings in the spring. The smell of wood smoke wafted through the air day after day. Brightly colored leaves fell, leaving behind a brown and gray landscape that turned white when the snow came. The cold poured down out of the north. The temperatures dropped so low, everything froze, including some of our animals.

As was usual, Joshua was around for a few weeks, then gone for a few more. On the seventeenth of January, I was racked with labor pains right after I got out of bed. I'd known my time was coming and had warned Mrs. Bannister to be ready for when I needed her. Sarah heard me cry out and came running up the steps to see if it was time.

"Dear God, this hurts," I wailed, grimacing in pain as I sat down on the bed. "Send Jesse to get Mrs. Bannister."

"He's not here today," Sarah said. "I'll run and get her."

I groaned and reached out, gripping her forearm. I shook my head and clenched my teeth. "No, I need you here."

"Well, what am I to do then?"

"Go get Dr. Foxcroft. Ask him to come here. Once he arrives, go get Mrs. Bannister."

"I will. Do you want to come downstairs?"

"No."

"Shall I bring you anything?"

"No, just get the doctor. I'll be fine. Hurry."

Sarah hustled down the stairs and was out the front door. I heard it slam behind her. I was grateful the children were at Martha's so they wouldn't see me in pain like this. I heard Sarah holler at someone, and I got out of bed, holding onto the wall with one hand and the bed with the other. I was sweating and opened the window to let the cold air in. Sarah stood in front of the house yelling at a boy down the road.

"Boy!" she yelled, "Boy! Come here!"

The boy and horse looked up at the same time and saw her. They trotted toward her.

"Do you know the Bannisters that live down toward the river?"

"No."

"It's down the road past the church, a white house with a fence around the front yard. I need you to go there and tell Mrs. Bannister that Mrs. Spooner needs her right now. Hurry! Hurry!"

He looked doubtful.

"Do you understand my directions?"

"I think so."

"Go up the road here and take a left. It's the only road that goes that way. At the end of the green, you'll find the house on the right. Go now and run. Leave your horse with me. Mrs. Spooner is having a baby, so hurry."

He handed her the reins and took off as fast as he could, slipping from time to time on patches of ice and snow.

Sarah led the horse to the front of the house, tied it to the hitching post, and came back inside.

"Are you alright?" she called from the east parlor.

"No, it hurts even worse than it did," I cried, falling back onto the bed gasping in pain. "Is the doctor coming?"

Sarah talked as she came up the stairs. "No. I did not want to leave you. So I sent a boy to the Bannisters' instead. She should be here soon."

I lay on the bed, sweating and clutching my belly as the pain rolled through me.

Mrs. Bannister arrived a short time later. I heard her running up the stairs. She came into the bedroom and threw her coat and hat on a chair.

"We'll have this little one out and crying soon." She ran a cloth over my forehead. "My girl will be here soon to help. Don't fret yourself now," she said. I took that as a reference to my last baby, poor John.

Later that afternoon, after pushing and yelling, breathing hard and sweating like never before, my baby girl made her appearance into the world. I didn't wait for Joshua but named her Bathshua, a variation of my name. I figured that since he had a Joshua, I could have a Bathshua.

Slowly, the snow melted, and the cold winds gave way to soft, southerly breezes that brought warmer temperatures. By early April, a few small signs of new life appeared—weeds were peeking out of the dirt along the roadways, the buds on trees began to open, and I saw geese and ducks flying north. The daily drudgery of my life ate away at my soul, and my depression deepened. Joshua was home more often than not, and my aversion to him grew greater by the day.

One day, I was working in the herb garden when he came up the stone walk from the front of the house. I knew he was there but paid him no mind.

He cleared his throat. I didn't look at him. "I am going to Chelmsford for at least two weeks. I should be back sometime in the first week of May."

I offered no response.

He waited for some sort of acknowledgment. I stood and put the scissors in the pocket of my apron, holding the bunch of herbs in the other hand, and turned to face him.

"I don't love you. I don't think I ever have."

"Oh," he replied. "This talk of war has upset you—"

"Of course it has! I think it is a stupid war, but what do I know?" I walked toward the house.

"Are we so much like your parents?" he asked.

I considered that for a minute. "Yes, we are. Although my mother cares deeply for the patriot cause while you care nothing about anything but yourself."

He walked past me, mounted his horse, and rode off.

The following day was even warmer than the day before. Martha came to visit, something she did less frequently now. The feelings between us ebbed and flowed as news of the various events of insurrection became more frequent with each passing week. Martha found me in the parlor with the children. Young Joshua, now five years old, was playing a game, Elizabeth, now eight, was embroidering the alphabet on a linen sampler, and the baby was fast asleep on a blanket on the floor.

"Why are you inside on such a beautiful day?" Martha asked.

"I don't know. I don't feel like doing anything today. Besides, I'm tired. The baby kept me up most of the night."

"You need to take the children outside. Fresh air will lift your spirits."

I nodded, thinking she might be right, that it would do me good. I picked up Bathshua, took Joshua by the hand, told Elizabeth to come along, and followed Martha out the back door.

"Isn't this better than just staying in the house?" Martha asked as they strolled around the yard.

"I suppose so."

Martha stopped, picked a small sprig of mint from the herb garden, rolled it between her fingers, and smelled it before offering it to me.

I cradled the baby in the crook of one arm and took the offered mint sprig. I took a whiff, then threw it to the ground.

"What's wrong?"

"Joshua is gone again."

"I thought you liked it when he was away."

"I do, but I'm lonely." I shook my head. "I guess I am starved for kindness and affection. We talked for a moment before he left," I said, looking down at the mint leaf. "I told him I don't love him."

"Did that come as a surprise to him?"

"No. It wasn't a surprise to either of us," I said with a loud sigh. "I just needed to say it."

We strolled a short distance, keeping the older children in sight as they played along the road. Suddenly, we heard the loud, heavy hoofbeats of a horse being ridden hard. We stopped and saw a man bent over the horse's neck, holding the reins tight, coming at us fast. We knew something was wrong. Switching the baby to my other arm, I flagged him down. He slowed to a trot as he came near, the horse blowing from its nose, foam around its mouth, eyes wild, ready to be off.

"What's wrong?" I asked.

"Redcoats attacked Lexington and Concord. The militia's needed," he said, kicking the horse in the flanks, bolting for the meetinghouse.

"Oh, dear God," Martha said. "It's war."

I felt my heart sink. "It's finally happened," I murmured, stunned. I stared at the wild daffodils growing by the side of the road. My mind was in a tumult. A chipmunk dashed across the road in front of us before skittering up a stone wall while the birds sang their spring songs.

"What are you going to do?" Martha asked.

The question snapped me back into focus. "What do you mean?"

"You could be in danger. Father's the leading loyalist in New England, and everyone knows you share many of his views. They'll be even more suspicious of you now."

"But he's gone, and what can I do? I have no power over any of these events." The baby began to whimper. I turned and walked a few paces before turning back. "I know you don't agree with me, but this is stupid. The king and Parliament are the source of all government for the colonies. Attempting a revolution will cause problems, both short- and long-term, for everyone. These people are too shortsighted to see that."

Martha looked sideways at me. "That includes me. And I don't agree with you," she said briskly. "The time has come, and it will end however it does." She began walking back to my home. "I need to get home. John will be going." She hurried to her carriage and was on her way in a minute, leaving me standing there with the children.

It was foolish of me, but I felt that I was the only voice of reason and moderation in town. I felt so alone. Not only did I hold far different political beliefs that isolated me from most of the other townspeople, my husband, useless man that he was, was not around either.

"Elizabeth! Joshua! Come along, we need to go home. Hurry!"

They came running and played hide-and-seek around my legs. "Stop that! Something's happened, and we need to get home."

Word of the battles spread like wildfire, reaching every corner of the region in an hour. Within two hours, three companies of men, under the commands of Captains Jonathan Barns, John Wolcott, and Leland Wright, assembled on the green in front of the meetinghouse.

I stood on the granite steps of my home and watched as the men paraded by dressed in faded brown, gray, or tan pants, and jackets, a motley mishmash of muted colors, muskets in their hands, on their way to Worcester to join with other troops for the march to Boston. They looked like a rabble, farmers about to play at war. But they were serious and somber, and I wondered how long they would be gone. I shivered and wrapped my arms around myself. Events moved about me like a whirlwind, and there was nothing I could do to stop it.

Joshua returned from Chelmsford two days later.

"What are you doing home so soon?" I asked when he came in the front door.

He rolled his eyes and looked at me as if I were stupid.

"I assume you are aware that Massachusetts is at war with Britain?" I asked.

"Of course I know that," he said. "What do you take me for? Why do you think I came home early?"

"An ass, that's what I take you for." I put my hands on my hips, bracing for a war of my own. "A cowardly little ass who spends most of his time with his head in a bottle of rum."

He gave me a cold stare.

"I don't care about any of it. I don't care which side wins. I don't care about the Loyalists or the rebels. It makes no difference to me at all. Life will go on no matter what happens." He opened the door and walked out. I followed him and stood with my hands on my hips, watching him walk away.

He came stumbling home towards midnight. I made sure all the doors were locked and that he couldn't get in. He started banging on the kitchen door, yelling all the while.

"Let me in! How dare you lock me out of my own house!" He said something else that I couldn't make out.

The noise woke Bathshua, who started crying. I went to the cradle and picked her up, rocking slowly back and forth to soothe her. I'd given the children and Sarah strict instructions that no matter what happened, he was not to be let into the house.

The banging and yelling faded after a few minutes. I assumed that he stumbled to the barn and slept on a pile of hay.

Early the next morning, when Sarah went to milk the cow, she almost tripped over him.

"I kicked his foot twice but he didn't move," she said as she put the bucket on the table.

"Leave him," I said. "Let him wake up with his face in the dirt."

CHAPTER 7

I WAS OUT FOR A RIDE ONE DAY toward the eastern part of town when I saw a group of men on horses and a large carriage coming in my direction. I stopped to let them pass, for the road narrowed at that point. The men on horseback rode by me, looking me over from head to toe. I heard a shout from one of the passengers and the carriage stopped. I couldn't for the life of me understand why until I saw a man stick his head out the side.

"Good morning, Mrs. Spooner," he said. I leaned over to get a better look at him and saw it was Sam Adams.

"Who's with you?" I asked.

"Why, Mr. Paine and Mr. Hancock. We're on our way to Philadelphia to the Congress."

Robert Treat Paine was at the other window.

"You know, if your father were loyal to our cause, and not with the king, he'd be with us now. He has a fine mind and passionate temperament, which I understand you've inherited. We'll be on our way. Perhaps we'll see you again," he said taunting me with a smile.

On the afternoon of June 18, word reached us of the battle on Breed's Hill in Charlestown. A man from Spencer rode into town with the news. Riders had been out all night spreading the word that the ragtag band of rebels had badly beat General Gage's troops. I was passing by Green's Tavern in the western part of town when I saw a commotion. I stopped my horse and sat listening to four men talking excitedly as they stood by the hitching post.

"What's going on?" I asked. They turned as one and watched me.

"You're Ruggles's daughter, aren't you?" one of them said.

"Yes."

"Why do you want to know?"

"I'm curious as to why you are so excited."

They looked at each other and laughed.

"Because there was a battle yesterday in Charlestown, and we beat the British. Killed a thousand of them, least that's what I heard."

"I heard it was more than that," chimed another.

They turned and started into the tavern, ignoring me.

I kicked my horse into a trot and made it home in a short time, determined to find out more. If the rebels had bested the British troops, it was a cause for concern. I was also worried about my father and hoped he'd not been involved in the battle.

I left my horse in the yard, telling Jesse to take care of it while I went looking for his mother.

"Sarah!" I yelled. When I didn't get a response, I went up the backstairs to see if she was doing something in the bedrooms. "Sarah!"

She came scurrying out of the children's bedroom. "What happened, Mrs. Spooner?"

"I'm hoping you can tell me?"

"I don't know what you mean."

"I heard there was a battle in Charlestown. Have you heard?"

"What? No! I haven't heard anything. Oh my!" she said.

"We're going to Cooley's to find out what's going on."

I had a bad feeling about it and didn't know what I'd find out, but I knew it wasn't good news for our loyalist cause. Seconds later, we were hurrying down the road to Cooley's. When we walked in a few minutes later, it was crowded and noisy, everyone talking at once. There was no place to sit, so we stood against the wall just inside the door. Two men I'd never seen before, one tall and the other short, each holding a large mug, were next to Sarah. I nudged her with my elbow.

"What's happening?" she asked the tall one.

"Haven't you heard, woman? There's been a big battle. We handed Gage his first of many defeats."

"That will teach him that we mean to fight for our freedom from British tyranny," said the short man.

"What else do you know?" I asked him. "Any details?"

"It lasted almost all day. They threw three waves of troops against us, and we beat them back."

"The rebels—I mean patriots—captured Boston? Is that what you're telling me?" I said, alarmed at the prospect, something I never considered possible.

"Well, no," the tall one said.

I spotted Cooley near the bar waving his arms.

"Alright, listen here! he yelled. "Listen here." The crowd quieted. "This man," he said putting his hand on the shoulder of the man standing next to him, "has everything we need to know. Let him talk now."

The man drained his mug and put it on the bar.

"Here's what happened. One of our men was at the tavern where a lot of the British soldiers eat. He was having breakfast just at dawn when a boy burst through the door, almost knocking over a table where two captains sat. He told them he'd seen men on top of Breed's Hill. The soldiers hustled out and down the lane to the water to find a small group of men looking up the hill. After hearing they were going to alert the soldiers on Copp's Hill, our man took off for the Green Dragon to warn our men of what was happening." He gestured at Cooley who quickly re-filled the man's mug.

"A short time later, the guns from one of the ships in the harbor started firing but stopped a little while later."

I looked around the room. People were either leaning forward listening intently or appeared deep in thought considering the implications of what we'd just heard.

"Everything was quiet until early afternoon when the first group of Brits tried to go up the hill. We beat them back!" A sudden, loud "Huzzah!" went up from the people in the room. He took another drink draining his mug that Cooley had refilled. "They tried twice more, and we beat them back again, but the third time we left. Let them chase us into the town, and they'll find out we mean to stop them!" Another loud cheer went up.

I backed out the door and walked home, hoping my father was alright.

Three days later, a young boy came to the front door. When I heard the knock and opened the door, he stood there, arm outstretched, holding an envelope.

"This is for you," he said, giving it to me and rushing off. I looked at it and saw the imprint of my father's seal in the red wax. I hurriedly opened it, closed the door, and sat on the divan. There were four pages, a longer letter than he'd ever written to me.

Bathsheba,

I'm sure you heard the news of the battle at Charlestown by now. I know you worry about me and want to assure you of my safety. It was a difficult day, but I was never in any danger, although I wish I had been. The news so far is probably filled with half-truths and rumor.

I was awakened by cannon fire. I jumped out of bed and ran to the east room where five large windows overlook Charlestown. I scanned the harbor with my telescope and saw smoke drift from one of the ships. The sun was just cresting the horizon when I saw the rebel fortification on the hill. Soon, all the warships in the harbor and the artillery on Copp's Hill began firing. The rebels moved back beyond the range of the cannon. I hoped for a decisive victory.

The firing stopped, began again an hour later, then ceased after a short time. Around 11:00 a.m., the bombardment began again, increasing in intensity, lasting twenty minutes. The cannonballs did not seem to do any damage.

I sent my servant to General Gage with a note that I'd join them if he needed me. He came back informing me that a captain took my letter and told him to leave. Can you believe such a thing? Me being ignored by a junior officer. Goddamn the impudent son of a bitch.

Barges filled with regulars crossed the river to begin the attack. Our troops landed, formed, and began marching up the hill. Through the telescope, I watched as the regulars approached, moving closer and closer to the rebel line without a shot being fired. When the regulars were almost on top of them, the rebels fired three volleys, decimating our ranks. Scores of regulars fell to the ground followed by a hasty retreat.

The regulars formed once more and marched up the hill. Still, they were pushed back. Dead and wounded men littered the hillside. As I watched the battle unfold, I realized I'd never been a spectator to a battle, but always a participant. It was maddening and frustrating.

Once more, our troops marched up the hill, finally breaking through the rebel lines and causing them to scatter.

When the afternoon finally ended, the rebels had fled, but I learned later that almost half our men were either killed or wounded. While it was a victory for us, it came at a great cost in lives. The battle had proved that Lexington and Concord were not just a skirmish. The war has begun in earnest.

Know that I think of you often and hope you and the children are safe. Be careful around the townspeople ... they're probably looking for a reason to banish you.

With great affection,
Your loving father

I sat there staring at the wallpaper. There was no turning back now. The war was here and could expand beyond Boston at some point. I realized I had to plan for it if it did.

The months that followed were filled with uncertainty. I waited for news, but none came. Boston was besieged; the rebels came and went from town passing by my front door almost daily. It was a stalemate.

CHAPTER 8

I WAS TEACHING ELIZABETH NEEDLEPOINT on a cold, snowy January afternoon as we sat in the east parlor. The fire burned nicely, its flames dancing along the tops of the logs. I put my needlepoint in my lap and watched the fire. I was very content after the ham and corn chowder with molasses bread we'd had for our early afternoon meal. I felt myself drifting off, my head nodding as my eyes closed. I sat up and resumed my needlepoint for a moment before nodding off again. The pleasant time was interrupted when Jesse came tearing into the house.

"Mother!" he cried, looking for Sarah.

"Jesse, come here," I said. He walked from the kitchen into the parlor. I felt a draft of cold air. "Did you leave the door open?" He hurried back to the kitchen; I heard the door bang shut.

He came back looking sheepish but obviously excited at some news he was bursting to share.

"What is it?" I yawned. I felt like going to bed.

"Tom Parker said a man is at Reed's and he's talking about cannon coming through. Colonel Knox took all the cannon from Ticonderoga and is bringing it to Boston. Least that's what Tom told me."

This news startled me. It was such an audacious measure that I couldn't believe they'd go to such lengths. I sat up straight, no longer tired.

"Did Tom say anything else?" I asked.

"Just that the man said Colonel Knox could use as many men as he can get, and that if anyone wants to help, they're coming through the Berkshire Hills."

I heard Sarah coming down the stairs.

"Was that you I heard hollering?" she said.

Jesse nodded.

"Well, what was it all about?"

I told her what Jesse related.

"Oh, dear," she said before rounding on her son. "Were you at the tavern? Who's Tom Parker? I've never heard of him."

"Tom lives on the other side of town," he said. "He's older than me."

Sarah didn't respond for a minute. "Go do your chores," she told him. He scooted off. She looked at me, shook her head, and went into the kitchen to begin preparing dinner.

Joshua came home a short while later and was in a talkative mood. He and I sat in the west parlor on each side of the fireplace. The logs crackled, and the flame shadows danced on the walls.

"Did you hear the news?" he asked. "The army is bringing cannon to Boston," he said without waiting for me to answer. He rubbed his hands together as he stood up in front of the fireplace. "Your daddy and all his British friends will be forced to leave Boston," he said with a smirk. "And won't that be a terrible thing?" He began laughing as if it were the funniest thing he'd heard.

"I thought you didn't care one way or the other," I said putting my needlepoint on the seat and standing up.

"Oh, I don't," he said taking my hands in his and smiling like a happy schoolboy. "But it means your father will suffer, and that makes me glad."

I pulled my hands away.

"Oh, and Mr. Gray and Mr. Morgan are joining us for dinner," he continued, referring to two of his business associates from Springfield. He took his watch out and checked it. "They should be here in two hours or so." He put the watch back in his waistcoat. "I wonder where your father will go?" he asked. "He can't come back here, for he'll be arrested. Hmm, where would he go?"

"Enough!" I said. "That is quite enough from you. I know the danger my father may be in and don't need you to keep bringing it up."

"Oh, Bathsheba," he said dropping into an overstuffed chair and stretching his legs out in front of him.

I sat there, fuming at his constant verbal prodding.

"You are your father's favorite, aren't you?"

I didn't respond.

"Is there anything you wouldn't do for him?"

"Go to hell."

"Oh, you're in fine spirits today, aren't you?"

"Go to the tavern and leave me alone."

He jumped up and adjusted his waistcoat and coat.

"I think I will. What a wonderful idea. I never would've thought of it myself, you know," he said with a chuckle.

I felt the urge to take the fireplace poker to him.

He went into the kitchen, whistling a happy tune. Through the open door, I saw him slap Sarah's wide bottom, causing her to jump and squeal before he headed out the kitchen door.

The feeling of wanting to hurt him didn't pass when he left.

I sat there pondering the situation, not only about the cannon, but also about Joshua. I realized with a jolt that this was the perfect reason for me to leave him and go to my father. I could take the children, although that could prove to be difficult. I'd need to travel fast to get to Boston in a single day, and that would not be possible if they came with me. I could leave them behind. They'd be well taken care of. Joshua, Martha, and Sarah would give them what they needed. Was it right to bring them into Boston where life was more difficult than elsewhere with the food and firewood shortages I'd heard about? No, it wasn't the right place for them. I could leave soon—tomorrow or the next day. If I left early enough and traveled hard, I could be there before nightfall. Maybe I could deliver the news, see my father, and be back in a couple of days.

No more than half an hour later, Joshua returned with a man in tow. The man looked to be in his mid-twenties and had brown hair sticking out from under his faded black hat, light blue eyes above a long nose, and a few days' stubble on his face. His clothes were a bit ragged although his boots looked new. A small well-worn leather satchel hung across his chest.

"This is Peter Wright. He's the messenger from Colonel Knox."

The man looked first at Joshua then at me.

"I really can't stay long," he told Joshua. "I appreciate your offer of hospitality but I have to get to Cambridge."

"Oh, you can sit and enjoy a real meal instead of the swill they serve at these taverns."

That did not seem to put him at ease.

"Besides, you have to meet my wife, Bathsheba. She's a loyalist, you know. General Ruggles's daughter."

Mr. Wright's eyes widened a bit as he looked at me.

Joshua noticed his gaze. "Haven't you ever seen a loyalist up close? Well, there she is!"

"Good afternoon, Mr. Wright," I said. "Welcome to my home." I saw Joshua's face go red when I mentioned that. Even though legally it belonged to him, it was my home. I intended to do my best to annoy my husband. "Please come in and sit down."

"I don't know," Mr. Wright said. "I think it best if I go."

"Sarah," I said loud enough for her to hear me from the kitchen.

She poked her head in the door. "Yes, ma'am?"

"Set three extra places. We're to have honored guests this evening." I turned to Mr. Wright. "Care for something to drink?"

"I'll have rum," Joshua said springing into action.

"I'll have one too," I said.

He looked at me askance, for I drank liquor only occasionally.

"Pour one for Mr. Wright too," I added.

"Please call me Pete. It's what everyone else does." I handed him his rum and motioned for him to sit in the chair to the side of the fireplace. He took his satchel and set it on the chair next to him.

No sooner had we sat down than Mr. Gray and Mr. Morgan arrived. Sarah served dinner a short time later. When we went in to dinner, Pete came in without his satchel. If he were bringing a letter to Washington, it would be there. When the men began an animated discussion about the rebellion, I excused myself and went back to the parlor. Closing the door quietly, I hurried to the satchel. I hesitated opening it, for I was taught to not snoop into the affairs of others. But I quickly discarded that thought.

The letter was the only thing in it. I looked around to make sure no one could see me, and after listening to the men's continued discussion, I took it out. It was not sealed, which surprised me. Wasting no time, I unfolded it and read:

Decm'br 17

May it please your Excellency,

I return'd here to this place on the 15th & brought with me the Cannon being nearly the time I estimated it would take us to transport them to here. It is not easy to conceive the difficulties we have had in getting them over the lake owing to the advance'd season of the year & contrary winds, but the danger is now past & three days ago it was very uncertain whether we could have gotten them until next spring, but now please God they must go. I have had made forty-two exceeding strong sleds & have provided eighty yoke of oxen to drag them as far as Springfield where I shall get fresh cattle to carry them to camp. The route will be from here to Kinderhook from thence into Great Barrington Massachusetts Bay & down to Springfield. There will scarcely be a possibility of conveying them from here to Albany or Kinderhook but on sleds, the roads being very much gullied. At present the sledding is tolerable to Saratoga about 26 miles; beyond there is none. I have sent for the sleds & teams to come here & expect to begin moving them to Saratoga on Wednesday or Thursday next trusting that between this & then we shall have a fine fall of snow which will enable us to proceed farther & make the carriage easy. If that should be the case I hope in 16 or 17 days' time to be able to present to your Excellency a noble train of artillery, the Inventory of which I have Inclos'd. I also send a list of those stores which I desir'd Col McDougal to send from New York. I did not know then of any 13 Inch mortars, which was the reason of my ordering but of few shells of that size. I now write to him for 500, 13 inch & also for 200, 5¾, & 400 of 4 ½ inches. As being if these sizes could be had there as I think they can, I should imagine it would save time & expence get them from thence rather than cast them. If sir, you think otherwise or have made provision for them elsewhere, you will please countermand this order. There is no other news of Colonel Arnold than that from Colonel McCleans having burnt the Houses round Quebec. Colonel Arnold was obliged to go to Point au Tremble about 6 miles from the City. General Montgomery had gone to join him with a considerable body of men & a good train of artillery. There are some timid & some malevolent Spirits which make this matter worse but by the different accounts which I have been able to collect I have very little doubt that General Montgomery has Quebec in his possession.

I am with the utmost respect Your Excellency's Most Obedt Hble Servant

PS—You will please Sir to observe that there are no carriages nor implements to the cannon nor beds to the mortars, all of which must be made in camp.

I folded it and put it back in the satchel. I picked up the needlepoint that I'd left on the divan and carried it with me back to the dining room.

"What were you doing?" Joshua asked, finishing his wine.

"Oh, I didn't know where I left this, so I just went to check. It was where I thought it was."

I was distracted through the entire dinner. I kept up the chatter expected of me, but my thoughts kept returning to the implications of the rebels in Cambridge soon having cannon to use against Boston. I worried about my father and wished there were some way to help him.

"Isn't that right, Bathsheba?" Joshua asked.

"I'm sorry. What did you say?"

"I said that if Washington gets the cannon from Ticonderoga, Boston will have to be evacuated, won't it?"

"Or surrendered," Mr. Morgan said taking a sip of wine.

"Or surrendered," Joshua said. He cocked his head to one side and smiled at me, obviously enjoying the torment of seeing me worry about my father.

Mr. Gray and Mr. Morgan left around nine o'clock, intending to be in Worcester in a few hours. The children were already in bed, and Sarah had gone home ostensibly to sleep but also to keep an eye on Jesse so he didn't go with the wrong boys, as she suspected he'd been doing.

All night long as I lay in bed, staring at the ceiling, I wrestled with the question of what to do, of how I could alert the people of Boston that they were in danger. Surely, I wasn't the only British sympathizer who knew of this development and had the power to do something about it. But I didn't know that for certain so I had to assume that I was. As dawn approached, I drifted off to the sound of Joshua snoring beside me.

I slept late and was awakened by the sound of the children playing. When I got downstairs, Joshua was already gone. Sarah gave me a cup of tea and a muffin. I sat at the kitchen table, yawning. I was having a hard time waking up until the thought of going to Boston jolted me fully awake.

The sky was cloudless, and the day was warm for that time of year, so after breakfast I dressed the children in their coats, and we went for a walk. While I watched them scurry about, I decided to leave and go to Boston. They were good children, and it was true that they would be well taken care of. I admitted to myself, as difficult as it was, that perhaps I didn't have the strong maternal feelings that I should. But on the way back to the house, I felt better, relieved at having decided. I planned to go in two days.

That night, I woke from a sound sleep to hear Elizabeth crying. I went to her room, where I found her coughing and with a fever. Joshua had left the day before, and Sarah had gone to Springfield to visit her sister for a few days, so I was alone with the children. I took care of Elizabeth; she felt better that night, but then young Joshua came down with the same malaise. The next day, I was sick too.

There was no mercy for me. The illness continued unabated for three days. Coughing and vomiting took most of my time. I cared for the children as best as I could, but I knew it wasn't enough. I wouldn't be able to go to Boston in time before the cannon arrived.

Sarah was back the next day and took care of all of us. I worried about her getting sick, but she said she'd be fine and proceeded to give us the care we needed. As I sat at the kitchen table on the fourth day of my illness, I realized that the only way to get word to my father was to send a letter. But I wasn't sure whom I could trust.

There were still some loyalists about, though they professed allegiance with the patriot cause. Two of them, Tom Jenkins, and Jack Williams, both of Brookfield, confided to me in early November that they were leaving for Boston soon to join the loyalists. They planned to go to Gloucester, buy a boat, and sail into Boston, thereby avoiding the rebels patrolling the road at Boston Neck. I had no idea if their plan would work, but I needed to find out if they were still in town. I hadn't seen either one of them in weeks. It took me three days, but I found out that they had already gone. Tom was single and would not be missed by many. Jack had a wife and two children. His wife, a devoted patriot, refused to leave with him, so he went alone. As far as I know, they never saw each other again.

I sat in my bedroom one afternoon and wrote the letter after considering whom I could trust to take it.

Dear Father,

Word came to Brookfield last week that Knox is bringing the cannon from Ticonderoga to Cambridge to use against you and the others in Boston to force a surrender or evacuation.

Knox has forty-two sleds of cannon and estimates arriving in a couple of weeks, no later than the middle of January. Even if he does arrive then, they have no gunpowder or shells of any size. He has requested these from a Colonel McDougal in New York. If you wonder how I know this, it is because I read the letter Knox wrote to Washington. His messenger stopped at the house, and I went through his satchel looking for information I can share with you.

Knox writes that the only news of Colonel Arnold's attempt on Quebec is that houses were burned, and that Arnold is at Point au Tremble. Montgomery went to Arnold with many men and artillery. Knox believes that Montgomery has taken Quebec.

Please share this information with General Gage and others who can use it wisely.

Desire it as I might, I cannot join you. I thought of leaving and taking this message to you in person but find that that can't be.

I miss being with you.

With sincere love and affection,
Your daughter,
Bathsheba

I folded it, sealed it in three places with wax, and put it in my dresser. I still wasn't sure whom I could find to take it.

I didn't have to wait long. The next afternoon, Joshua told me about Dick Andrews from the southern part of town, across the river, who was harassed unmercifully because he had declared that the king is the rightful ruler and rebellion is treason. Joshua thought it likely his house would be burned, or he'd be exiled for his beliefs.

Early the next morning, I went for a ride, crossing the bridge over the river while keeping an eye out for Dick. I knew who he was but had never spoken with him. As I neared his house, I saw him loading a small cart. I stopped and sat on the horse waiting for him to notice me. He talked to himself as he worked. I coughed; he looked up at me. He put a basket in the cart and came toward me.

"Mrs. Spooner, what are you doing here? This isn't any place for a lady like yourself. You might get in trouble talking with the likes of me."

I chuckled, thinking that if he only knew what I'd done.

"Hello, Dick. I hear that you've had trouble with some of the men in town."

He leaned an elbow on the back of the cart before scratching his chest. He shook his head. The pained look on his face was unmistakable.

"I was born here, buried my parents in the cemetery, and worked hard at everything I've ever done, and now, because I think these so-called patriots are wrong, they're going to push me out of town." He raised his palms. "I don't know where to go or what to do."

"You may not know, but I do," I said dismounting. "I need to talk to you for a few minutes."

We went into the house and sat on two rickety chairs that he hadn't put in the cart. I took the letter from my riding coat and held it in my hand.

"You must go to Boston, Dick. That's the only place for people who believe in the king's authority as we do." His eyes widened a bit when I said that. "Yes, I'm a loyalist too," I confided.

"But I don't know what to do when I get there. I don't even know if I'd get through." He scratched his head. "I don't have much," he said gesturing out the door toward the cart. "Do you think they'd let me in?"

I leaned over and touched his hand. "Yes, they will. You have to go and not just for yourself but for me." He was clearly confused. "Let me explain. I need to get this letter to my father, Timothy Ruggles."

"I know who your father is," he said.

"He's in Boston, and I cannot get to him. Because we believe as the British leaders there do, you must go for me. He must get this letter as soon as possible." I took four gold coins from my pocket. "These are for you," I said. His eyes never left the coins. I was fairly certain he'd never seen so much money at one time before. "It will help you when you get there." He held out his hand, but I closed mine. "Only if you agree to do what I ask."

He nodded several times and held out his hand again. I gave him the coins. He looked me in the eye.

"I have nothing to stay for," he said. "I'll take your letter."

"This is especially important, Dick. Far more important than you can believe. I'll not tell you what is in the letter. You don't need to know." I stood and stepped toward him. "You must leave today. This must be in his hands by the end of the day tomorrow. Do you understand?" I handed him the letter. He took it and held it tight.

Then he stood up, too. "I'll deliver the letter," he said. "I'll leave soon."

I wasn't sure he'd get through the rebel guard at the Neck, but he was my only hope. I shook his hand. "Thank you, Dick. When you get to Boston, tell the guard that the townspeople here ran you out of town, and that you want to be with your own kind. That should get you in. Tell them you must see General Ruggles."

I walked outside and mounted my horse.

He followed me.

"Leave now and travel fast," I told him. "Do not stop until you reach Boston." There was nothing more to say, so I wheeled about and headed home.

All that day and well into the night, I thought of Dick venturing to Boston. I had faith that he'd get the letter to my father, but I wasn't sure when that would be. If he stopped at a tavern on the way and drank up some of the money I gave him, I knew I'd never get a response.

I couldn't sleep; I lay in bed with my eyes open, my mind churning with what I'd done. It occurred to me that I was a spy. I had taken information from the rebels and had passed it on to the opposition. I smiled at the thought that I'd done something to harm the American effort at rebellion.

My thoughts turned to what could happen if I were caught. It wouldn't take much for Dick to give up the letter. The typical punishment was whipping, a hefty fine, or banishment. But these were not typical times, so what might happen was not beyond my imagination, but it was more than I cared to entertain. I'd acted and must bear the consequences, whatever they may be. I closed my eyes but did not sleep.

A few days later, I was playing a game with the children in the parlor when Jesse came tearing into the kitchen, leaving the back door swinging open in the wind.

"Mrs. Spooner! Mrs. Spooner! The artillery train is coming through."

My heart began to beat faster, and I felt a light sweat on my forehead. A jolt of fear ran through me at the thought of my having read Knox's letter, even though, at the time, I hadn't been caught.

"Colonel Knox and the artillery from Ticonderoga will be here in a few minutes," he said.

I'd met Knox once when I was fourteen and had gone to Worcester with my father. My father knew him, though he didn't like him. Knox was a fat, smiling bugger who had given me a lecherous wink. I never told my father about it.

I realized that Washington and his rebels were more resourceful than I thought they would be, and it was possible, I admitted to myself, that they could win the war. And then, where would I be?

I heard loud voices outside. Leaving the children to their game, I wrapped my thick wool shawl around my shoulders. As I stepped out the front door, I saw a group of men and horses coming from the west. I stood and watched as the artillery train went by. Many of my neighbors and other townspeople stood on the sides of the road, offering food, whiskey, and cigars to the men, who accepted them gladly. Colonel Knox, seeing me and knowing full well who I was, smiled and tipped his hat when he rode by.

"Bastard," I said under my breath.

I went inside, slamming the door closed.

The children looked up, startled by the sudden noise.

Sarah came in from the kitchen, a large spoon in her hand, to see what was the matter. "It's just the men going to Cambridge with the cannon," she told the children. She went back into the kitchen.

When word reached Brookfield that Boston had been evacuated, I knew that my father had gone, but had no way of knowing where. To my surprise, I received a letter from him three weeks later, brought by a rider from New York.

> *My dearest Bathsheba,*
>
> *I am writing these few words to make you acquainted with my safety. Evacuating Boston after the rebels forced us out with cannon was something I did not want to do, but it would not have been safe for me to stay. I'm at Staten Island and beginning efforts to bring together an association of loyalists. I know that soon I will be fighting against those who have shared Massachusetts with us. It may seem odd to you, but I find it a more difficult decision than I expected it to be. Fighting against men I know and once respected for their intellect and demeanor may be a personal challenge, but the usurpation of government is one of the greatest wrongs any people can do.*

I pray that you are safe and will write to you when I can. That may be infrequent. Do not write to me for it is too dangerous for you.

I am, as always, your loving father.

I kept the letter a secret, sharing it with no one.

He made no mention of my letter. I knew that even if Dick had made it to Boston, and Father had received it, nothing had been done to prevent Washington from using the cannon. My spying hadn't made any difference.

One evening during dinner two weeks after the evacuation, Joshua told us what he learned at Cooley's, where he'd spent a good part of the afternoon.

"What I heard was that Washington had two thousand other men work through the night to place fifty-nine cannon atop Dorchester Heights. They wrapped straw over the wheels to minimize the noise as they hauled the heavy cannon up the hill. They finished one hour before dawn and waited to see what Gage would do." He ate some potatoes and smiled at me. "I'm sure that Tommy Gage and your father shit their drawers when they saw what was waiting for them," he said with a cackle.

"I am going to Worcester to see my sister Mary, and will be back tomorrow afternoon," I told Sarah early the following week.

"Shall I tell Mr. Spooner when he returns?"

"I doubt he will be back before me, but if he is, yes, tell him."

Jesse saddled a horse for me, and a few minutes later, I was off.

It was a pleasant spring morning, and I enjoyed the ride alone, some time with no annoyances. It was horrible of me to think it, but I realized there were times when I wished I'd not had children.

I had brought Father's letter with me and was still debating whether to show it to Mary when I arrived at her estate.

Dr. Green was a strong supporter of the patriot cause. He provided Mary a good life on the large estate he owned on the northeastern side of Worcester. It was located on a hill overlooking a large pond with meadows beyond it. A large grove of elm trees surrounded the property, giving the home a stately appearance.

"It is good to see you," Mary told me as I walked into the entry hall. Mary's house was four times the size of mine. I envied my sister, for Dr. Green was a fine, upstanding man, a real pillar of the community, unlike my unpleasant, unkind husband.

"I never get tired of visiting you," I told her, smiling.

We settled into a small parlor at the back left of the hall opposite the wide mahogany staircase leading to the second floor. A servant brought us coffee and little pastries on a silver tray and put it on a side table.

"I have something to show you," I told her, deciding in a second about the letter. "A letter from Father."

"From Father?" Mary said, surprised.

I handed it to her. "I received it three weeks ago and have not told anyone else about it."

Mary looked at me for a moment, considering my strong political sympathies, knowing any prolonged discussion on the subject would bring about an argument she did not want. She took the letter but did not open it. "You do know that John is strongly for the patriot cause."

I began to say something, but Mary held up her hand. "I do not want to discuss it with you, for our ideas run in opposite directions, and discussions will only lead to us arguing. John is here and should be down in a few moments. I don't think I will mention the letter to him, for any word about Father or his association annoys him."

I drank my coffee while Mary read the letter.

"Staten Island?" she asked. "I assumed he would have gone to Nova Scotia with the rest." She folded the letter and handed it back to me before picking up her coffee cup. "He is ready to fight. Not surprising."

I let out a deep sigh and shook my head.

"What's wrong?" she asked.

"I wonder what my life would be like if I wasn't so much like Father. Would I be a better mother, be more compassionate, less judgmental? Of course, thinking about what might have been doesn't change what is."

She took my hand in hers. "Bathsheba, each of us is as we are. Our thoughts and experiences, our personality, make us what we are. Mother and Father are both strong personalities. You are more like them than the rest of us, except for John. He's just like Father. Make your life the best you can. Strive to be happy."

I was about to tell her my life got less happy with each passing day when John walked into the room.

"Bathsheba," he said enthusiastically, for I could tell he always enjoyed my company despite my allegiance to the Crown. I think that, in his view, my beauty, grace, intellect, and wit made up for my political shortcomings. I enjoyed his company as well, something that, at times, confused me, for I didn't like others who supported the rebels.

"John, it is very nice to see you."

"You should come to visit us more often. Shouldn't she?"

"You can visit us anytime," Mary said, patting my hand.

"That's truly kind of you. I will come more often in the future. It would be nice."

"How are things in Brookfield?" John asked.

"Dreadful. Joshua is away for weeks at a time. When he is home, he is at the tavern every day and ignores the children. We speak as little as possible. It is almost an unbearable situation."

Mary and John looked at each other. They knew it was not a happy household, but apparently had not thought it was that bad.

"There are times, and forgive me for saying this, that it would be better if he met with an accident on one of his trips and never came home."

"Oh, it can't be that bad," John said.

I looked at him, feeling sad and weary. "It's not good," I replied. "It gets worse every week."

Mary looked at me, perhaps understanding for the first time the depth of my unhappiness. John poured a cup of coffee and sat on the divan next to her.

"Is it truly that bad?" he asked.

"I am thirty-one years old, trapped in a loveless marriage to a man I cannot bear to be near. My children are growing up in a difficult household, much as we did. It is becoming intolerable. I lie awake at night, wondering if this is the way it will be for the next twenty or thirty years until I die. Contemplating that is like staring at a blank wall—there are no answers."

John and Mary had nothing to say to that, no comforting reply. Their silence told me they now knew that it was true, and they recognized the reality of my misery and unhappiness.

I remember clearly that it was July 18, 1776, when a rider from Worcester brought the *Massachusetts Spy* newspaper, which had printed the Declaration of Independence, to Brookfield. Word of his arrival spread quickly, and within two hours, a crowd of two thousand people from all parts of the town gathered near the town green to hear it read. I fought my way through the crowd to stand as close as possible to David Hitchcock, a member of the Brookfield Committee of Correspondence. People stared at me as I passed, wondering what a loyalist would want with a declaration of independence from Britain. The crowd was silent as Hitchcock signaled he was ready to begin. In a loud, booming voice, he read:

> In Congress, July 4, 1776. The unanimous Declaration of the thirteen United States of America, When in the Course of human events, it becomes necessary for one people to dissolve the political bands which have connected them with another, and to assume among the powers of the earth, the separate and equal station to which the Laws of Nature and of Nature's God entitle them, a decent respect to the opinions of mankind requires that they should declare the causes which impel them to the separation. We hold these truths to be self-evident, that all men are created equal, that they are endowed by their Creator with certain unalienable Rights, that among these are Life,

Liberty and the pursuit of Happiness. That to secure these rights, Governments are instituted among Men, deriving their just powers from the consent of the governed. That whenever any Form of Government becomes destructive of these ends, it is the Right of the People to alter or to abolish it, and to institute new Government, laying its foundation on such principles and organizing its powers in such form, as to them shall seem most likely to effect their Safety and Happiness. Prudence, indeed, will dictate that Governments long established should not be changed for light and transient causes; and accordingly all experience hath shewn, that mankind are more disposed to suffer, while evils are sufferable, than to right themselves by abolishing the forms to which they are accustomed. But when a long train of abuses and usurpations, pursuing invariably the same Object evinces a design to reduce them under absolute Despotism, it is their right, it is their duty, to throw off such Government, and to provide new Guards for their future security. Such has been the patient sufferance of these Colonies; and such is now the necessity which constrains them to alter their former Systems of Government. The history of the present King of Great Britain is a history of repeated injuries and usurpations, all having in direct object the establishment of an absolute Tyranny over these States. To prove this, let Facts be submitted to a candid world . . . .

I stopped listening and slowly made my way back through the crowd and headed home, dazed by what I'd heard. I must have been a lonely figure, walking the dry dirt road with my head down. I heard the roar of the crowd as Hitchcock read on. I stopped as a single tear rolled down my cheek as I grieved for what was lost.

"If only my father were here."

I walked slowly, not thinking about where I was going, my legs taking me home by their own accord.

CHAPTER 9

It was a cold, snowy February day in 1777 when a young man arrived at my doorstep too sick to continue on his way.

Sarah's son was at the well, fetching water, when he saw someone staggering along the road.

"He fell in the road right in front of the house," Jesse explained when Sarah opened the back door. Jesse had kicked it with his foot, sending a loud thump-thump throughout the house.

When I heard the noise, I was in the children's room and ran down the back stairs.

As I came into the kitchen, I saw Jesse holding the boy limp in his arms.

"He's very sick," Jesse said.

As if to prove the point, the boy broke into a loud, wet cough, doubling over from the force of it.

Sarah guided him to a chair near the fireplace.

The warmth was perhaps so welcome, so good, that the young man collapsed, barely conscious, slumping into a chair by the fire. After a few moments, he looked up and saw me. Neither of us could have had any idea how we would change each other's lives.

He had a ragged coat wrapped around him and was not wearing a hat. His hands and face were red and raw with the bitter cold, and his boots were tied together with strips torn from the hem of his coat. His hacking and coughing came from deep in his lungs. I put my hand to his forehead; he had a fever.

His clothes were soaking wet, and they steamed as he sat by the roaring fire. Jesse kept some clothes at the house so he ran and got them. They were about the same size.

Sarah and I peeled off the boy's tattered garments and saw the blue tint to his skin. His hands were numb, his toes dark blue, almost frozen. We put on the dry clothes and wrapped him in a blanket. Sarah, who mothered over him like a brood hen, fed him, a spoonful at a time, a small bowl of hot samp—a mush of ground corn and milk. He shivered, obviously needing warmth and rest. Assisted by Sarah, I helped him to one of the bedrooms and got him settled under a thick, warm quilt. Sarah made up a big fire to drive off the chill. He lay there in the soft light coming through the windows and looked at me. I could tell he was sliding into a deep and troubled darkness.

"Thank you," he croaked. It was apparent that his throat hurt. It sounded as if he had swallowed glass. "I'll be on my way tomorrow."

I stood next to the bed, took his hand, and rubbed it. I watched as he drifted off into a fitful sleep.

A howling snowstorm descended that night, the wind screaming around the eaves as the blinding snow blew every which way. There would be no traveling for him for a few days at least.

For the next two days, he stayed in bed, Sarah and I tending to him. The children were curious about him. They asked to see him, but I told them they couldn't, for he needed rest.

The third morning he was awake and alert when I went to see him. I stood with my hands on my hips, looking at him, knowing that he needed me more than anyone else at the moment.

"Feeling better?" I asked, putting my hand to his forehead. "The fever has broken."

"Yes," he croaked in a raspy voice, as he lifted his head from the pillow. "I slept well. What day is it?"

"You've been here three days," I told him. "It's Wednesday."

He fell back onto the pillow and put his right arm over his eyes.

I watched him for a moment, his fine features apparent even through the mask of sickness. I could see that he was older than I had first thought. "Are you hungry?"

"Yes."

"I'll tell Sarah to fix you a light breakfast. Do you want to go downstairs, or do you want me to bring it to you?"

He thought about it for a moment. "I want to come down, at least for a while. I need to move about."

I watched him get out of bed, groaning a bit with pain. I took his arm to help steady him. Slowly we went down the stairs. When we got to the bottom, he looked up, full of gratitude for my care and kindness. I led him into the east parlor and sat him at the dining table.

Sarah made him a light breakfast of a soft-boiled egg on toast, a weak porridge with healing herbs, and her special tea that included a mixture of rum, honey, and lemon.

He looked at the food as she placed it before him, eyes wide and ravenous.

"I'm starved," he said.

Sarah watched him closely. "Now," she said in her motherly voice, "eat slowly, a few bites at a time. If you gobble it, you'll get stomach sick, and I have no intention of cleaning that up."

"I'll take it slow," he said.

"Good. It will help get your health back. I've got some chicken soup on the fire so you can have a cup of that later if you'd like. When was the last time you had anything to eat?"

"The morning I came here." He coughed again and wiped his nose with a cloth I'd given him. "A woman gave me some cheese and a hunk of bread."

I sat at the table with a cup of tea and one of Sarah's pumpkin muffins. I nibbled at it, pinching off small pieces with my fingers and alternating each piece with a sip of tea.

"What's your name?" I asked.

"Ezra. Ezra Ross."

"Where are you coming from, Ezra?" I asked.

"New Jersey," he said around a mouthful of porridge. "I was with the army. We fought at Trenton."

"So, you're a Continental then."

"Yes. Enlisted with my brothers last year, right before the battle at Breed's Hill." I appraised him closely for he looked too young to be fighting in a war.

"How old are you?"

"I'll be seventeen next month."

"You're only sixteen?"

"Yes. My brothers are all older than me, but I convinced my parents to let me fight with them. Fighting in General Washington's army is a privilege."

"*You* fought at Breed's Hill?"

"Yes," he said, looking at me.

"You were fifteen when you enlisted?"

"Yes, I was. I may have been young, but I had no trouble fighting for the patriot cause," he said defiantly.

"Where do you come from?" I asked, taking another piece of muffin.

"Linebrook in Ipswich."

"You were walking from New Jersey to Ipswich? How long have you been on the road?"

"Almost a month. General Washington sent many of us home for the winter because we weren't well—there was smallpox and dysentery—and they couldn't feed us." He erupted into a loud, harsh cough and had to rest for a minute. "There weren't enough tents for all of us, so we took turns sleeping in them. It didn't do any good. It was so windy and cold we were never warm."

This gave me hope, since an army that can't feed itself is doomed to defeat. To support the war, taxes, as levied by the Provincial Congress, had increased every few months in Brookfield to the point where many people could not afford to pay them.

"You're too young to be fighting," I said.

He sat up in the chair and looked at me with a hard, determined stare that surprised me. "Our freedom is at stake. It is the very thing we fight for, and I fight willingly." He took the last spoon of porridge. "I am not too young."

"Where did you stay?" I asked.

"In barns and sheds when I could. Otherwise, in the snow in beds made of branches under pine trees."

The children came running in and sat asking him questions which he answered patiently.

I watched him as he talked with them. Even though he was sick, he was a handsome boy with blue eyes and a shock of brownish-red hair. He had freckles across his nose, and sensual lips.

After finishing breakfast, Sarah gave him another cup of tea and rum and instructed him to go back to bed when he finished it. As he took the last sip, he coughed again, deep and raspy, from his chest. Sarah was in from the kitchen in a moment, giving him another rag in case he needed to blow his nose or spit out phlegm, then helping him up.

"I think I will have Dr. Foxcroft look at you," I told him.

He reached and took my hand. "There's no need. I'll be fine in a day or two."

"You're not going anywhere until you are well."

After helping him back to bed, I sent Jesse to get the doctor.

An hour later, Dr. Foxcroft, wrapped in a heavy wool coat, appeared, trudging through the snow and up the stone steps to the door. I heard Sarah open the door before he knocked.

I came in from the east parlor. "Thank you for coming, doctor," I said.

He took off his coat and handed it to Sarah.

"Where is he?"

"Upstairs in bed." Sarah led him upstairs, while explaining what she and I had done for him. I watched them go up the stairs.

Twenty minutes later, Dr. Foxcroft reappeared. Sarah and I heard him coming down the stairs and went into the parlor to meet him.

"I bled him to get rid of the bad humor and balance him." He reached into his bag and took out a glass vial. "Give him this every four hours for the next two days. Mix a half teaspoon with a small amount of warm wine."

"What is it?" I asked.

"One of the best things for a cold—sweet oil, pennyroyal water, and spirits of hartshorn. He needs plenty of rest and light meals, soup, and crackers, or bread. If he is not better in three days, send for me."

Sarah brought his coat, and he left before I had a chance to pay him. Apparently, he did not want to spend more time at my house than he had to.

In three days, Ezra was up and around. His appetite returned, and he began to speak of leaving for home soon. I didn't want him to go. My motherly instincts, which I had thought were gone, were now in full force. I did know, however, that I wanted to take care of him because he was young and good-looking. And because he needed me, something no one older than my children had done in a very long time. It lifted my heart to be able to help him.

"Don't leave yet," I told him. "Stay until you are sure your strength is back."

He sat on the divan next to me. We were alone in the house. Sarah had gone to her home in the nearby town of Western, and the children were with Martha. I'd made a pot of tea and, as we sat in the parlor drinking it, I noticed, under his unshaven face, what a handsome man he would become. I looked at his strong hands that clasped the teacup; I took in his eyes, alight with a youthful glimmer. A sudden wave of desire fluttered through me, something I hadn't felt in a long time. I watched him as he walked to the kitchen for cookies that Sarah had made. He was a well-built man. My need for physical contact was almost overwhelming, and suddenly it burst forth, emanating from me in waves. I felt a warmth in my thighs and realized I wanted him, motherly instincts be damned.

"Are you alright?" he asked as he put the cookies on the table. "You're flushed."

I slid toward him until our thighs were almost touching. I could tell that he was frightened and excited at the same time. It was likely that no woman, except his mother and sisters, had ever been this close to him.

"I'm fine," I said as I put my hand on his arm.

He swallowed hard and started to move away.

"Don't. Stay right here."

The back door opened and in walked Joshua home three days early. Ezra and I stood up, and I stepped away from him.

Joshua came into the room and looked at us, unsure of what was happening.

"This is Ezra Ross," I said. "He was sick and needed help, so he stayed here. Dr. Foxcroft saw him, and he will be leaving next week for his home in Ipswich."

Ezra turned and looked at me, surprised at my statement since he had told me earlier that he planned on leaving the next day.

"Your wife gave me good care," Ezra said.

Joshua did not offer to shake hands. "Good," was all he said.

"Go to the tavern," I told him. "They'll be expecting you."

He raised his head and looked at me. "I'll go where I want, when I want." He left the room, went out the kitchen door, and mounted his horse. We watched as he went in the direction of the tavern at a slow walk. Most likely, Ezra did not know what to say, which was why he said nothing.

The mood was broken; I was angry at my husband's return.

Ezra stayed a few more days and prepared to bid farewell to me. We were alone again, the children having gone with Jesse. Sarah was visiting a friend, and Joshua was off somewhere, no one cared where.

We stood in the east parlor a few feet from the front door. Ezra seemed unsure of the situation. I sensed his anxiety and put him at ease before taking his hands and placing them on my hips before wrapping my arms around his neck.

"I am glad you found yourself at my door," I told him in a soft, seductive voice.

"I have to go," he said, taking his hands from me before swallowing hard. His fingers trembled. "I want to get home within a week."

I realized I had frightened him, for he was just an innocent young man. I dropped my arms before taking a step back.

"I'm sorry if I upset you," I said "but you've seen my life here. Caring for you has given me a purpose and made me feel things I haven't in years. I know you have to go, although I don't want you to."

"I have to leave now," he said, moving toward the front door.

"I know you do." I stepped forward and gave him a brief hug.

He tentatively put his arms around me, then turned and walked out the door.

I followed him and stood on the granite step. The day was partly sunny with a light wind; it would make for good traveling.

"Here," I said, giving him two gold coins for his ten-day trek to Ipswich. "If you ever pass this way again, please stop to see me."

He gave me a small smile but said nothing.

He turned and waved.

I waved, raising my hand halfway before moving it to my mouth while a little sob escaped me. I watched for a moment until he was over the crest of the hill and gone.

I doubted I would ever see him again. My life was back to the sad state it had been before he had arrived. As I stood on the steps, looking up and down the road, I remembered my childhood and how, for a couple of years at least, it had been wonderful and happy. Since then, my life had consisted of ever-increasing difficulties, things I didn't want to deal with, things that fate had forced upon me. I felt a grinding hollowness. Anger rose in me; I hardened with stern resolve before I went back in the house, determined to find a way out of my dreadful marriage.

Two weeks after Ezra left, I returned home from a few days' visit with my mother and found a Negro woman in the kitchen.

"Who are you?" I asked.

The woman looked at the floor and didn't reply.

Joshua came in from the parlor.

"This is Juba," he said, "I've hired her to help Sarah."

"Sarah doesn't need any help," I said, looking at the woman. She was young, no more than twenty, pretty, with a good figure.

I rolled my eyes and shook my head. I took Joshua by the elbow and led him into the parlor.

"Sarah does not need any help," I repeated.

"Ah, but there is where you are wrong. She's getting older, and it's difficult for her, you know that." He looked at the kitchen door. "Juba's very helpful and pleasant," Joshua said. "She'll sleep on a pallet in the upstairs storage room." He smiled at me. "Is it you don't like Negroes?" he asked with a sneer.

"No. It's just that I think you like this one too much."

In late July, I stood at the window in the east parlor watching the rain fall on a dreary afternoon. My thoughts drifted as they usually did on days like that to my marital mess. The previous night was like many others, but the memory was burdensome. After the children and I had finished dinner, we sat enjoying a quiet evening. I was reading a book, *Little Goody Two-Shoes*, to them. Our peace and quiet were interrupted by Joshua stumbling into the house in a foul mood after spending a couple of hours at the tavern. He ranted at me for a few moments before turning his wrath on the children. I still wince at the memory of them looking at me with the saddest eyes, as if trying to understand but unable to make sense of why their father treated them so harshly.

My thoughts then slipped back to a memory of when I was eight or nine, and Father had brought us an adorable puppy, a barnyard mix. He was the sweetest animal, always happy and ready to cuddle or play from the moment he opened his eyes each morning.

To make my children's life a little happier, three weeks after Ezra left, I got them a puppy, a spaniel, that they named Tulip. They loved her at first sight. It made me glad to see them so happy.

A little more than three months after Tulip came to us, the children and I were gone for the day. When we came home Joshua was there, but Tulip wasn't. He announced that he'd gotten rid of it.

"It bothered me," he said. "I never wanted it here in the first place."

Elizabeth and young Joshua both began to cry. They asked him over and over why he'd done this to them.

"What will happen to Tulip?" young Joshua asked.

His father ignored him.

I was so stunned I couldn't find the words to express my anger.

Young Joshua clutched my dress and looked up at me. "Why is Father like this?" Elizabeth asked, biting her lower lip, as tears streamed down her cheeks. "Why does he treat us so badly? Why can't he be nicer to us?"

My frustration boiled over at not being able to do anything about it. Joshua and I fought bitterly that night.

The rain fell as I hugged myself tighter, knowing that I had no answers for my children.

On an early August day, I was surprised at the sound of the tramp of many feet on the road. I looked out the window and spotted Ezra marching on the road with other men, all of them carrying muskets. I knew it was a militia regiment bound for some battle. Ezra spoke to a man for a moment, motioning to the house and nodding as the man spoke. As he stepped onto the walk, I hastened to the door.

My heart gladdened at his return. In the months that he'd been gone, he had changed. His face was fuller, he'd grown taller, wider of shoulder, more powerfully built, and more handsome. His eyes were keener; they met mine with a clear, warm regard and flashed with emotion. He looked like a man, not a boy. I wanted to touch him, but didn't, knowing that my husband was somewhere about town. He could be home again at any time.

"I thought I'd never see you again," I told him.

"I can only stay a couple of days," he said. "I'm off to the army for a four-month enlistment. My captain gave me permission to stay as long as I catch up with them. I told him you are a relative, that I wanted to see you before I went off to war again." He looked sheepish. "At least part of that is true."

"Why are you fighting again?"

"I have to. General Washington needs every man he can get. The British have taken Ticonderoga, and we have to stop them from any gains they make. Two of my brothers are already there. It's my duty."

I was torn between this man, a patriot who excited me so much, and my loyalties to the British.

"I thought about you," I told him.

"I thought about you, too."

I touched his hand. "That's good," I said.

"Yes, it is. I've thought of you quite a bit over the last few months. You were always on my mind. I wondered how you were, and if I would ever see you again," he said with an unmistakable warmth. He put his pack on the floor by the door and leaned his musket against the wall.

I took him by the hand, leading him to the east parlor. As we settled ourselves on the divan, he turned to look at me. "There's a great need for volunteers, and Ipswich was required to field men. I also got an eighteen-dollar bounty for enlisting."

"Oh," I said.

"While those are good reasons, the best one is that I could come through Brookfield again and see you."

I smiled, a surge of happiness enveloping me, an emotion I hadn't known for a long time.

"I despise the war, but I'm happy it brought you here again."

"You mean you wish the British would win?"

I looked at him in surprise, for he had never before spoken of my loyalty to Britain. I stood and walked toward the kitchen.

"You must be hungry," I said. "Come get something to eat. Juba will fix you something."

"Who's Juba?"

"A Negro woman my husband hired after you left."

Ezra enjoyed the food, obviously feeling content when he was done.

"Juba's very nice," he said.

"Yes, she is," I said, thinking of my success in preventing Joshua from molesting her.

The children were outside, so we joined them, and Elizabeth, who had become Ezra's favorite, rushed to him. He greeted the three of them warmly. We all walked to the center of town; it was a beautiful, though hot, summer afternoon. We strolled for an hour, making our way to Martha's, only to find she'd gone to Worcester. As we walked around, crickets chirped loudly, bees buzzed from flower to flower, and the world was full of life. It was a lovely afternoon.

I enjoyed the pleasant interlude, imagining what it would be like to be married to someone like Ezra. I longed to be rid of Joshua. With every passing day, my aversion to him had grown stronger. I enjoyed being with Ezra; it thrilled me. That, and the fact that someone wanted me in return. Though Ezra never acknowledged his feelings for me, from the moment he had walked in the door that day on his way to Ticonderoga, I knew that he had them. I could tell by the look in his eye.

"I'm glad you're here," I told him as we began making our way back to the house.

"Me too," he said with a twinkle in his eye.

CHAPTER 10

During Ezra's time with us in February while I had been nursing him back to health, Joshua had taken a liking to him, which surprised everyone. The day he returned to me, we had a wonderful dinner; the conversation was the most enjoyable I'd heard at our table for a very long time. With Joshua's blessing, Ezra settled himself into the upstairs room with the three sleeping pallets used for those travelers or business acquaintances of Joshua's who stopped by now and then for a night.

Throughout that first day and into the evening, I had felt the deep longing for Ezra return, the warmth running through me, leading me to try to find ways to be alone with him. He was receptive to my advances, seeming to want me almost as much as I needed him. But our efforts at intimacy were thwarted by the constant presence of people in the house.

The morning after Ezra had arrived, I found him in the barn brushing a horse. He loved horses and would spend hours with them if he could. The door was open, and I saw him with the jet black mare. I approached slowly, not wanting to startle him. He heard the hay crunch under my feet and turned. He placed the brush on the top of the stall wall and came to me. I slipped into his arms and we kissed, the passion we'd held for too long erupting in a second, flashing between us, igniting our desire. We kissed and fondled for a few minutes before young Joshua, all of eight years old, came running, hollering for me. We quickly adjusted our clothing. Ezra picked up the brush, grooming the mare just as Joshua came barreling into the barn, colliding with me.

"Mother, come in. You got something. A man brought you something!"

I felt my hair to make sure it was not disheveled, took my son's hand, and led him out of the barn. Before we reached the door, I turned and smiled at Ezra. He gave me an even brighter smile that was lit by the smoldering ardor of a young man finding his first love.

The next morning, he told everyone he must leave to get to New York. No one wanted him to go, but he had to report for his enlistment, and it was a week's walk. He bid good-bye to the children and Joshua, thanked Sarah and Juba, leaving his farewell to me until last. After gathering his pack and musket, he made a pretense of forgetting something he'd left in the barn, and the two of us went looking for it. As soon as we were inside, we embraced, kissing with affection and lust. We looked at each other—a moment of truth at last.

"Please don't go," I said.

"I have to."

"Come back to me," I said. "Stay of out harm's way and return as soon as you can."

"I will."

We held each other and I kissed him.

"I have to go," he said again.

I wiped a tear away and nodded. Ezra kissed my hand and was on his way, ardently promising me that he'd see me again as soon as he could.

"I'll be back when my enlistment is over."

I couldn't stop thinking and dreaming of him for days after he left. I felt young again.

A week after Ezra's departure, Joshua's behavior became more abusive, particularly to Sarah's son, Jesse, who, in turn, was less respectful to Joshua by the day.

Joshua sat at the table in the kitchen reading the *Massachusetts Spy*. Jesse brought in an armload of wood and began placing it next to the fireplace. Several pieces crashed to the floor with a loud bang.

Joshua stood quickly. "Stupid boy!" he yelled. "Can't you even bring in a load of wood without trouble?"

I saw Jesse glance at his mother, who was in the far corner of the room. She gave a slight shake of her head—a clear warning to be quiet. "Pick that up and stack it right," she said.

The boy picked up three pieces, but the largest slipped from his grip and banged to the floor again.

Joshua fixed him with a hateful stare and slapped him in the back of the head, hard enough that the boy's eyes watered. Joshua threw down the newspaper and stalked out to the barn.

"He's an old fart," Jesse said to his mother and me. "Thinks he is such a good man, but he's not. He's not a good man at all." He stacked the wood. "Bastard," I heard him mutter.

"Shhh, don't say that!" Sarah whispered. "He might hear you."

"Oh, so what?" He went back out to the woodpile to bring in more wood.

I started to laugh.

Later that day, I overheard Jesse talking with Sarah.

"If he keeps that up, I'll pummel him until he can't stand," the boy said.

Sarah nodded in agreement. She'd been the target of Joshua's venomous comments on more than one occasion in the past week.

"Be careful, and don't do anything foolish. But he has it coming, for certain."

I decided to take the children to Worcester for a few days to visit Mary and John. When we returned at mid-afternoon on Friday, the minute I walked in the door, I knew something was different, something was wrong.

I heard someone in the kitchen. When I opened the door, Juba was standing by the window, looking out.

"Where is Sarah?" I asked.

Juba turned her eyes downcast as she twisted a towel in her hands. "She's at her home," she said in a whisper.

I cocked my head to one side and looked at her as I wondered what reason there could be for Sarah not being there.

"Did Mr. Spooner send her home?"

Juba nodded.

"Where is he?" I asked.

"He left three days ago. I don't know where he was going."

"You've been here the whole time?"

"Yes." She started crying. "I'm sorry, ma'am, but there was nothing I could do. He made me."

I sat at the table and motioned for her to sit. She did, tears running down her face.

"What are you talking about?"

"I'm so sorry, so sorry," she sobbed. "I didn't want to, but he made me. He made me," she cried, her body shuddering with the force of her tears. "He told me to go upstairs to the guest bedroom. I said no, but he slapped me. He made me do it."

I knew the answer but had to ask the question. "He made you do what?"

She gulped air and covered her face with the towel. "He made me lay with him."

A cold fury swept through me, a burning desire to exact vengeance on the miserable excuse for a man I'd married.

"Was it just that once?"

She nodded and held up one finger.

I took her hand in mine. "It's not your fault," I said. Not knowing what else to do, I dismissed her. "Go up to your room and lie down."

Juba nodded and sniffled, wiping her tears with the back of her hand. She stopped at the foot of the stairs and looked at me.

"I'm so sorry, Mrs. Spooner. "I'll have to leave now and find somewhere else to go."

"We'll talk about that tomorrow. Go up to your room."

I intended to confront Joshua the minute he stepped into the house. I'd known he'd been unfaithful to me but never in my own home, as far as I knew. How dare he do this to one of our servants? My anger grew; I realized it was a bad situation that would not get any better.

I saw a heavy cast iron frying pan hanging from a hook on the wall. I picked it up, hefted it, feeling the solid weight in my hands. It felt good. I swung it hard, wishing Joshua was on the receiving end.

It was a week before he showed his face again.

"How dare you?" I yelled when he stepped into the kitchen. He stepped back and looked at me, a dangerous gleam in his eye. "How could you do that to her, you bastard?"

"I don't know what you're talking about," he said.

"You son of a bitch. Forcing her to have relations with you."

He smirked.

I slapped him hard, hard enough to make him stumble backward. He put out his hand to catch himself but hit the table, knocking a ceramic bowl to the floor, where it smashed into pieces that flew across the room. I took the frying pan from the wall and brandished it at him.

"Get out," I hissed. "Get out now." He stood near the door.

"It's my house," he said, "and I'm not leaving."

I wound up and threw the pan at him; it missed his head but caught him on the shoulder knocking him back against the door. I grabbed the fireplace poker and advanced on him. The anger I'd held for so long came screaming out of me.

"Get out or I'll beat you senseless."

He groped for the door handle and stumbled outside. He backed away, never taking his eyes from me.

"You'll pay for this," he hissed. He got on his horse and rode away.

I dropped the poker and sank to my knees. "Oh, dear God, how did my life get like this?" I asked, putting my head in my hands.

My husband did not return home for two weeks.

To add to my misery, word spread through the colonies of the American victory at Saratoga. On a crisp October afternoon, the brilliant fall foliage painted the rolling hills under a clear, hard blue sky, I walked down the road on my way to Waite's Tavern to meet a man who'd known my father on Staten Island. He'd gotten word to me that he needed to see me. Hearing hoofbeats, I looked behind me. A horseman came at a fast trot, stopping for a moment, the horse capering about.

"Did you hear? We won at Saratoga," he said excitedly, not having the slightest idea who I was or where my sympathies lay. "Burgoyne surrendered his entire army," he said grinning at the news. When I made no response, he turned and rode on. I stopped at the top of a small hill and considered the implications of the victory. I closed my eyes and shook my head, thinking of what it would be like to live in Brookfield if the Americans won. I feared that the American forces were gaining the upper hand and might soon win the war. My heart was heavy, and I was afraid.

I later learned that, when Burgoyne surrendered, it was agreed that his men would be marched to Boston and sent back to England, which I was glad to hear. However, the Continental Congress revoked that part of the surrender agreement, so the prisoners were to be marched to the towns outside Boston and forced to build their prison camps.

CHAPTER 11

I hugged myself, feeling the cold air wrap its fingers around me as I stood on the front porch watching Burgoyne's troops pass by on their march toward Boston. Six thousand men took three days to go through town. The prisoners came through in groups of a couple of hundred with stragglers at the end of every group. The men had no muskets or bayonets, only their uniforms and packs. The uniforms of the officers were fairly clean, while those of the infantrymen were filthy, caked with mud and stained with God knows what. They were a sight with their heavy red wool coats, the white straps of their packs crossing their chest, some wearing ragged black tricorn hats, others bareheaded. I thought of my father and how resplendent he'd looked in his uniform.

I watched as hundreds of townspeople came out and stood by the sides of the road watching the prisoners, sometimes taunting them with cries of "damn lobsterbacks!" or "bastards!" Some spit in the soldier's direction. The Continental soldiers guarding the prisoners did nothing to stop it.

The road turned into a quagmire, difficult to travel on foot, on horseback, or in a carriage. The plop, slop, plop sound of their footsteps through the thick mud continued all day.

I was about to go inside when three British officers approached me.

"Are you Mrs. Spooner, by chance? General Ruggles's daughter?" one asked in a clipped accent.

"Yes, I am."

"The tavernkeeper suggested we see you."

"Oh, why?"

"We are seeking shelter and food for the night for us and some of our men. The Continentals want no part of feeding us, so we must seek our own accommodations."

I looked at them for a long moment before making my decision. Joshua was in Charlton and would not be back until the next night. There was plenty of food to give them, and the officers looked weary and hungry.

"Yes, I'll help you. Come in."

They kicked and scraped as much mud from their boots as they could before entering.

"Oh, the warmth feels good," the shortest one said.

"How many men do you have?" I asked.

"One hundred eighty-nine, but there are forty or fifty needing food and shelter more than the others."

"Men can sleep in the barn. You three can sleep upstairs in the room at the end of the hall. There are three sleeping pallets there."

"Thank you very much. You have no idea how relieved we are to find someone who will help us."

One of the officers was short and very thin. He looked at me. "There are several other men that could benefit from your kindness. Is that possible?"

I considered his request for a minute. "Yes. They can sleep on the floor in the kitchen and the east parlor. However, they must get as much dirt off of them as possible before they come in. I don't want my house a dirty mess when you leave."

The officers looked relieved.

"I am Major Bronson. This is Captain Morgan and Lieutenant Bailey."

I nodded. "I am Bathsheba Spooner." I turned my head toward the kitchen. "Sarah, Juba, come here."

The two servants came out of the kitchen, Juba holding a large iron spoon and Sarah a knife in her hands. Sarah stopped at the sight of the officers, eyeing them suspiciously.

"These officers and some of their men will be staying here for the night. They will sleep in the barn, the guest room, and in the kitchen and east parlor. Prepare some soup, corn mush, and bread for them."

Sarah didn't move, and Juba slowly backed into the kitchen.

I turned and saw her standing there. "It's alright, Sarah. Now do what I told you to do."

Sarah turned and walked into the kitchen, where, a moment later, pots and pans began to crash and clang.

"I don't know how we can thank you," Captain Morgan said.

"You could begin by not having surrendered. Winning the war would be a good thing, too," I said, leaving them to get their men.

Fifteen men went to the barn while ten others stayed in the house. It was cramped but warm. Sarah and Juba gave the soldiers bread, cheese, soup, and corn mush for which they were grateful. The officers dined on roast chicken, cold beef, tongue pie, carrots, boiled potatoes, and sweet pumpkin tarts with the children and me.

"So what will become of you?" I asked.

Major Bronson finished chewing a piece of chicken before answering.

"We are to be sent back to England on the condition that we will not fight again in the war."

"Those were terms negotiated by General Burgoyne," Morgan added. "So your father really is General Ruggles."

I smiled at the mention of my father's name. "Yes, he is."

We talked after eating, Juba having cleared the table. Sarah was in the kitchen, washing the dishes, when I called for more wine. I told them of my father, his rise to power, his role in the French and Indian War, and his stubborn refusal to acknowledge the rebels' cause. After finishing two bottles of Madeira, they excused themselves and went to their pallets.

The men left early the next morning, all of them thanking me for my hospitality. Lieutenant Bailey smiled as he went out the front door. "We will do everything we can to win the war," he told me.

"Not if you keep surrendering, you won't," I said before stepping inside.

The next day, another group of officers approached me with the same request; I gave them the same assistance. By the late afternoon of the next day, all of the prisoners had passed through town.

Joshua was delayed for two days. I learned later that he had stopped at Waite's Tavern on his way home for a mug of hot buttered rum, which was where he heard what I had done.

I was sitting in the east parlor working on a needlepoint while the children played a game when I heard the pounding of hooves. Looking out the window, I saw my husband charge into the yard. The kitchen door slammed open, and he blasted into the kitchen.

"Where is she?" I heard him bark.

Startled, Juba dropped a pan; it banged on the floor.

"She was in the parlor," I heard her say.

The door to the parlor hit the wall when he opened it.

"You had British soldiers in this house?"

I turned and looked at him, unruffled by his question.

"Yes, I did. Twice, as a matter of fact. Do you object?"

"Yes, I object. Of course, I object."

"So, you are for the rebels." I turned back to my needlepoint.

"I am not for either side. I don't care who wins or loses. It makes no difference to me."

"Then what's the problem?"

"The problem is it cost me money. You are spending too much, and this is just over the top. How many of them did you feed?"

"Fifty or so. I gave them two meals each, so a hundred meals for whatever the cost."

"Damn it, Bathsheba. Business is not going well. You can't spend money like that."

"Leave me alone," I said as I went to the stairs to my bedroom.

I was dressing one morning when something outside caught my eye: a man in a British infantryman's uniform was walking the road. I could see that Juba was at the well, filling a large bucket when she looked up and saw him.

She asked him something. He had his hands inside his sleeves, his collar pulled up as high towards his head as it could be. He nodded. I saw that he had an unruly mop of red hair and he looked hungry. Juba pointed the way to the kitchen door, and they went out of my sight.

When I went into the kitchen, he was sitting next to the fireplace. Juba had given him some bread and cheese and was fixing him a cup of tea. He wolfed down the food and made as if to leave.

"Who are you?" I asked.

The man stood and bowed his head. "Alexander Cummings, of his Majesty's army," he said in a Scottish brogue. "But I'm called Alec. I'm from Larkhall in the south of Scotland and joined the army two years ago now."

I smiled. "And what did you do in Scotland?"

"I was a butler for a country gentleman for a year before joining the army."

"Really?" I saw a possible use for the man. "How old are you?"

"Twenty-two."

"You should be in Boston, shouldn't you?"

He waved his hand, dismissing the idea. "No one cares where we go. They don't want the expense of feeding and sheltering us. No one paid any attention to me when I left."

"Would you like to be my butler?" I asked.

He stood there, looking dumbfounded. I expected that my offer would certainly improve his prospects.

"Well?"

"I don't know if you'd want the likes of me in your house, a British soldier and all."

"I side with His Majesty."

He began nodding and smiling. "Yes, I'd like that very much."

I looked him over, noticing his dirty breeches and torn coat sleeve. "We'll get you some new clothes. Those will not do for my butler."

On the second Monday in November, I saw Ezra again. I was just inside the barn, running my hand down the neck of a chestnut mare, when I caught sight of a man approaching the kitchen door. My hand dropped to my side as I stood open-mouthed, looking at his back and his worn brown deerskin pants and gray jacket.

"Ezra," I said.

He turned at the sound of his name. When he saw me, he dropped his musket and pack and ran to me. We stepped inside the barn and embraced before he kissed me.

"I've missed you," I sighed.

He ran his hands over my clothing.

"Oh," I said, my breath coming in spurts. "Not here, not now." I composed myself and ran my fingers through his hair. "Thank God you're safe," I said. "Let's go in."

He followed me into the kitchen. The children, Sarah, Juba, and even Joshua, were glad to see him, relieved that he was unhurt. Ezra spent the next hour answering our questions and giving descriptions of the battles as he ate everything Sarah placed in front of him.

"The other men I was with kept on kidding me about being in a hurry to get home," he said around a mouthful of food. "I'll admit," he said, swallowing a hunk of bread, "that smell of fallen leaves reminded me of home. There were lots of brown oak leaves hanging on until the last, fluttering in the wind." He broke off another piece of bread. "One man kept telling me to slow down." He glanced up at me and I saw the need in his eyes and knew why he had hurried. "He asked if I was so homesick that I was going to run the rest of the way to Ipswich."

We all chuckled at the jest. "They didn't believe that I was stopping here. It's such a beautiful house they must have known it belonged to a rich man and lady. They thought I was kidding them." He took a long drink of freshly pressed cider and looked around at us. "They'd only seen a few houses like it before, all of them near Boston, and none like it since we'd left Saratoga. They didn't believe that I knew the people who lived here."

I felt a warm tingling running through me as I watched Ezra eat, careful to keep control of my reactions lest Joshua suspect something.

The next morning, Ezra said he'd slept well. We walked to the barn to visit the horses.

"Why are you so glum?" I asked.

"I realized last night that I've been away from home for a long time and miss it. I want to stay here, but I need to get home too. Do you understand?"

"I do," I said. "You just need someone to be with, the right type of person," I said in a sensual whisper, making sure I gave him a flirtatious smile.

"That would help."

"Would someone like myself do?" I asked, running a finger under his chin.

"Yes," he said, swallowing hard.

I put my hand gently on the side of his face moving my thumb back and forth across his cheek while staring into his eyes.

"We'll see," I said with a playful laugh, moving my hand to his upper thigh, giving him a start.

I needed to see Martha and visited with her for an hour or so. When I returned, Ezra was waiting for me like a puppy. He was adorable, and I wanted to have him right then and there.

After dinner, Joshua announced that he was taking Ezra to the tavern, that it might do to raise his morose demeanor, that it would cheer him. What Joshua didn't know was that Ezra was glum because he and I couldn't be together.

"I'll join you," I said.

"What do you mean?" Joshua asked. "You're not invited."

"Think of it this way," I told him. "*I'm* taking Ezra to the tavern. *You* can join *us* if you want."

He obviously didn't know what to say, so he stood there like a dumb ox.

We arrived at the tavern a little after six o'clock and sat at a table just past the fireplace in the corner. I heard the door open and saw Alec come in. He stood with a group of men near the bar. He got a mug and sipped it slowly as he looked around the room.

"Ephraim," I called to Cooley. "Two rums if you please."

"Make that three," Joshua said in a loud voice. Cooley brought them and put two down in front of Ezra and me, and handed one to Joshua.

"And who do we have here?" Cooley asked.

"This is Ezra Ross, late of the Continental Army. He is visiting us on his way home from Saratoga," Joshua said. Men from other tables looked up. Cooley looked at Ezra with a special interest.

"Fought in any of the other battles?" Cooley asked.

Ezra nodded before taking a sip of his rum.

Cooley and the other patrons waited for him to elaborate, but he didn't continue.

"What battles were they?" I asked.

Ezra looked up at the two men as if just realizing they were there.

"I was at Bunker Hill, New York, Trenton, and Saratoga."

A man sitting at the next table overheard him. "Did you say you were at Trenton?"

Ezra saw the man, an older sort, a pig farmer from the look and smell of him. Ezra nodded.

"What was it like?"

Other men had stopped talking and were listening to the conversation.

"It was cold," Ezra said, staring at the table, moving his finger around in a circle. "Awfully cold."

The men sat there waiting for him to continue, curious about his adventures.

"A snowstorm started on Christmas Day. We were on the other side of the river from Trenton waiting for orders."

Cooley walked over from the bar after throwing a towel over his shoulder. All the men were now facing Ezra. Joshua sat there obviously fascinated by the tales such a young man might tell. As I looked at Ezra, I could only think about undressing him.

"About mid-afternoon, we started for the river. Our packs were heavy with three days of food and plenty of ammunition, sixty balls for each of us. It was dark and raining when we reached the river." He drained his mug and looked around suddenly aware that there was no other sound except that of his voice.

Cooley took the mug and filled it. Ezra picked it up, took a sip, and wiped a hand across his forehead. "The river was high, the current was strong, and there was ice floating everywhere. I never thought we'd make it across alive."

A small log in the fireplace popped and fell onto the hearth. A man kicked it back into the fireplace with his boot.

"I heard the weather was bad," asked a man standing behind Ezra.

"It was horrible. Unlike anything you've ever seen. We made it to the river and had to wait for the others to get there, so we pulled down fence posts and started fires to warm ourselves. We couldn't keep them going. It started snowing but turned to hail, then rain, then the temperature dropped. Everything froze quick-like before it started snowing again. The wind blew the whole time. The snow came down so hard you couldn't see six feet in front of you. I remember everything was so quiet. There was no sound." He sat up a bit in the chair and put his arms on the table, fingers on either side of the mug.

"Did you think you were going to die that night?" Cooley asked.

Ezra snorted. "Five or six times. I was walking so slow that I thought if I didn't keep moving, I'd freeze to the ground." He chuckled, but it was a sad sound. "We made it across a couple of hours before dawn and walked for miles before reaching the town.

We ran across the field as fast as we could, racing the men next to us as much to stay warm as to be the first to reach the enemy." He drained the rest of his mug and put it on the table.

Cooley made no move to take it but waited like the rest to hear about the battle. "It was all over in less than an hour. Our guns were wet and frozen so they wouldn't fire, but we fixed our bayonets and charged. The Hessians ran, we chased them, they surrendered, and while it was still snowing, we marched back to the river and crossed to the other side." He held the empty mug up to Cooley.

Cooley grabbed it and hustled to the bar, filled it, and returned. "What happened then?" he asked, placing the mug on the table.

"I was so cold I didn't sleep for another day and didn't dry out for a week. That and sleeping out in all sorts of weather because we didn't have tents, made me sick, and that's why they paroled me in January."

The room was quiet for a moment. Someone threw a couple of logs onto the fire. Drinks were refreshed and men packed and lit their pipes; the good smell of tobacco smoke drifted around the room.

"Saratoga was better," Ezra said with a hollow laugh. "I helped General Arnold when he was injured. He fell off his horse right at my feet." People were crowding around again listening carefully as Ezra continued his tale, looking at the table while running a finger around the rim of his mug.

"I'll remember the day as long as I live. It was October 7th, and the dawn was crisp and clear. There was that sharp tang in the air when you know fall is here. Nothing much happened in the morning, but by mid-afternoon, they started firing at us. They were too far away so they didn't hit us, just wasted their ammunition. I was with General Learned's men, and we were in the center. Both flanks started moving towards the Brits, and we had to stay there. We were all itching to fight. By that time, our blood was up, and we wanted to finish this.

"Finally, the order came for us to attack. We faced the grenadiers, who were about two hundred yards away." He took a sip of his drink and looked at the men gathered around him. He turned to me and smiled.

"This officer came galloping at General Learned. He was going so fast I didn't think he'd be able to stop; I thought he'd run right into the general. Then I realized it was General Arnold. His horse never stopped moving. It pranced around, ready to run. General Arnold raised his sword and yelled for us to attack. He turned and rode right toward the British line.

"We all ran behind him, but we couldn't keep up. He ordered us to halt when we were about sixty yards away. Both sides aimed and shot at the same time."

Someone coughed and a couple of chairs scraped the floor as people moved their seats around. Cooley quietly filled mugs without being asked.

"I'd seen men die before but never like this," Ezra continued. "Two men to my right, a man was shot in the eye, and the back of his head exploded, spraying blood and brains on my jacket. The soldier next to me on the left was shot in the chest and fell at my feet." Ezra inhaled deeply and let it out. "I reloaded my musket while I saw big spouts of blood pouring out of him every time his heart beat. I thought I'd be killed too, then and there. The enemy fired again, and musket balls whistled through the air all around me, but none of them hit me.

"We followed General Arnold and overran their line and drove them back to two redoubts on either side. The general stopped right in front of me when his horse screamed and started tottering from side-to-side. It was shot in the leg. The general fell and the horse landed on his leg. He'd been shot in that leg too. He screamed as we pulled the horse off of him. I grabbed him by the arms while two others got his feet. I slipped and fell on a rock. I landed about two feet from the general's face, as close as me to you," he said to Joshua. "Even though he was shot, he looked right at me. 'Never give up,' he told me. We tied up his wound, made a litter, and got him back to headquarters."

No one said a word. I'm sure many in the room were thinking the same as me; I found it hard to believe that someone as young as Ezra had been through so much. My heart went out to him. I put my hand on his arm and squeezed it. He gave me a wan smile. Patting his shoulder, I stood up and went to the door.

Joshua looked at me with a steady measuring gaze. He was everything Ezra wasn't, and I despised him for it.

Two days later, I was finally alone with Ezra in the west parlor. He stood by the window looking out. I took his hand, pulled him away from the window, and kissed him.

"Do you want to defile my marriage bed?" I asked after breaking the kiss.

"Yes," he gasped.

I went into the kitchen, telling Sarah to take the children and Juba to her house and not to return until five o'clock. A few minutes later, the children were gathered up and gone. Joshua was away again and wouldn't be back for three days. I sent Alec on errands that would keep him busy until much later. I took Ezra by the hand and led him upstairs to the bedroom.

The afternoon sun shone through the windows, dappled against the walls through the leaves of the large pine tree outside. I stood watching him, with a burning need. I took off my clothes and cast them to the floor in front of the fireplace. I stood before him naked. I knew he'd never seen a woman fully undressed before. I watched as his eyes soaked in every part of my body. He trembled as I undressed him.

When we stood naked together, I kissed him gently while pulling him to me. We sank onto the bed, and he touched me. He ran his fingers through my hair, down my neck and shoulders to the swell of my breasts, then to my hips. Then I touched him. It was a shock, a pleasurable shock that caused his whole body to quiver. I watched him as he looked at me. He raised up to kiss me and the world fell away.

Ezra had sent a letter to his parents telling them he was staying with us. As he told me more than once, his parents were eternally grateful that I had saved his life. Their response, which he received two weeks later, told him to stay as long as he wanted, but to be home by mid-April to help on their farm.

During the next few weeks, Ezra helped around our farm and traveled with Joshua on several trips of a couple of days each. Joshua's liking for him increased, which irritated me and confused Ezra. I missed him when he was away and was glad Joshua was gone. Ezra and Alec become friends of sorts, as much as Continental and British soldiers can be, and spent some time together.

In the second week of February, I hadn't had my menses and began to feel as I had when I was first pregnant with my children.

"Oh, dear God, no," I said. "Please do not let me be pregnant." The realization began to settle upon me. I sat on my bed and put my head in my hands. "What am I going to do? What am I going to do?" I sat up and looked out the window at the hills in the distance, the leafless, gray skeletal trees matching my sudden mood. I remembered mine and Ezra's first time together when, in his excitement, Ezra did not follow my instructions to prevent pregnancy but had the next three times. I won't tell him, I thought. He'll leave if I do. Besides, if I am pregnant, being with him again will make no difference. I couldn't pretend the baby was Joshua's since we hadn't had relations in months.

I went downstairs and, while the children played quietly in the other room, knitted the wool yarn carded from our small herd of sheep. The repetitive motion soothed my mind and let me think clearly. As I sat there, the smell of the wool reminded me of my earlier years in Hardwick when my sisters and I spun wool and knitted. While I didn't enjoy it then, I looked back on it nostalgically. My hands moved, the needles clicked, and I became lost in thought. I knew something must be done about Joshua. I couldn't stand to live with the man any longer.

The next afternoon, I'd contrived to get everyone out of the house, and Ezra and I were together again, naked in my bed.

As I lay in his arms, I ran a finger over his lips and cheek thinking of what a fine lover the young man turned out to be. He stroked my thigh with the back of his hand.

"I never thought I'd be so happy," he said, turning on his side to face me.

I closed my eyes. Then I flipped onto my side and looked at him, full of happiness and gratification.

"It would be wonderful to be like this all the time, wouldn't it?"

"Yes, it would," he said, smiling broadly. "It would be perfect." I reached down and took the light blanket and drew it up over us. I snuggled down into his shoulder and began running a finger over his chest.

"Just think, all of this," I said, sweeping my arm around the room, "the house, the farm, and I would all be yours."

He sighed contentedly.

"But there is only one way for that to happen," I said.

He drew me close and put his hand on my lower hip. "And what is that?" he asked playfully.

"My husband must die."

He raised up quickly on one elbow and stared at me, his eyes wide in disbelief. "What?" he asked, wrinkling his brow as if he'd misheard me.

"My husband has to die."

He sat up and stared at me.

"If he is gone, then there is nothing to stop us from continuing this way," I said, smiling at him. "Think of all the fun we'd have. If Joshua were gone, we could be together as often as we wished."

"How would this happen? Is there someone you know who could do such a thing?"

"Oh, yes. You."

He sprung out of bed, startled at my suggestion. "Me?" he choked. "Are you crazy?"

"No, I'm not mad and yes, you. It would be so simple. All you have to do is put something I will give you into his drink and bid him goodnight. When you wake in the morning, all our troubles will be over."

He looked at me hard for a minute, as if trying to figure out if I was serious. Did I really want him to kill Joshua? He seemed to have grasped the idea that I was indeed intent on having my husband killed.

"No, no, I can't do that," he said.

I sat with my legs folded under me, hands on my knees, leaning forward toward him. He looked at my breasts as I moved.

"I can't do that, Bathsheba."

"Why not? You've killed men in battle."

"Yes, but they were strangers, men I didn't know at all, who were trying to kill me. I've spent time with your husband. He knows me and, as far as I can tell, doesn't wish me harm."

I lay back on the bed and stared at the ceiling. "I've spent far too much time with him," I said.

Ezra got out of bed, dressed, and gazed at me, lying there naked. He left the room. I heard him clomping down the stairs.

"What kind of life have I made for myself?" I asked. I thought of my situation; unable to get away from a bad marriage to a man I hated, three children that at times I wanted nothing to do with, and a young lover who got me pregnant in our first lustful encounter. And the war, always in the background, the chaos of war.

A week after discovering I was pregnant, the night before Joshua and Ezra left for Princeton to inspect Joshua's potash operation, I arranged for Ezra to meet me in the barn. Wrapped in a heavy wool cloak, I waited for him, my hand in the pocket of the silk apron I wore. He came, not quickly like he usually did, but at a slow walk, almost as if he were afraid of what I had to say. We hadn't been together since the night I asked him to kill Joshua. I waited until he was near me.

"I've come to the conclusion that you don't want me anymore."

His head snapped back. "What?"

"You don't want to be with me."

"But I do, you know I do."

I looked at him, searching for signs that he was lying. I saw none.

"We have no chance unless my husband is dead, and if you won't kill him, I will find someone who will, after you leave for home tomorrow."

His forehead creased, and he squinted a bit before cocking his head slightly to one side. "But I'm not going home tomorrow."

"You are unless you agree to get rid of him." I crossed my arms and waited for him to respond. "And you will never share my bed again until he is dead." I began walking to the door.

"Bathsheba, wait."

I turned and watched him for a minute as he considered my request.

"I'll do it."

I wrapped him in my arms and kissed him. I took a small bottle of poison from my apron pocket and gave it to him.

He looked at the brown bottle with a cork stopper, holding it up to the light.

"It's clear," I said. "So he won't know you gave it to him. You only need a small bit of this in his drink."

"How much is enough?" he asked.

"Just count to two when you pour it, and that will be plenty." I smiled at him, a happy smile. I was almost giddy with joy. The idea of Joshua gone forever made me happy.

"I'll give it to him tomorrow night when we get to Princeton."

I kept smiling until an idea popped into my head.

"Don't wait until tomorrow. Give it to him tonight at dinner."

"Tonight?"

"Yes, my sweet love, tonight. Why wait until tomorrow?"

He looked unsure at my suggestion.

That evening at dinner, the opportunity arose, and Ezra poured some of the poison into Joshua's wine. Ezra and I waited for him to drink, but he didn't. He looked at the glass and pushed it away. "Sarah!" he yelled. "Bring me some cider."

"You don't want your wine?" I asked. "How unusual for you."

"My stomach is upset. Has been all day. Wine just doesn't appeal to me tonight."

Ezra cast an apprehensive look at me, but I was not concerned. There would be other opportunities.

Early the next morning, before Ezra and Joshua set out, I took Ezra into the west parlor and closed the door telling Sarah that we were not to be disturbed.

"You have to get rid of him," I told Ezra.

He looked at me with sad eyes. I could see the indecision.

"I don't know if I can. I mean, what if he tastes it? He'll know I'm trying to poison him. What will I do if he finds out?"

"You have to. There is no other way for us to be together as husband and wife. Don't you see that? No one will miss him except Ephraim Cooley. You will have plenty of opportunities. Do it and be done. Come back to me when it is over, and we'll begin our life together."

He slowly shook his head, unsure if he would be able to carry out the plot.

"Don't you want to be with me?" I asked.

"Of course I do. Don't even question that, but there has to be another way."

"There is none," I said, my voice rising as my tone hardened. "If you love me, you will get rid of that vile man." I kissed his hand. "Do it for me."

He looked at the floor and nodded. "I will."

Joshua came in. Ezra quickly turned my hand and shook it.

"Ready to go?" Joshua asked.

"Yes, of course. I'll be right there."

"Hurry up. I can't afford to wait all day for you. Be done with this woman and come." He turned and left.

I closed the door when I heard him go out. I kissed Ezra, a deep passionate kiss designed to remove any doubts he may have had as to what he would lose if he didn't murder Joshua.

"Maybe I should stay," he said.

"No."

"But—"

"No," I said. "Leave and come back without him." I opened the door and watched as Ezra made his way to the yard where Joshua waited. They mounted the horses and were off.

With Juba's help, I got the children ready for church. We bundled into our warmest and finest clothes of bright reds, purples, and greens and climbed into the sleigh. In my hand, I clutched the Bay Psalm Book that Jedediah Foster had given me. Alec drove us to the church, where I greeted everyone I knew with a smile.

CHAPTER 12

On that unfortunate Sunday, February 8, 1778, the men must have started out early from Worcester in order to reach Brookfield by late morning.

I sent Alec out to the well for a bucket of water. I watched him because I was thinking of dismissing him. He didn't always do as I asked and that irked me. I wouldn't put up with that behavior from him or any of the other servants. He stood by the well, dawdling, so I put on my wool shawl and went out the kitchen door, intending to tell him to get busy or I'd get rid of him. I got only a few steps around the corner of the house when he moved toward the road. He spent a minute looking at two men who paused as they passed by. As he approached them, one of the men squinted at Alec, in the way people do when they think they know a person but aren't certain. I went down the walk, so I was only a few feet behind Alec.

"Cummings?" I heard the squinting man say. "Is that you?"

Alec stopped, looking hard at them.

"Buchanan," he cried dropping the unfilled bucket. "What are you doing here?"

"On our way to Springfield for work."

Alec looked at the other man, giving him a good look up and down.

"Who's this?" he said, cocking a thumb.

"Bill Brooks. He was with Burgoyne, too. We met at the camp in Rutland," he said, referring to a new prison camp being constructed to house some of the prisoners. "We walked by this house on our way to Cambridge. I remember it. What are you doing here?"

"I work for the woman who lives here," he said, waving a hand at the large house. "Come in out of the cold." He turned around and almost ran into me.

"Mrs. Spooner!" he said surprised. "I didn't know you were there."

"Of course, you didn't. Fill the bucket and come inside." I hesitated, giving the men a good look. "Your friends can come in too." I turned and went back into the house.

A moment later, they followed Alec into the cozy kitchen.

"The gentleman is away," Alec told them, "but Mrs. Spooner is in sympathy with the British cause," he said nodding in my direction.

They stood before the fire, hands outstretched, warming themselves.

"Ma'am, this is Jim Buchanan, a sergeant in His Majesty's army. This is Bill Brooks. They were with Burgoyne, too."

"How do you do?" I asked.

The men removed their hats and nodded. "Fine ma'am," Buchanan said in a Welsh English accent. Brooks said nothing.

"Get them some rum," I told Alec.

He dropped the bucket and water slopped over the side and splashed onto the floor. I shook my head and clenched my jaw. "Sarah will be serving our meal soon, so you can join us."

Alec served the rum, and they stood by the fire sipping it. I hoped that the rum was warming their insides as the fire was warming their outsides.

Buchanan was a good-looking man on the tall side with a firm jaw, long thin nose, hazel green eyes, and a head of thick black hair. Brooks looked like a weasel. He had a large nose, big ears, and dark beady eyes that continually darted around the room. He didn't smell good either.

Within a few minutes, Juba and Sarah arranged food on the table in the dining room. They followed me in. I watched as they looked around at the opulent furnishings taking in every detail. I knew that they hadn't been treated this well in their time in Massachusetts. Prisoners, who were free to wander about since the government couldn't afford to house and feed all of them, usually slept in barns or in the kitchen of those houses whose owners let them in. They ate whatever food they were given.

"Say hello to our guests," I instructed the children when they joined us. They were shy around new people and mumbled their hellos. Brooks shoveled the food down his throat as if someone were going to take it away. Buchanan ate slowly, obviously relishing every bite.

"This is wonderful," he said. "I'm sure I'll not get another meal like this soon." He used his fork, almost daintily putting a small piece of chicken in his mouth and closing his eyes while he chewed. "This is very good. Thank you again ma'am."

"Where are you going?" I asked.

"We're going to Springfield to look for work, but then on to Canada. I left my wife and son there," Buchanan said.

I gave him a curious look, wondering what type of man he was.

After eating, the children played a game while the three of us sat in the sitting room drinking my, or more precisely, Joshua's rum before a blazing fire. As the afternoon progressed, the weather turned, the beginning of a bad snowstorm.

"We'll have to leave soon," Buchanan said finishing his mug and elbowing Brooks, "if we want to get to Springfield before the snow gets too deep. Finish up and let's go." Brooks drained his mug in one swig. The wind whistled around the corners of the house as they prepared to leave. I made a fateful decision.

"You need to stay tonight. There's no use traveling in this blizzard. You'll only lose your way or freeze to death."

"Thank you, ma'am," Brooks in a strong Cockney accent, the first words out of his mouth since setting foot in the house.

"You don't talk much, do you?" I asked.

"Bill's the quiet sort," Buchanan said with a lopsided grin.

"Where are you from?" I asked them.

"I'm from London, Jacob's Island," Brooks said.

"I'm from Abergavenny. It's a little town near Cardiff," Buchanan told me.

"Well, you can sleep in the room with Alec. There are good pallets with heavy blankets."

"Thank you again, ma'am."

"Call me Bathsheba," I said.

"We will," Buchanan said, a warm smile breaking out on his face. "And you can call me Jim."

The weather the next day was no better, so they continued at the house. I sent Alec to Cooley's twice for rum, once in the morning and later, at dusk. He'd had to battle the snow and wind on foot, wrapped in a large, old wool greatcoat of Joshua's that I had given him.

That afternoon, after having drunk several mugs of rum, Buchanan and I were alone in the parlor. I was drunk for the first time in years.

"My husband is away, and he'll never be back," I slurred. "He will never be in Brookfield again," I said, giggling.

"What do you mean?"

"He mistreats me and the children. He spends all of his time at the tavern, and I am sick of him. A man, Mr. Ross, went with him and will poison him. He has an ounce of poison and will give it to him at a convenient time. He promised." I sipped from my mug.

"But he is your husband," Buchanan said.

"I hate him!" I said with a sudden, cold fury. Buchanan stared wide-eyed at my bold admission.

"I have to say, Bathsheba, that it's odd that a woman I don't know, though you've given us warmth and food and drink, would say such a thing to a man you just met."

I took another drink, looking at him over the rim of the mug before walking unsteadily to the window. Looking out, I saw the snow piling up, drifting against the edge of the house. It was still snowing hard.

I turned to him. "Give me more rum," I said, holding my mug out.

He filled it, and then his own, before settling back on the divan.

"You can't leave here until the snow stops," I said. "There has to be twenty inches on the ground now, and it's still snowing."

"I need to see where Brooks has gotten off to," he said. "We'll have to leave soon." He went into the kitchen.

I was right behind him, a bit shakily, and put my hand on the doorjamb to steady myself.

He turned to look at me. "Besides, your husband might be home in a while."

I threw my leather mug, splashing him with good rum before it bounced off the door.

"He will not!" I yelled. "I will never see him again, and I am glad."

He set his mug on the kitchen table and sat on the floor by the fire.

I left him there and went to my bedroom to rest.

That evening at dinner, I made sure I was calm and charming, laughing at the little jests I made and talking about the children, whom the men had seen only briefly. Soon, the conversation centered on Joshua.

"I've decided you must stay until we see if Mr. Spooner returns," I said between bites.

"When?" Brooks blurted around a mouthful of food.

"I don't know. Hopefully never."

Brooks swallowed and looked first at Buchanan and then at Alec for some clarification of my remark. Buchanan shrugged his shoulders while Alec nodded. I had thought that, since Alec knew Buchanan, it would be alright for him to join us at dinner, despite his being a servant.

For the next week, although it didn't seem that long, the revelry continued. Each day we ate and drank all day long. Buchanan and I talked for hours while Brooks was elsewhere most of the time, usually in the kitchen talking with Sarah and Juba, to whom he'd taken a fancy.

Alec attempted to limit the amount I drank. He came to me the afternoon of the third day and, when I told him to fill my mug, he took it from my hand instead.

"Mrs. Spooner, perhaps you've had enough."

"How dare you?" I said slapping him hard enough to leave my handprint on his cheek. He was stunned. He put my mug down and went upstairs. My hand stung so I shook it and sat down. Buchanan watched but said nothing.

On the morning of the eleventh day they were with us, under a clear blue sky, the sun shining brightly as its rays were reflected off the white snow, Buchanan and I went walking, the roads having been cleared by a horse-pulled snow roller.

"I've been thinking," Buchanan said. "Perhaps it is best if your husband does not come home."

I looked at him, trying to discern the reason for his change of mind.

"It's just that you seem so happy when you are not thinking about him, perhaps you are better off if he never returns. And if he does, there are other ways."

I pulled my cloak tighter about me and walked on, contemplating his words.

In mid-afternoon, Joshua returned. Alone.

I was shocked beyond words and tried to hide my dismay. After taking time to compose myself, I faced my husband, the familiar anger returning.

"Where is Ezra?" I demanded.

"He wanted to go home, so I lent him the horse. He said he'd been away too long and wanted to see his family again. I told him to bring it back whenever he could."

I sank into a chair, my dream vanishing before my eyes. The man I hated stood before me, and the man I loved let me down and crept off, not enough of a man to free me from my marital bondage.

Buchanan and Brooks came into the kitchen.

"Who are you?" Joshua asked. Alec came in from the barn having stabled Spooner's horse.

"He is Alec's cousin, and that is his friend," I told him. He had not been pleased with my decision to hire Alec in the first place, especially without getting his approval.

He ignored me and left, heading in the direction of the tavern.

Buchanan looked out the window and saw Joshua talking with Dr. Foxcroft.

"Wait until he finds out how much liquor he has to pay for," Brooks said.

"Who cares?" I snapped. "The man is a worm, and I have an utter loathing for him." I sat in a chair and put my hand to my forehead.

"Are you alright, ma'am?" Alec asked.

"I've never been so stumped in my life," I said, bewildered beyond belief.

Around eight o'clock, Joshua returned home and demanded that the men leave at once.

"Go. Now. I want you out of my house," he said pointing at them.

Brooks gazed at Joshua dejectedly. "Please, sir, can't we stay the night and go in the morning?"

"I think it best if you go now."

"It's cold, and we're hungry," Brooks said. "Won't you let us stay just this one night? We'll leave before first light."

Joshua considered this for a moment. "No. You've drunk twenty quarts of rum since you've been here. It's cost me a lot of money."

"Let them stay tonight, for God's sake," I exclaimed. "They'll be gone long before you get up, and you'll never see them again." I winked at Buchanan.

Joshua seemed to consider my comment for a minute.

"Fine. You can sleep on the floor in the kitchen. Sarah can leave cold biscuits for you for the morning."

The men went into the kitchen, leaving Joshua and me alone.

"If they don't leave in the morning, I'll go to the constable and force them to leave," he told me.

I ignored him.

Then Juba came to the door and motioned for Joshua to come into the kitchen. I followed him.

"What is it?" he growled, his patience running thin.

"I am leaving and need money."

"What are you talking about? You're not leaving here."

"Yes, I am, and you will give me money so I can."

"No, I won't. Mind your place. You are the lowest servant and will do as I tell you." He turned and walked away.

She glared after him. Demanding money from him had not been the best way to handle the situation.

I told her to come with me. We went to the front foyer as far away from the others as possible.

"Do you want to leave?" I asked.

"Yes," she said tearing up. "I can't stay here any longer." She straightened up and looked at me. "I thought he wasn't coming back."

My head snapped up at her comment. "What do you mean?"

"I heard you tell Ezra to give him poison."

"You must have misunderstood what I said."

"No, I didn't." She looked me in the eye. "You should have asked me. I would have done it and gladly watched him die." I grabbed her shoulders and shook her.

"Don't say a word to anyone about this. I will give you money. Just do whatever I ask of you."

It took a moment, but she nodded before going back to the kitchen.

An hour later, an acquaintance of Joshua's, Reuben Olds, who lived in a ramshackle house over the river, visited to discuss some business with him. He was about thirty years old, with a scruffy appearance, always looking like he needed a bath, haircut, and shave. They talked softly in the parlor, their low voices unable to be heard through the kitchen door. Alec, Buchanan, Brooks, and I were in there sitting at the table drinking more rum and nibbling on cheese Juba had made. After twenty minutes, Olds came into the kitchen and stood by the fire.

"He is afraid of you," Olds told Brooks and Buchanan. "He thinks you are going to rob him."

Brooks sat back in his chair, surprised. "Why would he think that?"

"Because he says that a silver spoon and a great deal of pewter are missing."

"What a fool," I said.

Alec was adding wood to the fire and overheard. "There is no pewter missing," he said. "And the silver spoon is where he left it." He went into the parlor to tell Joshua.

Buchanan looked at Olds.

"You've known him long?" he asked.

"Most of my life."

"What type of man is he?" he asked.

"An odd one. He worries more about his money and goods than anything else. Likes his rum. He needs to have it every day, sometimes all day long, like he can't face a day without it."

"Why does he think we will rob him? If we wanted to, we could have any time in the last few days."

"Maybe so, but he's a peculiar man, like I just told you," Olds replied.

Joshua called for Olds, so he went back to the sitting room. A few moments later, he returned shaking his head and grinning.

"He's got his money box, and he'll sleep on the floor of the sitting room tonight guarding it against you two." He chuckled. "Can you imagine any man doing that?"

Sometimes Joshua could act like an idiot, and this was one of those times. "He's probably had more to drink than normally," I said.

Buchanan opened the kitchen door a bit and, looking over his shoulder, I saw Joshua on the floor with the money box under his head. Buchanan shook his head at Joshua's foolishness.

"Here, have a mug," Alec said, giving one to me and then to each man before pouring himself a full one.

The next morning, after I arose, I learned that Joshua felt badly about how he'd treated them and had left five dollars for Alec to treat his "cousin" and friend to breakfast before they left. The three men made their way to Cooley's.

Before Buchanan and Brooks had left, Sarah said she'd asked where they were off to. They said they weren't sure, so she told them they could go to her house for a time until they could figure it out.

Buchanan told me later that they lounged about at Sarah's for several hours and were ready to be on their way to Canada, for he wanted to see his wife and son. They wanted to say good-bye to me and thank me for my kindness and generosity. Knowing Joshua was around, they went back to Cooley's in the late afternoon for some drinks. Dr. Foxcroft saw them there and invited them to his house. While he had no interest in hearing of the righteousness of the British cause, he was intrigued by their situation and wanted to talk with them.

Sometime after nine o'clock, I sent Alec to Cooley's for weak beer for the children; he found out that the men were at the doctor's house. He stopped there, and, while Dr. Foxcroft was busy with something else, he told Buchanan and Brooks that Joshua was in bed, and that they could come to see me. Alec then hurried home to tell me they were on their way.

I met them by the back door and told them to be quiet so as not to wake Joshua or the children. Sarah had gone to her house, so it was just the three of us. We had a light meal with several glasses of wine before I sent them to the barn with three heavy wool blankets each, for it was a bitterly cold night.

My sister Martha and her friend Mrs. Berry had visited a couple of days previous and asked Buchanan and Brooks to do work for them, so I accompanied them the next day. After visiting my sister, and the men having done the work they were hired to do, the three of us went to Green's Tavern in the western part of Brookfield, a few miles from my home. We stayed there drinking until late.

The blue-white moonlight illuminated the snow as we rode the three horses taken from Joshua's stable.

"I gave my handkerchief to Sam Woods," I said, hiccupping because of all I'd had to drink. "He's a British soldier."

"I know who he is," Buchanan snapped. "I told him to leave you alone. Don't you remember?"

I was swaying in the saddle. "No."

"You flirted with another man. Someone who knew you."

"Oh, yes. That's what's-his-name." I laughed at not being able to remember who the man was.

"He knew you well," Brooks said.

"People will talk about this for weeks, you know," Buchanan told me. "A woman of your rank, being with enemy soldiers, drinking in public, flirting for all your neighbors to see. It doesn't look good."

"I don't care!" I yelled. "I don't care what they think. The hell with them all." It seemed that for a long time I hadn't cared about much of anything until Ezra had come along. Now that he had left me, for surely that was what he'd done, I felt devoid of any emotion except anger. I supposed the excess rum did not help, but it blanketed some of the pain. We rode along in silence the rest of the way home.

In the morning, before Joshua was up and about, they scurried off to Gilbert's tavern, just up the road from Green's, and they stayed there until after Joshua had gone to Cooley's, and I told Alec to fetch the men. They visited for a short time, and I sent them to the barn for the night.

Jesse brought them plates of bread and cheese for breakfast, shortly after which, on my instruction, Sarah told them that Joshua was gone to buy oats and would be gone a good part of the day. We ate and drank until we were content, talking about their life back home, feasting on the best food and drink my horrible husband could afford.

Jesse, who at fifteen was a large boy for his age, had no doubt endured Joshua's verbal and physical abuse for too long, so he approached Brooks with an idea.

"When Spooner gets back, you can murder him and be done with it."

I jumped up and clapped. "Yes! Do it!" I said encouraging the plan. "The three of you!" My thoughts raced with excitement. "You can wait until he goes to bed, then kill him. You can throw his body down the well, so it looks as if he fell in getting water in the night."

Buchanan looked at me. "Would he go to the well in the middle of a winter night for a bucket of water?"

I didn't pause to dwell on the implications of his question. "It would be easy for the three of you," I said. "Do it, and it will all be over tonight." I was flushed with delight at the thought that my troubles could be over so soon.

Brooks stared at the floor in silence.

"Well?" I asked him. "Are you going to do it?"

"I don't know."

"What do you mean you don't know? You are a soldier. Killing should not be a problem for you. It is what you were trained to do."

He shook his head. "I can't. Not like that."

"I didn't think you were so faint-hearted." I sat in a chair and thought for a minute. "I know. You," I said, pointing at Jesse, "tell him that a horse is sick and when he comes to the barn, kill him then. Put his body under the horse's hooves, so it looks as if it trampled him."

"That won't work," Brooks told Jesse. "He won't go to the barn. That's what he has you for."

Jesse shrugged his shoulders and nodded agreement.

Brooks turned and looked at me. "If we don't kill him tonight, you going to throw us out onto the road with no food or drink?"

I knew he must be worried that a refusal to kill Joshua would result in losing the comforts they had come to enjoy.

It was the next night when Buchanan approached me as I was coming down the back stairs.

"We're leaving tomorrow morning," he told me. He hesitated before continuing. "I think's it's best if we're not here. Only trouble will come of our staying with you."

"Why?"

"We have to do something to earn a living. We can't sit around all day. You're wonderful to have us here and treat us so well, but we need to do work. I'm a blacksmith by trade, and Bill's a tinsmith. When we were at Sarah's house, I talked with the blacksmith down the way; he said he could use a hand, so we'll go there. Bill doesn't have the right tools, so we might go to Worcester to get them."

"But . . . but you said if Joshua returned home there were other ways to . . . "

He put a finger to his lips. "Let us not speak of that now."

In the morning, they were gone.

I felt restless and bored for the two days they were gone. The children annoyed me, Sarah burned a meal, Juba complained about my not helping her enough, and I didn't sleep well. The next day, I decided to go to the blacksmith's to see Brooks and Buchanan.

Jesse saddled a horse, and I set off. It was only a half-hour ride. I got there just as they were about to leave for Worcester. I dismounted and stood there for a moment, looking around for Buchanan. I saw him at the back of the shed, hammering what looked like a plow point. A few farmers were there, having various implements repaired, and no doubt all wondering what a fine lady like me, whom they all recognized, was doing at a place like that. Buchanan must have sensed that I was there, for after only a minute, he looked up and saw me. He put down his hammer, called over to Brooks, who was sweeping the floor, and the two of them walked over to me.

"He's gone," I said. "Come back to the house,"

Buchanan looked at me with curiosity. "Why didn't you send Cummings or Jesse? They could have come instead."

I ignored the question.

"There's no reason for you to be here when you could be near a warm fire drinking and eating. Come back to the house."

"No," he said. "We have to work. I told you that we can't lie around all day eating and drinking, as good as that is."

I handed the reins of the horse to Brooks before taking Buchanan by the arm and leading him away from the men.

"Please come back, Jim. Keep me company for a short time," I said, putting my hand on his arm. "I'm there by myself. And you know I need your help. I will make it worth your while." I knew he would understand my meaning without my having to explain.

He looked at the ground, moving the dirt and snow with the toe of his boot, before looking at me again. "Maybe we will." He looked back at Brooks. "Billy likes being there."

I mounted, taking the reins from Brooks.

"When?" I asked.

"We'll stop before nightfall."

I wheeled about, satisfied with myself for getting them to return. Then I rode away.

On the way back, I thought of how I could convince them to get rid of Joshua—*if* I could convince them. I felt the chance slipping away. My breasts were sore, and I had little appetite at times. It was only a matter of time before my condition became apparent.

The men stopped at my house but stayed for only a brief time before continuing on their way to Worcester to get Brooks his tools. There was no mention of getting rid of Joshua.

"Where will you be?" I asked.

"At Mrs. Walker's," Buchanan replied, referring to a well-known tavern at the north end of the main road.

"I'll meet you there tomorrow afternoon," I said giving him three Spanish dollars. "For your comfort." And, I hoped, as a down payment for the deed I hoped they'd do.

Buchanan shrugged as if he didn't care. He and Brooks began their walk to Worcester a short time before Joshua arrived home.

Mid-morning the next day, I approached Joshua as he was eating his breakfast.

"I need to go see Mary."

"No," he said without even looking up. "You can't use a horse. I heard about your ride to the blacksmith."

"For God's sake, I need to go see my sister. You begrudge me the use of one of five horses?"

"Yes, I do. You may not use one of my horses to go see your sister or for any other reason." He looked at me over the top of his reading glasses, his eyes flat and emotionless.

I glared at him, the anger boiling within me.

"You bastard," I said.

He smiled.

I made myself ready and walked to Josiah Weldon's house, two miles away on the Charlton road. He loaned me the use of one of his horses, an old gray mare. About halfway to Worcester, it began to rain. I pulled the hood of my wool cape over my head. After a time, the rain began to seep through; it was wet and cold against my clothes. The rain changed to freezing rain when I was a mile from the tavern; it coated me with a thin layer of ice. When I arrived at Walker's that night, I was soaking wet, shaking badly from the cold. I couldn't feel all of my fingers. A boy came out of the stable and took the horse. I gave him two pence with a hand that shook as if I had palsy.

The main room was warm and dry, and I sat near the fire, my clothes steaming from the wonderful heat as I shivered. I smelled the stew as it bubbled in the iron cauldron on the hearth. Mrs. Walker gave me a large cloth to dry myself.

"You'll catch your death if you don't dry out," she said.

I dried off as best I could with the cloth she'd given me.

Buchanan came down from the garret, saw me, and sat at the table.

"I need another," I told her, handing her the wet cloth. She brought me one that I used until it too was soaked through. The feeling in my fingertips returned as Mrs. Walker ladled a bowl of stew, brought me a wooden platter with brown bread and cheese, and handed me a mug of mulled cider. I ate some of the hot stew, feeling my insides warm a bit with each spoonful.

"Any trouble getting here?" Buchanan asked.

"Besides my awful husband not allowing me to use one of the horses?" I ripped a piece of brown bread and stuffed it in my mouth.

"He wouldn't let you take a horse? What an ass he is." He pulled a small piece from the loaf and popped it into his mouth. "Why?"

"He found out about my going to the blacksmith."

"Oh." He motioned for a mug of hot cider. "What did you do?"

"I borrowed one. He's probably wondering where I am."

"Didn't you tell him?"

"I said I was going to Mary's." I finished the last chunk of bread. "Now I suppose I actually have to go." I let out a breath and looked around the room. "Where's Billy?"

"He's out wandering somewhere."

I stayed until around midnight, then left to spend the night at my sister's, only a mile away.

I was back early the next morning and was told by Mrs. Walker that Buchanan was sick. I went up to the room where he slept.

"Jim?" He was dozing, in that place between being well and being sick, and looked up at me. "What is wrong?"

He coughed and spat a wad of phlegm on the floor. "Just a cold, I guess."

"You have to get better."

"I will. I need a day's rest is all."

The door opened, and Mary, Mrs. Walker's daughter, came in.

"Just need to get that broom," she said, pointing to one in the far corner.

I put my hand on his face, caressing him, feeling the stubble on his chin.

I saw her standing there watching us. "You can leave now," I said, dismissing her.

She hurried out the door, her heavy shoes clomping down the stairs.

After a half-hour with him, I made my way down to the main room and sat by the roaring fire, the comforting warmth spreading over me like waves. I needed Buchanan to recover. I did not know what I would do if he did not.

After a few minutes, Brooks came in and sat next to me. I could see that he, too, was worried about Buchanan. Without him, Brooks would probably be lost, always needing someone to tell him what to do and where to go. Buchanan was his sergeant, and Brooks always followed orders. He was not smart, never having learned how to read or write. He looked at me like a sad puppy. He knelt and put his arms around me, and rested his head on my bosom. He sighed deeply. I patted his head as I would a child's, gave him a brief hug, then pushed him away.

Buchanan had related a story to me that, on the troop ship to Canada, Brooks had stolen a shirt from another soldier. Accused, he jumped overboard to escape capture. He was fished from the sea and whipped.

A couple of hours later, Buchanan appeared washed and shaven, looking better than he had in days. He ordered a mug of rum to restore his spirits and took a chair next to me. I was relieved.

"I want you to get me some calomel powder," I told him.

"What for?"

"Elizabeth is sick," I said as Prudence, a helper of Mrs. Walker's, came to stir the fire. I waited for her to leave before continuing. "Have the apothecary give you enough for ten doses. After that, I need you to tell me when you plan to kill my husband so we can get it over with."

I gave him the money and he left, returning a short time later.

"The apothecary said to give her one dose every morning until she feels better. As for your other request, we need to get Billy's tools first, so we can be on our way and able to earn a living."

I nodded, taking the calomel from him, having no intention of giving it to anyone except myself in an attempt to induce a miscarriage when I returned to Mary's house. Once I arrived there, I took two doses; it had no effect on my condition other than to make me sick to my stomach. I didn't sleep well and begged off on Mary's wish that I stay another day.

I returned to Walker's Saturday morning and asked Buchanan what time he would leave for the blacksmith in Western.

"Shortly. We'll stop to get his tools and soon after that, we'll be able to be on our way."

I assumed that meant they would rid me of Joshua sometime in between. I began walking to the door but stopped as another idea formed. "When this is all over, I will write a letter to my father. Will you take it?"

"What?" he said. "Your father? Are you going to him?"

"I don't know."

Buchanan shook his head. "I don't understand why you want to get a letter to him. He has nothing to offer you, according to what you told us. Do you want me to go to Staten Island and hand it to him?"

"I don't know," I said, confused by his questions. "I just want to let him know that I'm well."

"But you're not," he said. "You're under a great deal of strain." He shook his head again, my intentions clearly perplexing him. "I could cross the lines and get there without any trouble, but it would take time."

"Never mind," I said, suddenly frustrated. Still, I left to get the paper and ink.

When I returned, Buchanan wasn't there. Prudence was cleaning the room, wiping tables, and sweeping the floor. I could tell she was watching me.

"What did you tell your sister about where you've been?" she asked. It was a bold thing to say, but she was evidently more curious than concerned about upsetting me.

"I told her that I dined at Mr. Nazro's shop and drank tea there." I gave her a sly look. "It was a pretty good lie."

Buchanan came back a short time later and sat with me.

"I need to go soon," I said. "Now remember, sergeant, once you're done in Worcester, be at my house so we can finish our business together." I looked into his eyes.

He nodded.

With a wink and a smile, I left him and headed home to Brookfield.

CHAPTER 13

When I got home, Sarah was puttering around the kitchen. I didn't even have the time to take my cloak off before she told me that Ezra had arrived the previous night, returning the horse he'd borrowed two weeks earlier.

"I was ironing when I heard a tapping at the window and there he was," she said. "He said he didn't want to see Mr. Spooner because he'd ridden the horse so hard it had hurt its back. I told him to put the horse in the barn and get into the milk room because Mr. Spooner never goes in there. I brought him a plate of warm bread, hard cheese, and cider. He asked where you were, so I told him that you went to see your sister in Worcester and that I didn't know when you'd be home. I gave him two blankets to keep him warm and told him I'd be out to get him in the morning."

Within a minute I was in the milking room.

"You came back," I said, kissing him on the cheek.

"I'm here to kill Joshua. I want to be with you." He took a wooden box, opened it, and showed me a brace of old, worn dueling pistols. "I'll challenge him to a duel and shoot him dead. It's the best way to get rid of him."

While it was legal and honorable, it was too uncertain a way for me. Joshua could refuse to duel because he was a coward, and then where would I be? The challenge would be all around town, and people would begin questioning why Ezra wanted to duel Joshua.

"That will never work," I told him.

"Why not?"

"He'd refuse you."

"What do we do, then?" he asked.

I stroked his hair and kissed him on the forehead. "I have another plan. Stay here tonight. You can come into the house tomorrow after he leaves." We kissed, and I returned to the house to ponder my next move now that Ezra had returned to me. And I was going to have his child.

Joshua was not an early riser, so Ezra shivered from the cold until mid-morning when my husband finally left.

"Go get Ezra," I told Sarah. "Then fix him some hot porridge and bacon."

After he wolfed down his food, I sent him up to the guest bedroom and told him to stay there until I came for him. Joshua was back at noon and dawdled around the house, annoying everyone as he usually did. He finally left for Cooley's in the late afternoon.

Shortly after Alec left to return Mr. Weldon's horse, Buchanan and Brooks arrived and came into the parlor where Ezra and I sat on the divan.

"Ezra, this is Sergeant James Buchanan and Private Bill Brooks of His Majesty's Army. This is Ezra Ross of the Continental Army."

Ezra eyed them with suspicion.

"They're here to help you and me," I told him.

He nodded and opened the wooden box and took out a pistol.

"Spooner will die by this tonight," he said, holding it up, rubbing his palm along the top of the barrel caressing it as he'd done to me.

Buchanan shook his head. "Don't be foolish. A shot will be heard, and people will come running."

Brooks stood opposite the divan staring at me, a silly grin on his face, for he liked being near me, watching my every move.

"If you help me," Brooks said to Ezra, "I'll knock him down and be done with it."

Ezra looked at Buchanan and me.

"I'll help," Ezra said.

"We'll keep a lookout," Buchanan said, knowing Joshua would be home from the tavern soon. The shutters were closed to keep out the cold and to prevent the sight of what was about to take place.

Sarah brought supper and mugs of flip to Ezra, Brooks, and Buchanan. Brooks went to the kitchen and asked for more flip. Sarah brought them another pitcher and a bottle of rum. They downed their liquid courage in a short time, getting drunker by the minute, each taking a turn looking out the front door.

I went upstairs and made sure the children were asleep. Then I went back down the staircase and stepped out the back door, hoping the cold air would help calm my nerves, for my anxiety increased with each passing moment. Joshua would be home soon, and I'd be rid of him. Shivers ran up and down my spine, and my hands shook.

A full moon had risen and its light illuminated the small drifts of snow along the sides of the road, which was covered with ice and snow. The moonlight sparkled off the jagged edges of ice from horses' hooves and wagon tracks, glittering like diamonds. The snow-covered fields shone white, while the distant tree-covered hills were dark.

I scurried back inside and opened the shutters of a window and saw Brooks watching down the road. My eyes followed his gaze; I saw a lantern bobbing in the dark as Joshua made his way carefully along the road.

"He's coming," Brooks said softly before ducking out to await Joshua by the gate.

Ezra and Buchanan were by the door ready to help Brooks when the deed was done. I continued to watch.

Brooks turned his head in Joshua's direction. He must have heard his footsteps crunching on the snow. Nervous and on edge, I opened a shutter a bit and saw Brooks jump out, startling Joshua. Brooks punched him several times in the face before my husband fell to the ground, crying out as the lantern flew from his hand through the air. I turned my head and covered my eyes. I couldn't watch; I felt nauseous and faint.

"What are you doing!" I heard Joshua yell. "Murder!" he screamed.

I winced at the word, but oddly enough, I felt like it wasn't real, more like a bad dream. I closed the shutter and sat on the divan, dazed and dumbfounded at what just occurred. I sat and waited, not sure of what would happen next.

I did not have to wait long.

"He's gone," Brooks said after rushing in. Ezra and Buchanan followed him out.

They came into the house a few minutes later. "It's done," Brooks announced. "He's in the well."

"What?" I was too stunned to process what he'd said.

"Jim and Mr. Ross shoved him in the well."

I gulped. "You can't leave him there. Take him out and bury him in the woods." They looked at me as if not understanding what I was saying. "You can't leave him there," I repeated. "It's our only source of water." I took Ezra's hands. "Please, get rid of him."

He shook his head. "I'm not touching him again."

"Brooks, you can do it."

He swayed a bit. "I'm too drunk."

I turned to Buchanan. "Will you help?"

"No. We're not moving him again. You want him moved, you do it. After all, we killed him for you."

Sarah, Alec, and Juba came in.

"He's dead," I said.

We looked at each other; the enormity of what had just happened settled upon us.

Juba did a little dance and smiled.

"I never liked him," said Alec.

"Neither did I," I said, a manic laugh escaping my throat.

We stood for another moment before Ezra, Brooks, and Buchanan began to move.

"You need to leave here," I said. I ran upstairs and got the money box, for I wanted them out of the house as quickly as possible.

I hurried down the stairs feeling out of breath, as if I'd been punched in the stomach. My hands shook, and I fumbled the box. "I can't open it," I said, handing it to Buchanan, who banged it with his fist three times before it opened, spilling paper money and gold coins all over the carpet.

"There has to be a couple hundred pounds," Buchanan said.

"More than that," I said dropping to my knees, furiously snatching up the money and handing it to Brooks and Ezra. When I got to my feet the three of them looked at me.

"You're going to give us all that?" Brooks asked his eyes wide in wonder.

"No, you fool," I snapped. "Not all of it."

I looked at Brooks and saw his clothes were covered with Joshua's blood.

"Take off your breeches, waistcoat, and shirt," I told him.

He hurriedly pulled them off, tossing them on the hearth.

"Sarah, go up to my bedroom and get a pair of Mr. Spooner's black breeches and coat."

Sarah looked at me questioningly but did as I asked. A few minutes later, she came down the stairs with the breeches, shirt, waistcoat, and jacket belonging to Joshua. She handed them to Brooks, who put them on.

"Get two ruffled shirts and handkerchiefs," I instructed her. I gave Buchanan and Brooks each a shirt and handkerchief before tossing Brooks's bloody clothes into the fire. We watched them burn.

After Brooks was dressed, I handed the men the money. They went to the front door.

Ezra came to me and held me in his arms. I kissed him and ran my hand over his cheek as I looked into his beautiful eyes. Buchanan put a hand on Ezra's arm.

"We have to go," he said.

Ezra took my hands.

"I love you," he whispered.

"I love you too. I don't know when I'll see you again," I replied my heart breaking at the possibility of losing him. I stroked his cheek. "We'll be together again, I promise."

He hugged me one more time before they stepped into the cold night.

Sarah and Juba went into the kitchen. Alec went up the stairs. I sat on the edge of the divan staring at the floor, shaking my head. I needed to get Joshua out of the well.

I looked up and saw Sarah standing there, nervously twisting her apron with her hands.

"I should go to the constable," she said.

"No! Please don't. I'll give you anything you want, but don't go. Not now."

She gazed at me for a long moment, her mouth twisted in disapproval.

"Alright," she said. "Not now, anyway."

"Thank you." I closed my eyes. "Will you sleep with me tonight?" I pleaded.

Sarah nodded and took me by the elbow and led me up the stairs and into bed.

Neither Sarah nor I slept well that night. I constantly stirred, turning from side to side and sighing. The thought of the horrible deed was too much to let me sleep.

CHAPTER 14

Early the next morning, I crept out of bed so as not to wake Sarah, who'd finally fallen asleep. I was groggy from lack of sleep and must have looked a mess. I'd slept in my dress, hadn't brushed my hair, or washed myself. No one else was awake.

I went to the well and stood there before casting a glance down, seeing my husband's stockinged feet. I grabbed them and pulled, but I couldn't budge him; I wasn't strong enough.

"Shit."

I tried again with the same result. I began to shudder with the reality of what I'd done.

"Oh, Joshua, why did it have to end this way? Why couldn't we have loved each other like a husband and wife should?"

I ran into the house, knowing that I had to come up with a story about his death.

I heard someone moving around upstairs; a minute later Alec made his way downstairs.

"Get a horse and go to Cooley's. Ask for Mr. Spooner. Tell them he never came home last night."

Alec cast a sideways glance at me and shook his head, but did what he was told, saddling a horse and galloping off to the tavern, keeping up the charade. I stood outside, waiting for him. He was back in a short time.

"Well?" I asked.

"Cooley was sweeping the floor when I went in," Alec said. "When I told him that Mr. Spooner didn't come home last night, he said Mr. Spooner and Dr. King left at the same time and that maybe he went home with the doctor. I started for the doctor's but turned and came back. There's no reason for me to go there."

"Put up the horse," I told him and went into the kitchen.

A short time later, as Sarah, the children, and I were eating breakfast in the kitchen, Ephraim Cooley and a few men arrived. Evidently, they were concerned about Joshua's well-being.

"Is Joshua home yet?" Cooley asked.

I stiffened for a moment.

"No," I said and began to cry.

The children were upset by the commotion.

"Mama, what happened?" Elizabeth asked.

"You're father didn't come home last night, and we're all worried about him."

"Where are the soldiers?" young Joshua asked. "They were here last night." He took a bite of toast. "Are they in the barn again?"

"Not now, my boy, not now."

Cooley went outside, and with the help of the other men, found Joshua's hat under a heap of snow. He brought it into the kitchen.

"Is this Joshua's hat?" he asked holding it by the brim.

I was startled. "Yes, it is." I went into the east parlor and stood at the window, doing my best to look as if I were in shock.

He went out again, and one of the men called to him. There were footprints near the well and blood on the well curb. Cooley peered down, saw Joshua's body, and raced away for the coroner, Tom Gilbert.

Jed Hankins, a ne'er-do-well who was often at Cooley's, took off at a run headed toward Dr. King's house. A few minutes later, Dr. King came running and arrived in time to see the men trying to pull Joshua from the well. He lent a hand, but they had trouble getting a hold of his lifeless bulk. As I went back to the kitchen, one of the men came in.

"Where's the biggest serving fork?" he said.

"What do you need with a serving fork?" I asked.

"To help get him out of the well, of course. Where is it?"

Sarah looked at me. I nodded, and she gave him the large fork from the drawer. I went back to the east parlor to see what they were doing.

The doctor used it to snag the edge of Joshua's cloak and they lifted him out of the well and laid him on the snow. His cloak had come untied; a small piece of its fabric was on the well curb, red with blood.

One of the men ran into the house. "They found him! He was in the well," he said before rushing out again.

Sarah grabbed the edge of the table to keep from falling over. The children turned to me, looking frightened and confused. Who could blame them? Their father was dead, murdered at the instigation of their mother. For a moment, I was dizzy and the world went black, as if I were spinning around and around. I clutched the back of the chair so I wouldn't fall. I began sweating and had a hard time breathing. After a minute, it passed.

The back door opened, and the men came in carrying Joshua's body. The children stood watching, stunned and crying. Sarah took them to the sitting room and closed the door.

"No! I can't look at him," I cried and ran up the back stairs. I charged into my bedroom and flung myself on the bed, sobbing. After a minute, I sat up and wiped my eyes. How was I to get out of this? What could I say in my defense?

I heard Sarah talking with someone whose voice I recognized as Tom Gilbert.

Then she came to my room.

"They want you to look at the body, ma'am."

"I can't."

"But you have to."

"No, I won't. I won't do it."

Sarah turned and left. I heard her steps as she went down the front stairs and then her voice as she relayed my refusal. I sat there for a few minutes until I realized I couldn't get out of looking at Joshua. I slowly made my way down the stairs and into the kitchen. I couldn't go into the dining room; my feet simply would not take me. I sat down and put my head in my hands.

Dr. King came into the kitchen after finishing the exam with the coroner.

"You must look at his body," he told me.

I closed my eyes and shook my head.

He took me by the hand and led me into the dining room. The knot of men moved aside as I entered. I kept my eyes down to the floor before looking at Joshua.

As I stood there, my little Bathshua, just three years old, came in and went to the table. She climbed onto a chair to look at her father. His skin was white except where bruised, his mouth open as if in a scream. His right eye was swollen and bruised and his nose was broken. There was blood on his lower face, a large gash on his right temple and his throat was black. Bathshua stayed a few moments as the men watched her. She said nothing but turned and went back to Sarah.

"Touch his forehead," Dr. King said.

I hesitated but then complied, laying my right hand on his head; the cold flesh startled me. There was a superstition that a corpse would color if the murderer touched it. The other men looked over my shoulder to see what happened. There was no change in Joshua's skin. Every man looked closely at me. I knew, from the look in their eyes, that they knew I had something to do with my husband's demise. How could they not? I hadn't hidden my dislike for Joshua. I had been much too vocal about it, which now had come back to cast doubt on me.

By Monday afternoon, the news of Joshua's death had made it to Worcester.

A rider was dispatched immediately to Brookfield to inform the constable that he should bring Sarah, Juba, Alec, and me to Worcester for questioning. When he arrived, we learned that Ezra,

Buchanan, and Brooks had been arrested and had immediately confessed to the crime—and had implicated me.

We were put into a sleigh driven by Cooley and accompanied by the constable and three other men on horseback. With the snap of the reins and a sudden jolt, we began the fateful journey to Worcester.

On the way in, I tried to keep up the appearance of normalcy and spoke to the others as if nothing had happened. I didn't know what else to do. A light snow began to fall, and I opened my palm to catch some flakes.

"It sure isn't like Christmas day." I smiled as I looked at my servants, hoping to allay their concerns for their safety and well-being. We watched the countryside go by; we saw a crowd gathered outside Waite's Tavern. As we passed, the people stared at us. I took Sarah's hand in mine, held it for a moment, then patted it. It was a poor gesture of comfort but all I could offer at the time.

Alec sat to my left and looked at me. His eyes narrowed, his brow creased. He said nothing, yet the turmoil he felt showed plainly on his face. I let go of Sarah's hand.

"Ephraim," I said. "It would be good to see my father right now." My thoughts were a tumult, and I felt myself falling even though I sat upright. I didn't know what was happening to me. For a moment, I didn't know where I was. I shook my head and took a deep breath. "It has been four years since I've seen him and only received a few letters from him." I was quiet for a moment, as I tried to complete the thought. "It's sad, don't you think, for a daughter not to see her father?"

Cooley looked back at me but didn't say a word.

"It would have made all the difference in my life. I know it would have. If only I could see him again." I looked at the snow-covered fields and wished with all my heart my father was there with me to help me with the mess I'd created. I missed him so much.

We traveled several miles when, near the Spencer and Leicester town line, I reached out and touched Cooley's arm. He perhaps did not feel it at first through the thick wool coat he wore. I tapped his arm harder. He turned around.

"Sarah, Alec, and Juba are innocent. I paid them to say and do what I told them to. I would suffer ten deaths before anything should happen to them."

"That's not for me to decide," he said. "It's up to the sheriff what to do with them."

As we were descending the hill into Leicester, I tapped Cooley's arm again. He shifted the reins to look back at me.

"You did your duty, Mr. Cooley, and it is right that you did. This whole thing is my fault. I instigated it, and I am responsible for every part of it. If only Ezra had not gotten sick and come to our house, everything would have been alright, don't you think?"

He turned around without answering.

We arrived at Brown's Tavern just after midnight, where Ezra, Buchanan, and Brooks had been taken. The seven of us sat under guard until the morning. We were given something to eat and drink before being questioned together. I held up my hand when the constable began asking Ezra questions.

"I am the cause of this sad affair, and none should suffer because of me. I began thinking about killing Joshua over two years ago, and when poor Ezra showed up at my door, sick as could be, seeking nothing but care and sustenance, I began thinking of a way to make him my accomplice."

I began to cry softly, thinking of how I had robbed him of the prime years of his youth. "If Joshua had only showed me some affection and care, and not been such a drunkard, I would not have thought of harming him, which I repent with all my heart. That he could but live again." I talked for quite a while, detailing the plan of how to get rid of my husband, explaining the parts played by Ezra, Buchanan, and Brooks. I told them that Sarah, Juba, and Alec had done as I'd instructed, that I'd paid them to do it, and that they were innocent.

"I am so sorry for involving you," I said, looking at the three soldiers, Ezra included. "I should have left him and gone to my father," I added more to myself than anyone else. "It would have been better, though I would have missed the children."

"No, Mrs. Spooner," Sarah said. "I don't think you would have missed the children. If you did, it wouldn't be for long. You were living the life you wished you had, instead of the one you do have."

As we sat there, the constable questioned Ezra, Buchanan, and Brooks.

"What time did you leave Brookfield?"

"It was about eleven o'clock," Buchanan said looking at me for confirmation. I nodded, for that was about right. "We arrived at Mrs. Walker's tavern around four."

"The door was locked," Ezra said, without even glancing over at me. "So I knocked. I didn't hear anything, so I knocked again a little louder. When we still didn't hear anything, Brooks shoved me out of the way and pounded on the door. It was loud enough that it drowned out the creaking of the sign over the door."

"Mrs. Walker finally came to the door," Buchanan said, picking up the tale. "When she opened it, she asked what we were doing here at that time of the night." He took a sip of cider before he continued. "The Springfield guard is after us,' I told her. I said that Mrs. Spooner met us in Leicester and told us that the guard was searching houses. It was a dumb excuse but the only thing I could think of at the moment. I knew Mrs. Walker was suspicious of us."

"She kept looking at me," Ezra said. "She asked what I was doing with these two." He nodded at the two British soldiers.

"She asked me why I was dressed so nice," Brooks said. "She kept looking at my shoe buckles." Everyone looked at Brooks's shoes; I recognized Joshua's silver buckles.

"'Have you seen Mrs. Spooner?' she asked me," Ezra said. "I didn't say anything, except that I'd like a bed. She pointed at the stairs and told me that there were two pallets empty."

"And you two?" the constable asked looking at Buchanan and Brooks.

"We drank flip," Brooks said. "Big mugs of flip."

"Three pitchers," Buchanan said, "and we got good and drunk." He wiped the back of his hand across his mouth. "Then I went to bed."

"And what about you?" the constable asked Brooks. "What did you do?"

"Him?" Mr. Brown cried out. "He came here looking for rum. Lots and lots of rum."

Brooks dropped his head as if in confirmation of his need for drunkenness.

"What happened when he got here?" the constable asked the innkeeper.

"Well, let's see. I was getting food for three men who were at that large table," he said, pointing to one near the fireplace. "This one," he said pointing at Brooks, "was at that table on the other side of the room." Brown watched him now, looking at Brooks as if he were a new species of bug. "I never saw him before, and I didn't like the looks of him. What manner of man wants a mug of rum for breakfast? When I asked him if he had any money, he put down a gold coin. This one," Brown said digging it out of his waistcoat and handing it to the constable, who examined it closely. "He had another mug, and when he got up, he stumbled. The three men and I saw those fancy shoe buckles and the fine clothes he's wearing and knew they didn't belong to the likes of him." We all looked at Brooks, who looked ill and withered under Brown's tale. "He showed us his watch."

"Where's the watch?" one of the constable's men asked.

Brooks took it out of his pocket.

"Is that your husband's?" the constable asked me.

"Yes," I whispered. I saw in my mind's eye the moment when I had given it to Brooks. It seemed like a year ago, although it had been just a day.

"I threw him out," Brown said. "He got nasty, demanding more rum when we knew he'd stolen those things. I grabbed him by the scruff of the neck, hauled him to the door, and shoved him outside."

"What did you do?" the constable asked Brooks. When he didn't answer, the constable kicked him in the leg. "What did you do?"

Brooks looked up, blinking his eyes as if he'd been asleep. "I went back to Mrs. Walker's and had more flip." He scratched his chest and gave a loud burp.

Shortly after dawn, the seven of us were taken to jail. The men were put into a room on the first floor; Sarah, Juba, and I were in a room on the second floor. All day long, people crowded around the jail, standing under the windows, calling to us, shouting questions and generally causing a commotion. This upset me greatly, for I wanted to be alone with my guilt.

That afternoon, the pastor of the Old South Church, which was a short distance up the road from the jail, visited us.

"I'm Reverend Thaddeus Maccarty. As part of my pastoral duties, I provide comfort and spiritual care to prisoners." He was tall, almost six feet, with a slender build, ruddy cheeks, and a stern visage. His black eyes penetrated as if seeing into my soul. Dressed in his black waistcoat, greatcoat, breeches, and stockings, he was an impressive looking man. I noticed he had two Bibles in his hands.

Sarah was pacing back and forth, while I sat on the thin straw mattress. I'd lifted the hem of my dress into my lap and now twisted it back and forth with my fingers, while Juba sat on the floor in a corner.

"I will do all I can to give you the opportunities and benefits possible for salvation," he said. "I advise you to make your peace with God so you will be prepared for your happy appearance before your judge, the great God, and his everlasting mercy. To help you prepare for that moment, I've brought you a Bible to help you reflect on the possibility of salvation."

I began to cry. Sarah comforted me as best she could and held my hand. We stayed that way for a moment before I looked at him, a trail of tears down my cheeks.

"I've made some terrible choices in life," I sobbed. "And now I must pay for them."

"Now, now," Maccarty said. "Let's talk of your future situation and the need for you to find everlasting grace."

"Oh, I would love to be wrapped in everlasting grace when I die, but after what I've done, I cannot believe it," I said.

"If you repent, sincerely repent, ask forgiveness of Almighty God, and spend the time between now and the moment of your death seeking spiritual help, you may be able to achieve what so many seek." He coughed twice and looked at Sarah and Juba. "And you," he said, "were accomplices to assist in this terrible deed?"

"Sarah and Juba are innocent," I said quickly. "Everything Sarah did was because I asked her, promising money and goods for her help. Juba had no part in it at all. It was I who instigated this dreadful happening." I wiped my eyes with the heel of my hand.

As if in prayer, Maccarty folded his hands around the Bible he was holding. "Would you like to confess your sin to me?" he asked

I looked at him and felt a sudden anger, a determination stir within me. I stood and walked toward him until we were no more than a foot apart. "No," I said, locking my eyes onto his. "I confess to the crime, but any confession of sin I give is between my Maker and me."

He looked away, probably wondering what kind of spiritual solace he could possibly give such an unrepentant woman like me. "Think about it," he said. "I will visit you every day to help guide you along the path to salvation in your final days."

"How did you find the men?" Juba asked. She'd hardly said five words from the time we'd left my house.

The reverend cocked his head and looked at her. "Mr. Buchanan has accepted his fate but is sorry for his part in the murderous deed. Mr. Brooks was sullen and angry. Mr. Ross was upset and fearful."

Mr. Ross—my Ezra—the boy I had loved, the boy I had ruined. I placed a hand over my slightly bulging belly and lowered my head.

"They all expressed an earnest desire to spend the remainder of their days repenting to achieve everlasting grace," the reverend continued. "Mr. Cummings did not say anything. He just sat, staring at the other men."

Reverend Maccarty then went to the door and called for the guard. Before leaving, he gave me a quick glance and said, "I'll be back tomorrow."

I lay on the bed and covered my eyes with my arm, wondering how I'd ever gotten into this situation.

CHAPTER 15

SARAH, ALEC, AND JUBA were granted immunity from prosecution and released. I made a request of Sarah before she left.

"When you get home, please tell the children I love them and am deeply sorry for the terrible things I've put them through. I was so caught up in myself that I never considered what this would do to them." I took a deep breath, let it out, and covered my eyes. "I'm a horrible mother."

Sarah did not disagree. She put a hand on my arm. "The children will not be at your home any longer," she said gently. "No one will want to stay there, not after what happened."

I slowly realized she was right. "Will they have been taken to Martha's?" I asked.

"I'll check on my way home. That's most likely."

The following Saturday, the door to my room opened and Martha came in. Her manner was circumspect and distant.

"Joshua was laid to rest yesterday," she said. "His children, your children, saw their father buried after he was brutally murdered by those men, those . . . rough soldiers who came to you because you are for the British—just like Father."

"Ezra came because he was sick." I walked toward her, but she took a step backward. "I didn't ask any of these men to my house. But Ezra, oh, Ezra."

"And what have you done to him? Got the boy involved in your murder scheme is all." She took a deep breath and moved along the wall toward the window, as if she needed fresh air. "How long did you plan this?" Anger flashed in her eyes as they drilled into me.

I said nothing.

"What did you do to coerce Ezra into helping with your plot? Did you seduce him?"

"It didn't start that way."

"You trollop!" She stiffened her back and moved toward the door again.

"Was Joshua's family there?" I asked.

Martha hesitated, as if deciding whether to stay and answer my questions or leave and be done with me.

"No," she said after a minute. "No one from his side was there."

"What about the children? Are they with you?"

She put her hands on her hips, bit her lower lip and shook her head.

"You never cared about your children. Why start now?"

"That's unfair! I love my children."

"Unfair? Who are you to talk about something being unfair? You murdered your husband."

"Don't say that!"

She walked in a tight circle then stopped. "All I'll say is that the children are taken care of. You no longer need to concern yourself with their welfare. You've given them a horrible experience that will haunt them the rest of their lives."

I sat on the bed and put my head in my hands.

"Reverend Fiske gave this to me when I told him I was going to see you." She handed me two pages with writing that I recognized as his. "It's the funeral oration he gave. He thought you might find comfort in it."

My hand began trembling and the pages shook as if being blown by a strong breeze. I threw them onto the bed.

She was still for a moment. "You're no longer my sister, Bathsheba. I want nothing more to do with you." She banged on the door. "Guard!"

The door opened, and my sister was gone from my life.

I paced the room from one end to the other, back and forth, back and forth, until I grew weary. I picked up the sheets of paper and went to the window for the light. I leaned against the wall and read:

> *The bloody tragedy so lately acted among us in the shocking murder of one of our friends, neighbors, and respectable citizens, whose mangled remains are now before us, as it forces our attention, astonishes our minds and affects our hearts, so it ought to be improved by us for the purposes of religion to make us wiser and better. To promote this end is the design of the present discourse. God grant that the design may be answered.*
>
> *What is the possession of wealth without domestic peace and the sweets of conjugal affection and confidence? What are elegant apartments; what is a house full of silver and gold to a man, if his house will not afford him a quiet retreat, nor a safe shelter, nor a single friend? We sincerely pity the distressed friends of the murdered victim and would give them all the consolation in our power. We would not designedly add to their grief with too minute a detail of the affecting circumstances, but would rather help them improve the melancholy providence and especially would commend them to a compassionate God, whose consolations are neither few nor small.*
>
> *So premeditated, so aggravated, so horrid a murder was never perpetrated in America and is almost without a parallel in the known world. Is it not shocking that men should be so hard-hearted and cruel as wantonly to spill the blood of a fellow creature? More shocking still, that they should spill the blood of an innocent person, one that never injured them. Yea, that they should do this in cold blood, and lie in wait, watching an opportunity to put their bloody design*

into execution? But the crime is greatly aggravated when the deed is committed by a professed friend, and the murderous purpose is concealed under the guise of esteem, affection, and an obliging carriage.

Let us sympathize with all that are distressed by this awful event. The virtuous friends of the murderers, as well as of the murdered, deserve our compassion and our prayers. The innocent children so suddenly bereft of their father, yes, I may say of their mother, too, demand our pity and ought to never be reproached with the infamy of the mother, much less with the tragic death of their father. And sure I am, the condition of the unhappy murderers loudly bespeaks our anxious concern and earnest supplications at the throne of grace. That they may not, after their hardness and impenitent hearts, treasure up unto themselves wrath against the day of wrath but may be brought to a pungent sense of their deep and aggravated guilt, and may abhor themselves and rent as in dust, that their souls may be plucked as brands out of everlasting burnings.

Finally, this complicated scene of wickedness should make us all weary of such a world, which is a theatre for such bloody tragedies to be acted upon, and to long after that better, that heavenly country, where all is security, all is harmony, all is perfection, and all felicity. Why so attached to this state of trouble, uncertainty, disappointment, distraction, and abounding wickedness! Let us look out and prepare for a happier abode, where no bloody hand shall reach us, where are durable riches and joys of evermore.

I let go of the papers and watched as they drifted to the floor. I put my head against the wall and thought of my childhood and the happy times I'd had. The first memory made me smile, something I'd not done in what seemed like a year.

We had been living on Cape Cod, and I was supposed to be helping around the tavern my parents owned, but I ran away to see the ocean. It was a warm, sun-filled, mid-April afternoon, and I ran along the beach as a salty wind blew off the rolling blue ocean.

I remember running along the wet sand, chasing the gulls and terns as they swooped low over the beach. Martha was calling for me, but I paid her no attention. I was having too much fun. I ran away from her when she tried to catch me; I laughed at her as I ran to the water's edge. When I stopped to pick up a shell, she caught up to me. She took me by the hand, and no matter how much I wriggled to be free, Martha wouldn't let go. I looked back at the water, seeing the waves roll to the beach. The memory faded like a handful of sand blown by the wind.

I sat on the bed and felt very alone.

The clothes I wore were dirty and becoming ragged. I was angry at being kept in the small room; it was cold and drafty. I had only one blanket, and it was not enough. My pleas to the sheriff fell on deaf ears until one day I couldn't take it any longer.

I went to the door. "Guard, tell the sheriff I want to see him."

To my surprise, the sheriff appeared in a few minutes.

"Yes?" he said, sticking his head in the door.

"I need new clothes. These are dirty."

"And what do you want me to do about it?"

"I want a chest of clothes brought from my home. If you give me a paper and ink, I'll write a list. One of the constables can bring it to Brookfield. My servants will gather the things I need and bring them to me."

"No."

"No what?" I asked moving toward him.

"No, I'll not send a constable to Brookfield for the likes of you. You're a murderer, and you get no special treatment from me." He closed the door behind him.

The next day Reverend Maccarty came to visit. I asked for his help. Within a short time, I had the paper and ink I needed. I wrote out the list and gave it to him.

"I'll make sure it gets to your servant Sarah as soon as possible," he said.

"Thank you, reverend. It means a great deal to me to have you interested in my welfare."

"I'm interested in more than your physical welfare, Bathsheba. I am interested in your eternal salvation perhaps, I think, more than you are."

Two days later, I heard a noise outside the jail and looked out the window. Sarah was climbing down from a wagon; I recognized my clothes chest next to where she'd been sitting. A young man I didn't know was with her.

"Oh, Sarah, thank you," I whispered.

A few minutes later there was a loud banging on the steps. The door opened and the young man and Sarah carried the chest into the room, dropping it with a thud in the corner near the bed. Sarah was breathing heavily. The young man looked at me for a moment before running out the door and down the stairs.

"Who was that?" I asked while Sarah caught her breath.

"A boy who works for Cooley. No one else would help me. I would have had Jesse do it, but he's in Springfield with my sister." She sat on the bed as I opened the chest lid and pulled out a new dress. I shucked off everything I was wearing and put on fresh garments for the first time in weeks. It felt good to be halfway clean again.

"How are the children?" I asked.

"Not well," she said. "They're angry and confused. Bathshua cries much of the time, Joshua doesn't say much to anyone, and Elizabeth, well, she just sits in the chair and stares a good part of the time, least that's what Martha says. The children are with her."

My heart sank at the news. What had I done to my poor children? Words were useless to me now. There was nothing I could do to change what happened. A heavy depression settled upon me like a black fog.

"Juba's gone to your sister's," Sarah said.

"She went to Martha's?"

"No, to Elizabeth's. All the way to Hingham. Martha told her what a good servant Juba was, so Elizabeth hired her."

"I haven't spoken to Liza in a long time," I said.

"Well, with her husband, why would she talk to you?" Liza's husband was a rabid patriot who intensely disliked my father and me. He'd make sure that Liza never communicated with me again. Another sister gone from my life.

"And in Brookfield?" I asked.

"Oh, there's bad talk about you everywhere. I went to Cooley's a week ago, and when I walked in everyone stopped talking and just looked at me. I left and went home." She sighed. "People don't like me either 'cause I'm helping you." She heaved herself off the bed. "I'll never hear the end of it, I'm sure."

CHAPTER 16

On Tuesday, April 21, 1778, a grand jury was impaneled and found a true bill against the four of us.

> *April Term, 1778. The said William Brooks, James Buchannon [sic], Ezra Ross, and Bathsheba Spooner are brought and sit to the bar here, by the Sheriff of Worcester County, and arraigned; and upon their arraignment they severally plead, that they are not guilty, and thereof they put themselves, for trial, on God and the Country.*
> *All., H. SMITH, Clerk.*

The trial began at 8:00 a.m. on Friday, April 24 in the meetinghouse, a short distance from the jail, since it could accommodate more people than the courthouse.

Robert Treat Paine, a signer of the Declaration of Independence and attorney general for the State of Massachusetts Bay, acted as the prosecuting attorney. Levi Lincoln, just six years out of law school and inexperienced in trial law, was appointed to defend Ezra, Buchanan, Brooks, and me. Just from that, I knew it would not be a fair trial. I had met with him only once for just a short time, during which he asked me several questions.

"Since you confessed, there's not much I can do," he told me. "But I will try my best. In case you're interested, the justices are

William Cushing, chief justice, Jedediah Foster, Nathan Peaslee Sargent, David Sewall, and James Sullivan."

I cringed when I heard that Mr. Foster would judge me. How could it get any worse?

A jury of twelve men was selected and sat to our right. Mr. Paine and Mr. Lincoln and the clerks sat at a large table in front of the judges. The people in the courtroom remained silent, listening to every word. I felt everyone staring at me. I turned and looked at them, recognizing several.

The four of us stood facing the judges, as was the custom, for the length of the trial. I was allowed to sit a few times so as not to bear the burden of being on my feet the entire time. It was the one consideration I received. The bailiff, standing to the left of the platform on which the judges would sit, preceded the justices, and called the court to order:

"The Honorable, the Chief Justice and the Associate Justices of the Superior Court of Judicature, Court of Assize of the State of Massachusetts Bay. Oyez! Oyez! Oyez! All persons having business before the Honorable, the Superior Court are admonished to draw near and give their attention, for the Court is now sitting. All rise!"

The five justices, clad in black flowing robes and white powdered wigs, led by Chief Justice Cushing as the presiding officer of the court, walked into the room and onto the platform. They sat in large wood and leather chairs at a long table with an ample supply of paper, ink, and quills for each justice. My heart sank when I saw Mr. Foster. I thought of the Bay Psalm Book he'd given me on my wedding day. He sat, stone-faced, staring at me.

Above the witness box was a sounding board, a large, ornamented piece of wood to amplify the sound of the witness's voices so they could be heard as well as possible. Near us, a large mirror was placed so that the judges and jury could watch our expressions as we listened to the witnesses.

Then there was silence as the justices looked at the jury, the lawyers, clerks, and reporter and those in attendance, which included many provincial and local government officials.

Chief Justice Cushing cleared his throat, adjusted his spectacles, and addressed the crowd that overflowed out to the street. "Bailiff, close the doors." Ezra, Buchanan, and Brooks stood there, looking ahead and not moving as if they were made of stone. I turned to watch as the bailiff made his way to the front door of the meeting house and, after some pushing and shoving, got all the people who did not have seats out of the building before making his way back to the front of the room.

"We will have order today. Any outbursts will not be tolerated," Cushing said. He turned to the court clerk. "Read the indictment."

The clerk stood and spoke in a loud voice so all could hear:

"At the Superior Court of Judicature, Court of Assize, begun and held at Worcester, within and for the County of Worcester, on Tuesday the twenty-fourth of April, in the year of our Lord seventeen hundred and seventy-eight. The Jurors for the Government and People of Massachusetts Bay, in New England, upon their oath present that William Brooks, resident at Charlestown, in Middlesex County, Laborer, James Buchanan, of the same Charlestown, Laborer, and Ezra Ross, of Ipswich, in the County of Essex, Laborer, on the first day of March last past, feloniously, wilfully and with malice aforethought, assaulted Joshua Spooner, of Brookfield and that William Brooks, with his right fist, struck Joshua Spooner to the ground then, with both his hands and feet, struck him in and upon his back, head, stomach, sides and throat, resulting in several mortal bruises, of which Joshua Spooner instantly died. And that James Buchanan and Ezra Ross then and there were present, aiding, assisting, and abetting William Brooks, to the felony and murder to be done and committed. That they feloniously, willfully, and of malice aforethought, killed Joshua Spooner. And that Bathsheba Spooner, of Brookfield, in the County of Worcester, widow, late wife of the said Joshua Spooner, not having God before her eyes, but being seduced by the instigation of the Devil, did incite, move, abet, counsel and procure the accused in the murder of Joshua Spooner."

He placed the paper on the table and looked at the justices.

Cushing addressed the jury. "You must return a verdict of either guilty or not guilty after hearing all of the testimony and weighing all of the evidence. We will now proceed with opening statements. Mr. Paine."

Robert Treat Paine was not a good-looking man, having an angular face with a long nose, mouth like a slit, bushy eyebrows, and dark, hard, resolute eyes. Dressed in a tan waistcoat and breeches, white stockings, black shoes with gold buckles, and dove gray coat, he was the image of a well-to-do man of power and prestige. He stood and picked up a sheaf of papers from the table.

"Thank you, Mr. Chief Justice and Associate Justices. If it may please the Court." He moved to the side of the table and stood squarely facing the jury.

"The men standing before you," he said, stabbing an index finger at the defendants, "signed a confession, a lengthy, detailed document specifying their part in the crime, admitting their guilt. They stated," he continued, looking at the paper in his hand, then reading from it: "'William Brooks went out and stood within the small gate leading into the kitchen, and as Mr. Spooner came past him, he knocked him down with his hand. Mr. Spooner strove to speak when down, but Brooks beat him with a club, took him by the throat, and partly strangled him. Ross and Buchanan came out, and Ross took Mr. Spooner's watch out and handed it to Buchanan. I, Buchanan, pulled off Mr. Spooner's shoes, and Brooks and Ross then took him up and put him into the well head first.'"

He set the paper down. "We will hear from fourteen witnesses who will testify as to the accused being at Joshua Spooner's residence, and give testimony of discussions between the accused with the goal of murdering Mr. Spooner. We will also explain the events which transpired that led to this terrible incident that deprived a well-known and well-respected member of not only Brookfield but of the state, a man who dedicated himself to his business and family, of his life."

He put his hands behind his back as he paced. "That Joshua Spooner was murdered is not in question. He was killed in a most despicable and cowardly manner. The defendants Brooks, Buchanan, and Ross attacked and killed him on the night of the first of March, beating him most severely about the head, neck, and torso. Brooks strangled him until unconscious then kicked him in the head and chest causing gashes and cuts from which his blood flowed, leaking into the ground near the well into which Brooks and Ross stuffed his body. Imagine being beaten to that point where your life is ebbing away only to be shoved into a well and drowned because you are incapable of being able to remove yourself from the well. The enormity of the crime cannot be dismissed. It was all at the urging and encouragement of his wife and mother of his children, Bathsheba Ruggles Spooner, who had an utter aversion to her husband and made plans to have him killed. She was the conspirator who set the entire incident in motion."

I shivered at hearing his words, and envisioned Joshua's cold, lifeless body in front of me.

He rubbed his hands together while looking down, then raised his head and approached the jury box. "She planned his murder for many months, cajoling and attempting to seduce some men into carrying it out while promising to pay the defendants large sums of money and valuable belongings of her deceased husband."

He looked at me for a moment. "She is a woman without a soul." A gasp ran through those seated, all on the edges of the benches. "She cannot have a soul to commit such a heinous crime. She is a seducer of souls."

I stayed composed, trying to show no sign of emotion, merely taking in what he was saying. I brushed a lock of hair from my face and watched Paine do what he could to convince the jury to find me guilty. "We will prove beyond a reasonable doubt that these four conspired and acted to cause the death of Joshua Spooner."

He looked at the judges. "Your Honors."

Justice Cushing looked at Mr. Lincoln.

"Mr. Lincoln."

"No opening statement, Your Honor."

I was aghast. Trying to do his best apparently meant abandoning me from the outset.

Cushing instructed the clerk to call the first witness.

Alec walked to the witness box and sat in the chair.

I knew from accompanying my father to the courthouse when he'd been Chief Justice of Common Pleas, that each justice had the authority to ask the witnesses any question in an attempt to obtain information or to clarify a previous statement.

Justice Cushing began the questioning, the attorney's role to provide opening and closing arguments and in some cases, to cross-examine the witnesses.

"How would you describe the two weeks before Mr. Spooner's death?" Justice Cushing asked.

Alec was hesitant to answer and stared at his feet for a long moment. I could tell that being questioned by such an eminent person made him nervous, and he was afraid he would somehow say the wrong thing.

Justice Cushing rapped the gavel once. "Answer the question."

Alec looked at me, a mix of emotions on his face. "It was odd," he said.

"How was it odd?" Foster asked.

"Brooks and Buchanan came and went as they pleased and were given the best food and drink. They were treated very well for soldiers."

"Did you know Brooks and Buchanan in Burgoyne's army?" Justice Sargent inquired.

"Yes, I did. I knew Buchanan in Canada. We were not in the same regiment, but I did speak with him from time to time."

"What did you think of him?"

"That he was a scoundrel."

I saw Buchanan's fists clench and his face grew red, his anger clearly growing as this squirt of a soldier, a private, as he'd once told me how he thought of Alec, denigrated him.

"Was Mr. Spooner there?" Foster asked.

"No, he was not. He'd gone to Princeton with Ross," Alec said, nodding in the direction of Ezra. "When he came home, he found Brooks and Buchanan there. Mr. Spooner asked that I sit with him because he did not like the look of Brooks and did not want him in his house."

Paine nodded and waved his hand, indicating Cummings should continue.

"Mr. Spooner told Mrs. Spooner to get rid of them and that if she did not, he'd call the constable to do so."

"So Mr. Spooner was concerned with his safety at that time?" Judge Sewall asked.

"Yes, sir. The next morning, they were in the barn, and Mrs. Spooner told me to bring them food. She brought them some too, as did Sarah."

"How long were they there?"

"They stayed in the barn for two days and nights."

"So they were there until Mr. Spooner was killed?" Cushing asked.

"No, sir. They left on the Thursday before and came back Saturday night. I saw them there Sunday night."

"Was Ross with them?"

"No, sir. He came before they did. He wasn't with them."

"What happened next?" Foster asked.

"Mr. Spooner went to Cooley's as he did every night he was home. I went outside, and Brooks was there and, not seeing too well because of the darkness, asked if I was Mrs. Spooner. I said I was not. He told me to get Mrs. Spooner. I said I would not. Brooks then told me that Mr. Spooner would not come home a living man that night."

The people in the courtroom began murmuring about this, a direct confirmation of Brooks's intent.

Justice Cushing wrapped the gavel a few times. "Order!" he yelled.

Justices Foster and Sargent were writing notes as the questioning proceeded; they looked up at the sound of the gavel.

"What happened then? Be as precise as you can be." Cushing said.

Alec looked confused.

"Do you know what the word precise means?"

"No, sir."

"Give as much detail as you can."

"When Sarah, Juba, and me went into the sitting room, I smelled burning wool and went to see what was happening. I saw Mrs. Spooner, Brooks, Buchanan, and Ross in the parlor burning clothes. They started putting on other clothes, Ross putting on Mr. Spooner's pants and breeches."

"How did you know they were Mr. Spooner's?" Sergeant asked.

"I'd seen him wear them many times and knew they belonged to him." He coughed and shifted himself in the chair.

Paine resumed his walk across the room and stood on Alec's right side.

"What else happened?" Judge Sullivan said.

"A month or so before, Mrs. Spooner asked me to kill Mr. Spooner. She said if I did, she would make a man out of me."

"What do you think she meant by that?"

"That she would take me to her bed."

I flushed at the memory of that moment. I had told him that. I felt that if I had to take him to bed to get him to kill Joshua, then I would.

"What else?" Foster said.

I turned and looked at the crowd. People sat on the edges of their seats listening to every word, taking in the salacious bits of information, ready to relay it to everyone they knew.

"The next morning, she told me to go to Cooley's to ask if anyone had seen Mr. Spooner because he had not come home last night. I took a horse and rode there. Cooley told me that he'd left at nine o'clock with Dr. King and that I should go there to see what happened to him."

"How did Mr. Cooley seem when you told him you were looking for Mr. Spooner?" Cushing asked.

"I think he was concerned about him. He was Cooley's best customer."

I saw Cooley sitting in the third row and nodding every time his name was mentioned, silently confirming the details of Alec's testimony.

"I started to Dr. Foxcroft's, but I went only a little way before turning for the house because I knew what happened to Mr. Spooner and that going to the doctor's wouldn't serve any purpose."

Cushing looked at the other judges.

They said they were satisfied with the witness.

"Mr. Lincoln, do you have questions for the witness?" asked Cushing.

"No, your Honor."

I began to feel a burning resentment against Mr. Lincoln.

"You may step down," Cushing told Alec.

He went to the second row and sat with Sarah.

The bailiff then called Sarah. She was dressed nicely, in a dress I'd given her. She was a moderately sized woman with a stout figure, brown hair, dark brown eyes, and full lips. I could tell she was nervous, sitting in the witness chair, looking around uncertain as to what to do.

Cushing tried to put her at ease. "Mrs. Stratton," he began, "were you aware that Mr. Spooner was killed that night?"

She looked at me. I was composed and attentive and gave her a slight nod.

"Yes . . . yes. I did know."

"How did you know?"

"Mrs. Spooner told us." She fidgeted, glancing at the five judges, all of whom were staring at her. The meetinghouse was packed to the rafters with people, which must have made her even more nervous. She looked down at her hands in her lap.

"How did that happen?" Sewall asked.

"We were all in the room together and she told us." She sighed and trembled.

"What did she do then?"

"She asked me to sleep with her, and I did. For hours, though, she tumbled about, tossing and turning. At some point, I told her that I was going to tell the constable, for it wasn't right."

"What did she say to that?" Foster asked.

"She sat up in bed and told me that if I kept it a secret, she would give me a great deal of money. Then she lay down and went to sleep, at least for a little while."

I shook my head for I hadn't slept a wink.

Paine, sitting at the table, was writing his notes. He looked up at her.

"So," Foster continued, "Mrs. Spooner knew her husband was dead, killed by the three men standing there." He pointed towards Brooks, Buchanan, and Ross.

"Yes," she answered softly.

"Yet she told you not to say anything."

"That's right," she said.

Cushing looked at the other judges, indicating he would resume the questioning.

"Who was at the house the night of Mr. Spooner's death?"

"Well, there was Mrs. Spooner, Alec, Ezra, Buchanan, Brooks, the three children, me, and Juba."

"So, there were ten people at the house that night?"

"Yes, that's right. Ten."

"Doesn't that seem odd? Committing a murder when there are so many people there?"

"Yes, it does, but that is who was there."

"Tell us what happened that night."

She looked at me again; I saw the sorrow in her eyes. She took a deep breath, let it out with a loud whoosh, and glanced at me again, seeming to be on the verge of tears.

"Mrs. Spooner told me to bring food to Buchanan and Ezra, which I did. Brooks was outside, waiting for Mr. Spooner. I saw Mrs. Spooner show the men Mr. Spooner's money box. Then Mrs. Spooner asked me to go up and get Mr. Spooner's black breeches. When I came down, she was giving money to the men. Buchanan had a handful of paper money."

"What did you do then?"

Sarah began wringing her hands together and looking around the room. She took another big breath and wiped her eyes with her hand.

"I asked Brooks what he'd done. He told me, 'His time is come.' I also saw a ring that belonged to Mr. Spooner on Buchanan's hand. Mrs. Spooner gave them more money, and they left."

"Thank you, Mrs. Stratton."

"Mr. Lincoln?" asked Cushing.

"No questions, Your Honor."

"You may step down."

Juba was called to the stand. A whisper of conversation went through those assembled. I knew for a fact that a Negro had never testified at a murder trial in Worcester County and possibly all of Massachusetts. The jury and judges watched Juba; they were seemingly captivated by her dark skin, bright eyes, and demure countenance.

Cushing began the questioning. "You are a servant in the Spooner house?"

"Yes, sir," she said in a clear and strong voice.

"What did you think of the night of Mr. Spooner's murder?"

She glanced down at her hands before looking at him. "It was terrible. All those people in the house and the confusion."

"What is your impression of Mrs. Spooner in relation to her husband?"

"Mrs. and Mrs. Spooner hated each other, and Mrs. Spooner made no secret that she wanted him dead."

Cushing looked at Paine, who shook his head.

"Mr. Lincoln."

"No questions, Your Honor."

Cushing called for an hour break for a meal, and the room emptied quickly.

When the trial resumed, the bailiff called Dr. Jonathan King to the witness chair.

Cushing began the questioning. "Dr. King, tell us about the night Mr. Spooner was murdered."

"I sat with Joshua that evening, talking while he sipped his mug of rum. It was his fourth mug of the evening.

"'I almost don't want to go home tonight,' he told me. He said that trouble awaited him.

When I asked if it was Bathsheba, he said that it wasn't just her. He said it was the soldiers that kept hanging around, eating him out of house and home. He said they drank twenty quarts of rum when while he was gone. He said he could only imagine the argument he and Mrs. Spooner would have later."

"Mrs. Spooner has a fiery temper?" Mr. Foster asked his eyes once more boring into me.

"Yes, your Honor. She inherited all of her father's worst qualities. His temper, his obstinacy, his penchant for profanity."

"What else happened?" Cushing asked.

"He told me that his Negro woman was angry with him. That she was demanding money so she could leave." He coughed and cleared his throat.

"Joshua pulled his watch out, a beautiful piece engraved with his initials. He checked the time before wishing me goodnight. I checked my watch also. It was almost nine o'clock. The last thing he said to me was that he was going home to see what mess awaited him.

"I watched him as he put on his heavy cloak, and settled his wool hat on his head before grabbing his candle lantern. He lit it with one of the small wooden sticks for lighting pipes that Cooley kept next to the pipe rack for customers. Once he had the candle burning, he took the lantern and adjusted his cloak with the other hand. Cooley was wiping down a table and looked up as Spooner was about to open the door. I was debating whether to have another drink or leave, when he opened the door and let in a gust of bitterly cold wind. He pulled the cloak tighter about him, smiled and nodded at me, and left."

All of the justices, except Cushing, were scribbling notes as he spoke.

"What happened then?" Justice Sergeant asked.

"The sun was only a half-hour high when I heard Mr. Spooner was drowned in the well. So I rode there. The others who were there before me found his hat and cloak. There was blood on the ground near the gate not more than six or seven feet from the house. I saw a three-foot wooden club standing up against the house and supposed that was what they'd knocked him down with. I helped them get him out of the well. With the tine of a large serving fork, we drew up his cloak and then hooked him up from the bottom by grabbing him under the left arm. He came up headfirst."

All the justices, as well as Paine and Lincoln, looked up at the same time. They stared at the doctor, unsure they had heard him correctly.

Cushing cleared his throat. "He came up headfirst?"

"Yes."

"There has been testimony that he was put in the well headfirst and that his feet were sticking out." He looked at Dr. King. "You heard that testimony?"

"Yes, sir, I did."

The events of that night were a blur and, for the life of me, I couldn't remember whether Joshua was in the well feet or head first. It didn't matter. He was dead.

The room buzzed with the murmuring of the crowd. At the same time, Foster, Sewall, Sargent, and Cushing looked at each other, seeming to understand that, if Dr. King's testimony was correct, Joshua might have been alive when Ezra and Buchanan had put him into the well, and that he'd somehow attempted to get out but was unable to. Or someone had taken his body out and placed it back in feet first.

I was emotionally numb and didn't care.

"Continue," Cushing said.

"When he was out of the well, I noticed a great bruise on his nose and that the bone was all broken to pieces. His left temple was very bruised, which must have been from a heavy blow, and there was a gash on his head an inch and a half long. His throat was very black, and his chest was bruised, too. We found one shoe in the bucket. His watch and buckles were gone, and a few dollars were in his pocket. None of the family went out to look at him after he was brought out of the well. They were in the kitchen, eating their breakfast as if nothing had happened. Cummings passed by but did not turn his face toward the well. When the body was brought into the house, no one except his little daughter would view him. Mrs. Spooner was told to touch him, and she went and laid her hand on his forehead but removed it quickly and said, 'Poor little man.'"

I could still feel how ice-cold Joshua was. I shuddered with the memory.

The questioning continued for hours, until well after dark, with twelve more witnesses providing testimony of the day-to-day details of the weeks leading up to the murder. I felt bad for Ezra, Buchanan, and Brooks having to stand the entire time. Ezra turned to me at that moment.

"My feet are asleep. I can't feel anything," he said.

The bailiff came over and cuffed him behind the ear. "Be quiet," he said.

After the testimony ended, Paine walked to the jury box, stood a few feet from it, and looked each juror in the eye.

"You have heard the testimony of those with knowledge of the Spooners' life in Brookfield, the events that transpired, the men of low station involved in this wretched deed, and the planning, cajoling, and seduction Mrs. Spooner engaged in to have her husband murdered. It is your duty, your obligation, to return a verdict based on the evidence and testimony as you have seen and heard. There is nothing else you need to consider.

"It is clear that all four of them participated in the murder, for it would not have happened had she not planned it, if Buchanan and Brooks had not spent time at her home, and if Ross had not arrived. But, as you have heard, Mr. Spooner was beaten viciously and thrown down his well to die but may have had enough strength left to attempt to get out of the well, which he was not able to do."

He looked at the floor and shook his head. "There is clear proof from the hours of testimony, as well as a full confession, as to the guilt of the accused. There is no reasonable doubt at all. A verdict reflecting the guilt of the accused is now your duty."

At the end of the presentation of the prosecution's case, Cushing again called for a brief recess, instructing Mr. Lincoln that he would begin upon the return.

The bailiff told the four of us to sit; he offered us a small basket of bread, cheese, and hard-boiled eggs. We ate only after he and two of his men took us outside to the outhouse. It was painful having to hold things that long. As we began to eat, Brooks sat downcast, nibbling a piece of hard cheese.

I observed them—otherwise good men who'd made a tragic mistake and would now pay for it with their lives, all because of me.

"No one cares about us," Brooks said.

"We're far from home," Buchanan replied. "Why should anyone care?" He looked around the room at the few people chatting together as they waited for the procedures to resume. "We are going to die and be buried here. No one will know or care who we are." I flinched at the cold finality of his words. "I just wish I could get word to my wife. I'll die and she'll never know that I did or the reason why."

"We should have kept walking when Cummings asked us to come in," Brooks said.

"But I knew him," Buchanan said.

"So?"

Ezra groaned. "It doesn't matter what you did or didn't do then. We are here now, and we are going to die because of what we did to Spooner."

"At least you got to bed her," Brooks said with a coarse laugh, cocking a thumb at me. "I thought of it many times myself. I think you would've given it to me if we'd had more time, you and I."

For a minute, I didn't know what to say.

"You are fooling yourself if you think that, Billy boy," Buchanan said with a snort. "She's a fine woman and wouldn't have done that with the likes of you."

I snapped my finger against Brooks's cheek so that it stung. "The thought of taking you to my bed never crossed my mind. Even if it had, I wouldn't have because you're a little shit of a man."

Brooks stopped chewing and put his hand to his face. His eyes gleamed with hatred.

"If you only hadn't taken care of me when I was sick. That's how it all started," Ezra said, putting his hand on my knee. "I'm so sorry." He gave me a weak smile.

"You told us before," Brooks said, "that she made you better. So what?" He scraped the floor with his foot. "It's your fault we're here and we're going to die." He stood up and gazed at Ezra for a minute. I could see the rage building in his face, his body tightening like a spring before he launched himself and began pounding Ezra about the head and neck. What remained of the food landed on the floor and was stepped on.

"You bastard!" Brooks cried as Buchanan tried to pull him off Ezra.

I grabbed Brooks's ear, twisted it hard and pulled. He let out a cry of pain that I was glad to hear.

The bailiff came running over and grabbed Brooks, hauling him over the bar and dropping him to the floor where he lay in a heap, his breath rasping in and out.

CHAPTER 17

When all had returned, and the judges, clerks, bailiff, and attorneys were in their respective positions, the trial resumed.

The spectators were still, awaiting every word. They no doubt were curious as to what type of defense Lincoln could present that might have any chance of persuading the jury to find a verdict of not guilty.

Judge Cushing turned to Levi Lincoln.

"Mr. Lincoln."

Lincoln stood in front of the judges. "Mr. Chief Justice and Associate Justices. If it may please the court."

He was a tall, thin man with a long nose, broad forehead, curly brown hair, and intelligent blue eyes. His maroon waistcoat, set off by a white shirt, light gray breeches, and dark gray coat, was the mark of his station in life—a relatively new lawyer early in his career who was attempting to look his best at the most important trial of his career thus far, possibly ever. I was eager to hear how he might spare me my life. He faced the jury.

"The importance of this case cannot be overstated. It is one of the most significant in the judicial history of Massachusetts, and perhaps one of the most difficult cases ever committed to an American jury. As such, there are exceedingly high public expectations that the verdict will be fair and just." He walked to the railing in front of the jury box, put his right hand on it, and looked at the jurors for a moment. "It is a novel case, having many facets that have not been addressed in this province or perhaps in any of the other American colonies. This is the first capital trial since the establishment of the new government and must be taken most seriously for, as inhabitants of Massachusetts, we must demonstrate that justice was indeed done. The case is remarkable in its nature if you consider the number of people, and the persons involved, the manner of the commission of the crime, its rise, progress, and consequences."

He folded his hands in front of him. "I must suggest to you such principles of law, with such observations on the evidence, as will enable you to determine the quality of each defendant's conduct in this matter on which you are to form a judgment. You are apprised of that important duty you are called upon to discharge in this trial. You must banish all prejudices, all public indignation, the enormity of the offense, all opinions derived from hearsay, their profession, connections, and put aside all political sentiments. You are to give your verdict according to the fair result of the evidence. You are to suppose them innocent so far as they are not proved guilty by the evidence that has been given in the trial."

He began pacing.

"A great principle of the law is at work here, that all prisoners, regardless of the crimes of which they are accused, are innocent until proven guilty. It must be proven beyond any reasonable doubt. If there is any doubt in your mind, any doubt at all, as to the guilt of these four," he said waving his arm in our direction, "then you must find them innocent.

"They are accused of murder. Murder is where a person, of sane and sound mind, with discretion, kills another, with malice aforethought. An accessory before the fact of murder is he who, being absent at the time, does yet procure, counsel, or commend. For, if present, it is aiding and abetting, but even if only one person does the act, they are all principals in the deed."

He turned to us. "To determine whether the prisoners have been guilty of the crimes they are charged within the indictment or not, it will be necessary that you keep in your mind the evidence against each one separate and distinct. It is required that you be convinced that each one was designedly influential in Spooner's death, both of which facts must be proved by such evidence as not to leave the shadow of doubt in your minds, for if you are unable, you *must* acquit them."

He turned back to the jury. "The fact of killing is not denied, that it was a murder, is confessed. But it does not necessarily follow from that, that Buchanan, Brooks, and Ross are the murderers, which must be proved before you can convict them, for you can't infer, from the murder itself, which of them did the killing, where it might have been only one of the three. Could not all the facts take place as testified, and yet it not be to that degree which this indictment supposes?"

He turned from the jury and walked back to the table, looked at his notes, then turned again and resumed his former position.

"It is not my business to defend either of the British prisoners against the charge of guilt; all have been wicked, have been guilty to some degree. The gist of your inquiry—and the proof of nothing else is your purpose—is whether they are principals or accessories. Everything that is proved respecting Ross is entirely innocent in reference to the crime charged in the indictment. I'm sure the circumstances all taken together don't afford proof, probability, or even suspicion of there being a desire in Ross to hurt Mr. Spooner."

It was late and people were beginning to tire. I turned and watched the jurors. Several rubbed their faces while others stretched, not taking their eyes off of Lincoln.

"Is there anything in the nature of things that Ross did that necessarily implies the existence of all those circumstances that constitute murder? Is not innocence perfectly consistent with those facts proved? And it is a rule that no man's guilt can be proved by any evidence that is compatible with his innocence.

"If he had a design against Mr. Spooner's life, did he not have frequent opportunity to kill him at his own house, or Princeton, or on the road by poison, by strangling, by weapons? The matter had long been in agitation, and his not doing it shows he had no real design but only that he would keep on good terms with Mrs. Spooner. It goes further and proves that he not only had no such design but that he was determined not to do it. Why did he not do it, when in so many instances, places, opportunities, and means favored it? The omission proves not only an absence of design to do it but a determination against it.

"The confession of a criminal can rarely be turned against him without avoiding the end for which he had given it. There have been instances where a murder has been declared that has not been committed, and the confession of goods stolen that were never out of the possession of the owner.

"It is unjust and dangerous for confessions that have been influenced by fear, or with the misdirected hope of mercy, to have much weight. Besides, the evidence of words ought to be received with great caution and distrust, especially those that are spoken in confidence, or the hurry and agitation of an anxious mind that is pressed by leading questions. The words may be very innocent when spoken, yet criminal when related; much depends upon the time and circumstances."

Lincoln looked at the justices for a moment before gazing at those in attendance. Raising his finger for emphasis, he began pacing back and forth in front of the jury.

"If one comes informally to the alliance, though he did not stop the felony, he is neither principal nor accessory. Ross's going to Brookfield was ignorant as to what took place—he knew nothing of the appointment made at Walker's, or of Buchanan and Brooks going there.

"What makes one an accessory is one's commanding, counseling, abetting, and procuring another to commit a felony. And therefore, words that sound as if giving permission do not make an accessory. So, if A says he will kill Mr. Spooner, and B says you may act at your pleasure, for me, this does not make one person an accessory. Does the evidence about Ross amount to more than this?"

I perceived that a couple of the jurors were bored and wanted him to be done with his defense. I could tell they'd already made up their minds of our guilt.

"Is there not as much evidence of Ross's repenting and countermanding as there is of the fact that he ran away?"

Several of the jurors looked at the mirror to see Ezra's reaction to Lincoln's points. He sat there, stone-faced, not showing any emotion. I saw them turn their gaze to me as I fidgeted, my legs tired and sore from standing. I pushed up a strand of hair with my finger and stared back at them.

"The prosecution labels him an accessory because it gives countenance, encouragement, and protection to their case, and if he is not an accessory, it does not help their case," Lincoln said.

"If he is a principal, he must be present with the design to assist if needed. You must be convinced of this by proof beyond all reasonable doubt that there was be an evil design to the crime committed. Merely being in the company of others, being present, without a design of having anything to do with it, although he did not endeavor to prevent it, is punishable—but not as murder. He might be present for many reasons without the design to assist in the murder."

Robert Treat Paine made some notes while he shook his head, obviously not agreeing with Lincoln's contention. Paine looked at Cushing and saw him put his hand to his face as he listened intently.

I put a hand on Ezra's forearm and squeezed it gently.

"Spooner was dead when Ross went to him and took him by the leg. That doesn't prove Ross guilty of murder." He walked to the window on the opposite side of the room, tapping his finger on his chin, contemplating what to say next.

Turning, he paused for a long moment and looked at the justices, the jury, and those assembled before walking to stand before the jury box. "You must be convinced that Mrs. Spooner was of a sound mind."

I had no idea what he would say about my part in the affair, but I put my hands on the railing in front of me for I began to feel faint.

"If the conduct is irrational, if it is what could not be directed by a person in the exercise of reason, then there is the best evidence of a disordered mind. Conduct is the only evidence of a person's state of mind. Disorders of the brain operate variously. There is a difference between a fool and a person distracted. Mrs. Spooner is either a fool or a distracted person."

Heads turned to watch me. I looked at the justices and jurors, smiling faintly.

"What end would the murder of Mr. Spooner serve? Would any advantages to Mrs. Spooner arise from his death? By his death at best, she orphaned their children by depriving them of a father, widowed herself, and subjected herself to the burdens of supporting herself and the children. Would she have successfully planned the murder, with a design of having it occur, if she were in the exercise of reason?

"If it is said she could not live with her husband, could she not have separated, could not have gone to her father, whose favorite she was, or to her sisters or brothers or her other friends? There, with her speech, intellect, and engaging appearance, she might have had any gallant she pleased, not someone such as Ross. If she was capable of murdering her husband, she was sufficiently advanced to have embraced this or any course of life. But what was the necessary consequence?

"Is it possible that she would ever entrust such an affair to strangers and foreigners, to women and boys, that she not have had some motive, some means, someplace fixed on, some confidant, some hope of impunity before she would have engaged in this if she had been in her senses?

"Was it possible to conceal the matter, considering the number of people employed? And to hide each of his or her character, situation, and profession with no plan made to conceal what was to transpire, no story agreed upon, no place to flee to, no evidence of their fidelity? Could she, therefore, have had any confidence in them or their behavior? She is seen in company with them the night before at Walker's. After the murder, she gives the murderers her husband's watch, buckles, waistcoat, breeches, shirts, etc. and even puts them on, then to be worn in the eye of the world, where they are well known to be Spooner's clothes, where it is known that the quality and fashion of the clothes don't belong to the persons wearing them, they being low and vulgar. Is this the conduct of a woman in the exercise of reason? There is all the evidence of a disordered mind."

As he spoke, I realized he was probably close to the truth. I had been disordered, so caught up in my hatred of my husband that I'd lost all track of everything else.

A few of the jurors leaned forward, their interest piqued. It gave me a glimmer of hope.

Lincoln's eyes glinted with the passion of his argument. He raised his arms and turned his hands, palms up.

Justice Foster sat watching me. He shook his head, and sighed deeply. He turned his attention back to my attorney, who inhaled deeply, and began anew.

"It is incredible that it should ever enter the head of a person of so much capacity, so much cunning, to entrust an affair so heinously criminal to strangers and foreigners who, had they escaped detection, would probably have boasted of their feats after they got away to the enemy, the British." He dropped his arms and began pacing again in front of the jury box, stopping at every turn to look at them.

"Must she not have had some motive, some proper means, some plan fixed, some chosen trusty confidant, or some reason to hope to accomplish or conceal the crime of so detestable an action before she would have engaged in it if she had been in her senses? It was perpetrated in the heart of a populous town, near neighbors where it must be discovered by the morning, liable to be heard at the time of it, by the people abroad, by the children, by the servants.

"Is it possible she would commit so atrocious a crime and run so great a hazard from no motive? It is said she was upon ill terms with her husband. This is to trump up one crime that there may seem to have been a motive to have perpetrated another from. But to whom did she commit the execution of it, whom did she make use of as her accomplices, whom as her confidant, whom did she trust with the management of the villainy that so dearly affected her reputation, her safety her life, her children, the lives of others, and the happiness of her friends? The answer is strangers and foreigners. But was a woman who is known to have so much sense, such high intellect and learning, so stupid, if in the exercise of her reason, to put such a heinous act in the hands of such persons? If she were rational, would she have given them so much money?"

It was apparent to me that now the jurors' attention was flagging. They'd listened to hours of statements and testimony, and most likely were quickly reaching the point where they no longer cared about Lincoln's arguments.

"In summation, as you begin your deliberations, remember that this is the first capital case since the beginning of the new government. All of the other colonies are looking to us to see that a fair verdict is returned, one that is based upon the evidence and witness testimony presented. You must be sure beyond a reasonable doubt and must be unanimous in your decision.

"The defendant in a court of law has no burden to prove his or her innocence. He or she is innocent until proven guilty.

"During this case, you heard from fourteen witnesses. Are all of the witnesses reliable? Could their testimony not have been tainted by long affiliation with Mr. Spooner or prejudice against Mrs. Spooner or her father? When considering what you have listened to, the law requires you to keep an open mind.

"Mr. Ross had ample opportunity to cause Mr. Spooner fatal harm. Why didn't he? What prevented him from committing the act? Because he was unable to harm the man who was his acquaintance. Why did he not poison him in Princeton? What part did he play in the events of that night of Mr. Spooner's demise? He lifted Mr. Spooner's foot while Brooks placed him in the well. He did not commit the act, Brooks did. If anything, Mr. Ross is an accessory to the act and should not be judged as a perpetrator in the first degree.

"Was Mrs. Spooner in her right mind? What person in the exercise of reason would have planned a murder that would cause her to lose her children, her wealth, her social standing? Why would she entrust it to three men whom she has known for so little time? What person acting with reason would not establish some escape plan, some alibi, some means of covering the act? Would someone of a sound mind urge such a horrible act be committed in a house containing ten people? Would a person with a sound mind not leave such a difficult situation instead of resorting to murder? She could have gone to her father, but did she? She did not. She could have gone to any of her sisters', but did she? She did not. She could have gone to her mother's, but did she? She did not.

"Instigating a murder with many people present, having no plan or alibi, depriving herself and her children of shelter and sustenance, I ask you again, are these the actions of a woman in her right mind? They are not.

"If there is any doubt in your mind, any shred of reasonable doubt, you must find her not guilty."

It was approaching midnight when he finished his closing argument. I was weary and hungry, no doubt as was everyone else in the room.

Cushing looked at Robert Treat Paine.

"Mr. Paine, do you wish to make a closing statement?"

"No, Your Honor. The defense rests."

Chief Justice Cushing gave the charge to the jury.

"You are to assemble here tomorrow morning at eight o'clock to begin deliberations as to the verdict. Speak to no one about what you have heard or seen here. You are dismissed."

The jury filed out of the jury box and made their way toward the doors into the cool night.

Then the judge said, "Constable, take the prisoners back to the jail."

The four of us were guided out of the building and taken back to our cells. I crawled onto the mattress and fell asleep.

The next morning, after everyone else was seated, the four of us were led in. The room smelled less of the human odor unavoidable in large gatherings of people sitting for an extended time. And it was filled again. Justice Cushing did not order the bailiff to close the doors; people streamed outside, down the steps, and into the street where hundreds more had gathered.

The jury deliberated for forty minutes. We stood at the railing, watching and waiting, as the justices talked amongst themselves. Mr. Paine and Mr. Lincoln sat at the attorney's table, each scribbling notes and talking to the clerk now and then. I tried to catch Mr. Lincoln's eye but he didn't look my way.

Finally, the bailiff came into the room and spoke in a low tone to Justice Cushing. The justices sat imposingly in the chairs, their full authority on display. When the jury was brought into the room and seated, Cushing looked at them.

"Have you determined a verdict?"

"We have, chief justice."

"Give the verdict to the bailiff."

My heart was hammering in my chest as the piece of paper that would determine my future was handed by the foreman to the bailiff who delivered it to Cushing. The room was silent, the air eager with anticipation. I could feel the intense excitement flowing through the crowd.

Cushing read the verdict to himself, and then motioned for the other justices to move to a separate room to decide our sentence. They returned in less than ten minutes. Cushing looked at the bailiff, who motioned to the four of us.

"Defendants all rise," the bailiff said.

We stood at the bar facing the justices.

Cushing sat magisterially, the paper folded in his hands.

"James Buchanan, William Brooks, and Ezra Ross, you are hereby found guilty of the murder of Joshua Spooner. Bathsheba Spooner, you are hereby found guilty of being an accessory to the murder of Joshua Spooner. The four of you are hereby sentenced to be hanged by the neck until your bodies are dead. Your execution date will be determined by the Council of the State of Massachusetts Bay. This trial is concluded."

I hung my head, and my shoulders quivered as I began to cry, but it was only a moment before I regained my composure.

Brooks pounded on the bar, presumably angry at the judgment; Ezra stared blankly, as if in disbelief; Buchanan showed no emotion whatsoever.

"Justice is done!" someone yelled to the crowd outside.

A loud cheer went up from the people assembled in front of the courthouse.

"If I could only undo all that I have done," I whispered.

When the sheriff and his men took us outside, the crowd went silent. They watched us with an unnerving intensity. Ezra was in the lead followed by Buchanan and Brooks. I was last. The air was still; the only sound was a single loud "Caw!" from a large raven sitting on the meetinghouse roof.

CHAPTER 18

Two days after our sentencing, my brother Tim came to see me. It was a welcome surprise. I hadn't seen or heard from him since before that fateful night in March. The guard, a large, foul-mouthed lout of a man, banged on the door so loudly I jumped with fright.

"Visitor," he said as he shoved the door open; it slammed into the wall.

I guess I'd been dozing because it took me a moment to realize where I was. As I sat up, Tim came in. I jumped up and hugged him, for it was so good to see him.

The guard grabbed the door and banged it shut so hard the wall shook.

"I'm sorry I haven't come to see you before now," Tim said, looking around for a place to sit. Because there was no furniture but the bed, he went to the window and leaned against the wall facing me. "I heard that Martha came to see you."

"Yes," I said, "and announced that she is no longer my sister."

He shook his head. "That's Martha. She's changed quite a bit since the war started, not that I see her that often."

"And should I ask about mother?"

"No. No need. She will not come you see you. She's as obstinate and irascible as always. You are gone from her life."

"And you?"

He considered his response.

"I never liked Joshua. From the first day he came to dinner, I didn't like him. There was something about him that didn't ring true." He shook his head. "I don't know how Father settled on him. I tried to talk to him about there being a better man for you than Spooner, but he didn't let me get five words out before he told me to stop, that he didn't want to hear my opinion." He reached into his coat pocket and brought out a paper, folded in half, the wax seal broken. "This is from Father." He handed me the letter. I took it with trembling hands and read it slowly.

My dearest Bathsheba,

I just received a letter from Tim telling me what happened. Remember to be strong in the face of all adversity. I want to go to you but cannot. If I were to set foot in Massachusetts, I would be arrested and imprisoned. Did you murder Spooner? Tell me that isn't true. Tim told me about three soldiers being arrested for helping you.

I am sorry for what I have done to you. My heart is breaking knowing that if I had not insisted you marry Spooner, this would not have happened.

I am powerless to help you and can offer nothing that will make your situation any better.

Please forgive me, Bathsheba. I humbly beg for your forgiveness.

Your loving father

I dropped it onto the bed and began pacing. After a moment, I stopped and turned to him.

"You sent Father a letter?" I asked. "How did you do that?"

He was nodding his head before I'd finished asking. "What happened was this. A rider galloped into my yard and hurried into the kitchen. He was yelling for me, but I wasn't home. He started going through the house until he came upon Mother. Her eyesight is failing and she couldn't see who he was, so she accosted him, yelling for him to get out."

"Who was it"

"Amos Jenkins from Brookfield."

"I didn't think he cared for me one way or the other," I said.

"He may not, but he delivered the news of your arrest. Our cousin Will came while he was there," he said, referring to our cousin Will Ruggles, constable of Hardwick. "I was on my way home and saw Amos and Will on the road; they told me the news. I got home a few minutes later and rushed in to find Mother in the parlor, her hands on the back of a chair. She was shaking her head, her jaw clenched, squeezing the chair so hard I thought she'd break it."

"What did she say?"

"Twice she asked, 'Oh Bathsheba, what have you done?' then went to her bedroom. She has not mentioned you since."

We were quiet for a little while.

"How did you get a letter to Father?"

"I went to Western to talk with Isaiah Fowler who, like me, feigns loyalty to the patriot cause, but has well-hidden British sympathies. I told him I needed to get a letter to Father as soon as possible. He said he knew people who could get it to him, and they did."

I sat lost in thought, wondering where my father was at that moment and if he was thinking of me as I was of him. I picked up the letter, reread it, and put it on the bed with a loud sigh.

"How did you get the letter from him?" I asked.

"Well, it took four couriers, spies actually, to get it to Isaiah. One of them was intercepted shortly after he landed in Connecticut, but he'd already given the letter to another man. He'd been suspected of smuggling messages and military plans to Loyalists for some time and was finally caught."

"What happened to him?"

"He was arrested as a spy and hanged."

My throat felt tight when he said that. The same fate awaited me. I just didn't know when it would be.

"I'm sorry," Tim said. "Why didn't you come to me? I would have helped you."

I shrugged and began pacing again. "I don't know," I told him. "I honestly don't know."

He stayed for a while longer. Before he left me to return to Hardwick, I held him in my arms for a long time. I never saw him again.

CHAPTER 19

On Friday, the ninth of May, I learned how long I had left to live. The sheriff opened the door to my cell, stuck his head in, and looked at me with his beady little eyes.

"You have four weeks to live," he said. "The fourth of June is your last day. Four weeks from yesterday." He offered the message along with a smirk and then closed the door.

Having nothing else to do, I stood at the window, watching people passing by, when I heard voices outside the door. I recognized the sheriff's, and though the other was familiar I couldn't place it. Before I had time to consider it further, the door crashed open and there stood a man I least expected—John Avery Jr.

"You killed my brother," he said, stepping into the room.

I didn't respond; I didn't know what to say. You consider your stepbrother your brother? Do you know he mistreated me for years and deserved to die? That he was a horrible drunkard who spent more time with a mug of rum than with the children and me? That he raped me on our wedding night? There was no good reply to his statement, so I said nothing.

He sauntered around the room, then turned to the sheriff. "You may go," he said dismissively.

The sheriff gave him a long hard stare before slowly closing the door. Avery ran a finger along the wall and studied the dust on it before brushing it off his hands. He looked at the chest with disdain, decided not to sit on it, and instead stood by the door. "I brought the death warrant. Let me read it to you."

"There's no need. I'm to die on the fourth of June. That's all I need to know."

"Oh no, Bathsheba. I insist you hear it."

Only then did I realize he had the paper in his hand. He unrolled it and read.

DEATH WARRANT, STATE OF MASSACHUSETTS BAY, THE GOVERNMENT AND PEOPLE OF THE STATE OF MASSACHUSETTS BAY.

To the Sheriff of our County of Worcester, Greeting:

Whereas William Brooks, resident at Charlestown, in the County of Middlesex, laborer, James Buchanan, of the same Charlestown, and Ezra Ross, of Ipswich, in the County of Essex, now prisoners in our jail in Worcester, were, by the jurors of Worcester County, at the Superior Court of Judicature, Court of Assize, held at Worcester on April 24th last, found guilty of feloniously, wilfully, and with malice aforethought, killing and murdering, against the peace of the government and the law of this state, Joshua Spooner of Brookfield. And that Bathsheba Spooner, of Brookfield, widow, late wife of the said Joshua Spooner . . .

He lowered the paper and fixed his harsh eyes on me a moment before continuing:

. . . not having God before her eyes, but being seduced by the Instigation of the Devil, maliciously, willfully, and with malice aforethought did incite, move, abet, counsel, and procure, the aforementioned Brooks, Buchanan, and Ross to murder Joshua Spooner.

William Brooks, James Buchanan, Ezra Ross, and Bathsheba Spooner, pleaded not guilty and were by the verdict of our jurors, convicted and thereupon were, by justices of our said court, adjudged to suffer the pains of death.

He looked up and smiled, a smile of terrible joy. "This is the part I like best:

> *We command you therefore that, on Thursday, the fourth day of June next, between the hours of twelve and four of the clock in the afternoon, you cause the said William Brooks, James Buchanan, Ezra Ross, and Bathsheba Spooner, to be conveyed from the jail in Worcester, where they now are in your custody, to the usual place of execution and there to be hanged by the neck until their bodies be dead. This shall be your sufficient warrant; fail not at your peril, and make return of this writ, with your doing therein, into the Secretary's Office of said State, at Boston, on the tenth day of June next:*
>
> *Witness the Major Part of our Council, at Boston, this Eighth day of May, In the Year of our Lord, One thousand Seven hundred and Seventy Eight. By their Honors' Order, John Avery, Deputy Secretary.*"

He gave me a sinister smile of sweet revenge when he finished. "That wasn't so difficult now was it?"

"Get out, you bastard!"

"Now, now, there's no need to get so upset. I wanted to make sure you heard it from me." He smiled once again, so full of hate that it caused me to shudder. "You broke your promise to me."

"What promise?"

"The promise you gave me the day of your wedding. To be a wonderful wife to Joshua. Do you remember?"

I spat at him. "Go to hell."

He nodded and went to the door.

"Guard!" he yelled then looked back at me. "I'll leave you now to contemplate your fate. You've lived up to your Biblical namesake. An adulterous relationship with a man and then implicated in your husband's death." He stood waiting for the guard to open the door. "I'll be at your execution. I want to see you die." The door opened, and he left.

The next day, Reverend Maccarty returned to the jail and met with the four of us, spending time alone with me first.

"My dear," he said, sitting upon a rickety chair I'd badgered the sheriff into finding, "I heard the Council has approved the sentence. I will pray to our God for you, and you can join me in seeking the salvation of your soul."

I stared at him.

"Reverend," I said, taking his hand, "I will pray from now until the hour of my death, which will be in twenty-seven days, for God's forgiveness."

He put both hands around the Bible he carried with him always, the cover well-worn and some of the edges of the pages slightly tattered. "Perhaps if you confessed to Almighty God, He would hear your petition all the better."

I stared straight ahead for a moment before changing the subject as I always did when he mentioned my confessing to God.

"I do miss my children," I said, getting up and walking to the window. It faced the courthouse where my father had been chief justice for twelve years. In the few times I'd accompanied him to the courthouse, I'd never thought I would be in the jail I'd seen many times.

"I am sure you do," Maccarty replied. "I can arrange for them to visit if you'd like."

I turned to face him. "I've thought about that, and while I would like to see them one last time, I don't want their last memory of me confined in this wretched room. The children should remember me for the fine times and the love I gave them." I sat on the edge of the bed and began to cry. "I do so miss them!" I wept for a moment before wiping my eyes with the heel of my hand. Sniffling a bit, I looked at the minister. "I'd like to be alone."

He nodded and stood. "I'll be back tomorrow so we can continue to pray for your salvation and the forgiveness you want and need." He knocked on the door, and the guard let him out.

As the door opened, I thought of freedom, of not being confined but able to walk about and ride Invictus on a pleasant sunny day, through the meadows and fields as I'd done when a child. As the door closed, my heart was heavy with sadness, and the quiet weight of my sorrow lay upon me. I lay on the bed and wept.

The reverend was back again a short time later.

"I just spoke with the men," he told me. "Ross says he is afraid he won't be prepared to meet his Maker. The other two feel the same way."

"Do any of us ever have enough time to be prepared?" I asked.

"They said they'd do anything to have more time to prepare for the awful day that awaits them. They asked what they can do; I told them the only thing is a petition for more time."

"Of course," I said. "I never thought of it." I became excited at the prospect of not dying soon.

"I told them that I'd write it."

I nodded in agreement.

"I also said that it must be from all four of you. If it is just from the three of them, the Executive Council won't consider it, but reject it out of hand." He took my hand.

"If it's our only hope," I said, "then let's write the petition and get it to the Council."

"Then you are you in agreement?"

"Yes," I said softly. "Yes, I am." I opened my mouth to say something else, but closed it again.

"What's the matter?" he asked.

I shook my head and turned away from him for a moment.

"I am pregnant," I said.

He did not seem to know what to say. He pulled the chair from the corner and sat on it.

I lowered myself onto the edge of the bed. "I've known for a while. I am almost five months along."

"You are quick with child?" he asked. "You feel it move?"

"Yes."

He took a deep breath and looked at me. "What are you going to do?"

"I will request a stay until the baby is born."

"I will help you with that."

"Thank you, but I can write this myself. I think my words will carry great weight."

"I am sure they will," he said. "I will add a notation to the petition informing the council of your situation. They will want an examination by midwives."

"Yes, I know."

He hesitated in asking the question. "Was it lawfully conceived?"

I stared at my hands, folded in my lap, my mind far away, reliving the moment of Ezra and me in bed for the first time. How sweet and innocent he was.

The reverend waited quietly.

"Yes, it was," I said in a whisper.

"But you said you had an utter aversion to your husband and had grown away from him, that you even detested him. How can it have been lawfully conceived under those circumstances?" He drew near to me and put his hand on my arm. "Is your husband the father?"

I stood and walked about the room. He waited a few moments and, realizing I was not going to tell him, called for the guard to let him out. As he was about to walk through the doorway, he studied me with a critical eye, shook his head, and took his leave.

He returned an hour later.

"The petition is written," he said holding it in his hand. "It will be sent by messenger to the Council in Boston this evening."

"Let me see it," I said extending my hand. He hesitated a moment before giving it to me. I read it slowly.

PETITION OF THE PRISONERS FOR A REPRIEVE

To the honorable the Council of the state of Massachusetts Bay, in New England:

The humble petition of James Buchanan, William Brooks, Ezra Ross, and Bathsheba Spooner, most humbly show that your poor petitioners, fearful of their unpreparedness to appear before their Maker and judge after perpetrating so horrid a crime, and they were informed by the sheriff the time of their execution would be on the fourth day of June, do therefore most earnestly pray that you would be pleased to grant them some longer time than the before mentioned, which, should your honors in your great goodness grant them, they hope, and through the divine assistance and blessing upon the means used, trust they shall improve it to the most valuable purposes, it is a matter which concerns their everlasting salvation.

They most humbly submit to your honors' goodness, and as in duty bound, they will ever pray, &c. &c. &c.
James Buchanan
William Brooks, his X mark
Ezra Ross
Bathsheba Spooner
Worcester Jail, May 20th 1778.

"I added that it is the right thing to do and made mention of your condition," he said.

I continued reading.

Mr. Maccarty's most dutiful respects wait upon the honorable board, begging leave humbly to represent to them, that he has had many opportunities to know the state of the above-named prisoners; that he has found the men all along, and especially since their condemnation, to be much affected with their deplorable condition, freely acknowledging their heinous guilt and the righteousness of the sentence pronounced against them. They appear to be very humble and penitent to be much in earnest that they may make their peace with their Maker much engaged in acts of devotion, and eager to embrace all opportunities, both public and private, for religious counsels and instruction. For which reasons Mr. Maccarty presumes humbly to desire, that the prayer of their petition, as above, may be granted. And in that case, he can assure your honors on his behalf, and the behalf of his brethren in the ministry, that all suitable endeavors will be used with them, in order, if it shall please God to succeed them, that they may be prepared for the solemn scene before them. And as to the unhappy woman, he would beg leave further to represent, that she declares she is several months advanced in her pregnancy, for which reason, she humbly desires, that her execution may be respited till she shall have brought forth.

Worcester, May 20, 1778.

"Please get me a quill and ink," I said.

"Why?"

"I want to add a note of my own." Reluctantly, he left and was back in a short time handing me the small bottle of ink and a goose quill. I sat on the floor and put the petition on the top of the chest. Considering what to write for a moment, I finally scratched a short message.

The above application is made at my most earnest request.
Bathsheba Spooner

One week after our petition, John Avery came to see me again.

"So, you claim you are pregnant?" he asked, cocking an eye at me. "You're a lying Tory bitch. Pleading your belly to avoid execution. It's been done many times before, but it won't work this time." He smiled that horrible smile. "How many days do you think you have to live?" His question caught me off guard for we hadn't heard the judgment of our petition. "You may not know, but I do."

I noticed that he had papers in his hand.

"Are you going to read me whatever those are?"

He looked at the papers for a moment.

"No, I'll let you read them. I was not in favor of either one of these and voted against the petition but you probably guessed that. Here," he said offering me the documents.

I grabbed them out of his hand, sat on the end of the bed nearest the window, and read.

REPRIEVE.
THE GOVERNMENT AND PEOPLE OF THE MASSACHUSETTS BAY IN NEW ENGLAND.

To the Sheriff of our County of Worcester, Greeting:
Whereas, William Brooks and James Buchanan, of Charlestown, Ezra Ross, of Ipswich, and Bathsheba Spooner, of Brookfield, in the County of Worcester, widow, now prisoners in our jail in Worcester, were, at our Superior Court of Judicature, Court of Assize, convicted of murder, and was thereupon adjudged to suffer the pains of death: and a warrant issued out by the major part of the Council of our State, requiring you to put the sentence thereof in execution the fourth day of June next: but it hath been represented to us, that the said William Brooks, James Buchannon, Ezra Ross, and Bathsheba Spooner, are desirous of further time being allowed them to prepare for death, we, of our special grace and favor do hereby direct and command you to suspend and delay the execution of the sentence of our said court until Thursday, the second day of July next, at which time you are to proceed to execute the said Warrant in manner and form as therein is directed.
Witness the Major Part of our Council, at Boston, this Twenty-eighth Day of May, in the Year of our Lord, 1778.
By their Honors' Order,

"Thank God," I whispered. Another four weeks to make my case for a stay of execution.

"And my request for a stay?"

"Read," he said.

I tossed the reprieve at him and it fluttered to the floor. I read the second paper.

WRIT DE VENTRE INSPICIENDO.
THE GOVERNMENT AND PEOPLE OF THE
MASSACHUSETTS BAY IN NEW ENGLAND.

To the Sheriff of Worcester, Greeting:
Whereas, Bathsheba Spooner, late wife of Joshua Spooner, of Brookfield, in County of Worcester, stands attainted in due form of law before our Superior Court of Judicature, held at Worcester, on the third Tuesday of April last, being accessory before the fact to the murder of Joshua Spooner, for which she has received sentence of death, and a warrant has issued, in due form of law, to have the same sentence duly executed on the fourth day of June next; and whereas, it has been represented to us in Council, by Bathsheba Spooner, that she is quick with child: And we, being desirous of knowing the truth of the said representation, do command you, therefore, that, taking with you two men midwives, and twelve discreet and lawful matrons, to be first duly sworn, you come to the said Bathsheba Spooner, and cause her diligently to be searched by the said matrons, in the presence of the said men midwives, by the breasts and belly, and certify the truth whether she be quick with child or not, and if she be quick with child, how long she has so been, under your seal, and the seals of the said men midwives, into the Secretary's office of Massachusetts Bay, at or before the 25th day of June next, together with the names of the matrons by whom you shall cause the search and inspection to be made; hereof fail not, and make true return of this writ, with your doings hereon.
Witness the Major part of the Council of Massachusetts Bay in New England, at Boston, this twenty-eighth day of May, A. D. 1778.
By their Honors' Order,
John Avery, Deputy Secretary.

"It must have caused you a great deal of pain to write these," I said flinging the paper at him. It landed on the floor next to the first. He picked them up and looked at me.

"Even if you are pregnant, which I doubt, I will see that you and your unborn child die for what you did." He rolled the papers into a tube and went to the door. "Guard!" He tossed me a baleful look before leaving.

Reverend Maccarty, upon hearing the news, came to see me.

"The reprieve is granted," he told me. "I've already seen the men. They are pleased beyond expression and prayed with me."

"Yes, I know of the reprieve," I said.

His smile faltered and he cocked his head to one side. "How do you know?"

"John Avery came to see me yesterday. He told me the new date of execution is the second of July." I smiled at him. "Well, more than a month was gained."

"And you know about your being quick with child?"

"Yes, I read that also. I'm to have twelve matrons and two men midwives exam me to confirm that I am pregnant." The thought of them examining me in such an unpleasant way settled heavily upon me. But if it was necessary to save my baby's life, then I would willingly endure it and much more.

CHAPTER 20

Sheriff William Greenleaf was a large, raw-boned man with an oversized head, cropped graying hair, and long arms with big hands and knuckles. He'd had a run-in with my father, as many people had, when Father was Chief Justice of the Court of Common Pleas. Greenleaf was an enthusiastic patriot and despised me for being the daughter of a powerful loyalist. I knew that he would choose matrons who did not like me.

They came to my cell the morning of Thursday, June 11th. Once the more than a dozen of them had crowded into my small cell, the sheriff swore them in. Each of them vowed that their testimony would be true.

"These are the matrons I've selected to examine you to see if you are quick with child," he said. "You may begin," he told Josiah Wilder, a man midwife, whom I knew through my brother-in-law.

"Hello, Josiah."

He ignored my greeting.

"When did you first miss your menses?" he asked.

"Four months ago."

"So February?"

"Yes."

The matrons stood around in a circle, some scowling at me.

"Were you sick in the stomach?"

"Yes." I stared at him. "I've given birth to four children. I know what it feels like to be pregnant, and I am."

A few of the matrons scoffed, causing Wilder to turn and look at them.

"Was it lawfully conceived?" asked Hannah Brooks.

I fixed her with a sharp glance. "Yes," I said.

"Take your clothes off," Wilder ordered.

The midwives and matrons watched as I removed my clothing. I stood before them naked, without shame or embarrassment. Even in jail, I was superior to them even when naked. I suspected that the women did not like me, for I was much finer and prettier than any of them. For the most part, they were short, stout, and plain, several with gray hair. I was everything they were not.

Each of the matrons took turns looking at me before they groped my swollen breasts and felt my rounded belly. Three of them looked in my mouth. My gums felt thick, and I'd spit a small amount of blood in the last couple of days as I had with my earlier pregnancies.

When Molly Tatmaw put her hand on my stomach, I know she felt a movement. The baby kicked once.

I inhaled in surprise. "There! Did you feel it?"

Molly looked up at me. "I didn't feel anything," she lied, before putting her ear to my belly.

She must have known there was a fetus inside me; she must have birthed hundreds of children over many years. She squeezed my breasts so hard it caused me to wince in pain.

Elizabeth Rice examined me next. The baby kicked then also. I knew she'd felt it, too, but she did not acknowledge it, either.

After each of them performed their examination, they were as stone-faced as statues. None of them showed any sign of their findings.

"Lie down," Wilder told me.

I lay down on the mattress and put my feet on the bed with my legs apart, waiting for them to begin. Elijah Dix gently spread my legs and put his fingers into me, trying to feel movement. When he removed his fingers, he looked at them. They were covered with a thin whitish excretion, another sign I'd had with Elizabeth and Bathshua. Each of the matrons took a turn putting their fingers, or in the case of Molly Tatmaw and Elizabeth Rice, most of their hand into me, hard enough to cause me to cry out in pain. I suffered their harsh examination quietly. When they finished, Wilder told me to put my clothes back on, and the midwives and matrons left the room.

As the lingering pain from the examinations coursed through me, I thought about Molly Tatmaw and Elizabeth Rice. If I remembered correctly, they each had a long-standing grudge against my father. He had told me that Tatmaw's husband had allegedly stolen money from Brown's tavern when another man owned it. Father had ordered Tatmaw's husband to repay the tavernkeeper the money, which he refused to do, stating his innocence. Father then ordered that he receive ten lashes of the whip and spend five days in jail. Molly hated him for that, and now I knew she'd found a way to get her revenge. Elizabeth Rice had a similar story—her father claimed that my father had cheated him out of some land he owned in Oakham. I doubted it was true, but it didn't matter to me. She, too, now had a chance to even the score.

And so they lied.

When I learned that my petition for a stay of execution was denied, I stood at the small window looking down at the people passing by, enjoying their freedom. I clutched my arms around my belly as if to protect my child from the dangers it faced. I thought of how my baby would die with me. I closed my eyes and wept from the bottom of my soul.

But I couldn't sit by without making another effort for a second examination to prove the truth of my claim. I wrote another petition to the Council.

May it please your honors. With unfeigned gratitude, I acknowledge the favor you lately granted me of a reprieve. I must beg leave, once more, humbly to lie at your feet, and to represent to you, that though the jury of matrons that were appointed to examine into my case have not brought in my favor, yet that I am absolutely certain of being in a pregnant state, and above four months advanced in it, and that the infant I bear was lawfully begotten. I am earnestly desirous of being spared till I shall be delivered of it. I must humbly beg your honors, notwithstanding my great unworthiness, to take my deplorable case into your compassionate consideration. What I bear, and clearly perceive to be animated, is innocent of the faults of her that bears it, and has, I beg leave to say, a right to the existence that God has begun to give it. Your honors' humane Christian principles, I am very certain, must lead you to desire to preserve life, even in this its miniature state, rather than to destroy it. Suffer me, therefore, with all earnestness, to beseech your honors to grant me a further length of time, at least, as there may be the fairest and fullest opportunity to have the matter certainly ascertained—as in duty bound, during my short continuance, pray.

When I finished, I told the guard to bring the sheriff.

He stared at me with idiot indifference.

"Get the sheriff, damn you."

He hesitated to go.

"Now! I have something I have to give him."

He turned but took his time going down the stairs.

Some time later, the sheriff opened the door. "What do you want?" he asked.

"I have another petition I want you to deliver to the Council." I held it out for him to take.

He looked at it without taking it. "I don't have to take it."

"Please. If not for me then for my unborn child."

"Ha! Still pleading your belly. It won't work, you know," he said.

I extended my arm. He grabbed the paper from my hand and strode out of the room.

Two days later, he informed me that Dr. Green was also to examine me as he was the leading physician in the county. The sheriff also chose Josiah Wilder, Elijah Dix, Hannah Mower, Elizabeth Rice, and Molly Tatmaw.

Six days before my scheduled execution, the midwives spent over an hour examining me again. It was a gentler exam than the first. They left me wondering what they'd tell the Council. John Green came to see me that afternoon.

"You'll be pleased to know that Josiah Wilder, Elijah Dix, Hannah Mower, and I all know you are pregnant, and we have written to the Council. I'm sure they'll give you a stay now. I can't see how they couldn't."

I appreciated my brother-in-law's kind words but had no hope that I wouldn't die in a few days.

"What of the other two?"

He sighed loudly. "They think you aren't pregnant and sent a separate opinion." He ran a hand through his hair. "I don't know what will happen. They are spiteful, vindictive women."

I nodded and put my hand on his arm.

"Thank you, John." I kissed his cheek. "Why hasn't Mary been to see me?"

He stared at the floor for a minute before responding.

"She loves you so much it rips her apart that you're here. She doesn't know if she has the strength and courage to see you. You are her favorite sister, you know."

I sat down heavily on the bed. "I wish she'd come, if only for a few minutes."

"She cries for you every day. I don't know if she'll agree to come visit you. But I'll ask."

"Thank you," I whispered.

The thought that Mary loved me so much that she couldn't face my plight made me lie awake all night, thinking of her and of what'd I'd done. I'd broken her trust, and for that I felt awful. But I hoped she'd see me once before I died. Just a few minutes alone with her would put me at peace.

CHAPTER 21

I LEARNED THAT MY PETITION had been denied.
Reverend Maccarty was disturbed by the news, as he thought the Council would show some decency and Christian principles towards me. He, after all, was entirely convinced of my pregnancy.
"I wrote a letter to the Council," he told me. "I made a copy if you'd like to read it."
I shook my head. "No, thank you."
He started to say something then stopped. He put a hand to his chin; I could see he was deep in thought.
"I told them that people that are acquainted with your circumstances are exceedingly affected with it. I am fully satisfied of your being in a pregnant state and have been so for a considerable time. And it is with deep regret that I think of you being executed, till you have brought forth, which will eventually, though not intentionally, be destroying innocent life. I told them that, since an experienced midwife visited you this week, examined you, and found you quick with child, I think justice ought to take place upon you as well as the rest, but that you be respited for such a time as that the matter may be entirely cleared up. And that I have no doubt it will be satisfactory to everyone. I also stated that I wrote it of my own accord, and not at your desire, that you had no idea I was petitioning them again.
"I also told them that I should be very sorry if they should consider me as over-officious in the matter. But that principles of

humanity and Christianity, as well as a desire that righteousness may go forth, had prompted me to make this application on your behalf."

"Thank you, reverend. You've been good to me. I know I don't deserve it, but I do appreciate your efforts." A thought struck me. "Would you ask Dr. Green to visit with me today?"

"Yes. Of course I will."

That afternoon, John came to see me.

"You came," I said.

"Of course, I did. You asked that I visit. Why would I not?"

"I need to talk with you," I said. "It is a matter of great importance to me, and I don't want anyone else to know about it. Will you agree to that?"

"It would be best if I knew what I was agreeing to."

"My petition for a stay has been denied so I must be ready, and I will be. When I am dead, I want you to perform an autopsy to prove that I'm with child and that, in addition to my life, they'll have taken that of an innocent infant."

He looked at me for a moment.

"Are you sure this is what you want?" he asked.

"I've given this a lot of thought, and yes, it is what I want." I leaned toward him. "If you don't want to do it, I understand. I will find someone else, perhaps Dr. Dunning."

"He's an old codger who hates you." He nodded, his eyes downcast. "So, yes, I will do it." He let out a long sigh.

"You don't know how much this means to me," I said, standing up.

"Can I tell Mary?"

I bit my lip and thought for a moment. "Yes, tell her."

"She may come to visit you to try to talk you out of it."

I gave him a faint-hearted smile before hugging him. He put his arms around me for a moment before leaving.

CHAPTER 22

THE FATEFUL DAY CAME. Ezra, Brooks, and Buchanan went to the Old South Meetinghouse for Reverend Maccarty's sermon. I was too ill to attend. I stood in the warm cell, it being noon on a hot, muggy day staring out the window. Craning my neck, I saw clouds beginning to tower in the western sky.

The reverend had come to see me that morning to give his execution sermon and to say good-bye.

I was calm and humble, professing my faith in the Savior. Reverend Parkman of Westborough, who'd accompanied Reverend Maccarty, asked if I would like to be baptized. I said that I never had been, and I agreed. It was done immediately.

"When we consider your sex," Reverend Maccarty said, standing at one end of the room as if in the meetinghouse and talking as if there were hundreds of people in attendance instead of just Reverend Parkman and me, "the respectable figure that in times past you made in life, your connections, and your many agreeable qualities, it is with grief that I behold you a prisoner of death, about to be led forth to execution.

"Though you have not been disposed to confess to me, I hope you've done so upon your bended knees to the omniscient God, who cannot be deceived. You are indeed looked upon by man, as guilty, as the author and procurer of the bloody deed. I am loath to dwell upon some very aggravating circumstances of that tragic affair, but I would hope that under a deep sense of your guilt, you have been earnestly applying to God for pardoning mercy and grace. That from a sense of your unworthiness before him, of your ill desserts, your lost, perishing condition as a sinner, that you have been earnestly seeking the face and favor of God. The death before you, though shameful, will yet be safe and joyful. And you shall ascend this day to be with God in glory. This is what I earnestly wish and pray for on your behalf, and I shall continue to do so till your soul shall take its flight into the eternal world. And so I bid you a solemn and final farewell."

When they'd left, I sat and considered that in a short time my life, and that of my unborn child, would be over. Surprisingly, I'd slept well the night before and wasn't frightened at the prospect of dying but calm and at peace with my fate.

I dressed in my wedding gown and waited to die.

CHAPTER 23

I HEARD A COMMOTION OUTSIDe. After the sermon at the meetinghouse ended, people streamed to the jail. In their midst, I saw Ezra, Brooks, and Buchanan standing below the window. There was a knock on the door and Sheriff Greenleaf entered.

"It's time," he said.

I stood and followed him. Two of his men walked behind me. As we went outside, the harsh sunlight blinded me for an instant. I then saw Ezra, Brooks, and Buchanan looking at me. Oh, poor Ezra! I hadn't seen him in three months, and he looked haggard. I ignored the guards and went to him. I wanted to hug him, but instead I took his hands in mine. We didn't speak. I looked into his eyes and saw acceptance. He squeezed my hands and smiled a heartwarming, lovely smile that touched my heart as nothing had in all the months we'd been imprisoned. One of the sheriff's men placed a hand on my elbow. I gave Ezra's hands one last squeeze and let go. I ached to think that he was going to die without knowing that his child was inside me.

We stood, the sun beating down on us as a great crowd assembled, all wanting a good look at we who were about to die.

Many of the sheriff's men were lined up on either side of the road to keep the teeming horde at bay so they did not interfere with the proceedings.

The sheriff came out of the jail and slipped the nooses around the men's necks, as was the execution custom. A two-wheeled open cart in front of us contained four coffins. We stood that way, each of us staring at the coffin that would hold our mortal remains.

Ezra bowed his head in prayer while Brooks looked around at the crowd. Buchanan stared at the coffins as he chafed under the noose, moving his head and neck in an attempt to relieve the raw fiber cutting into his flesh. He laughed.

"I won't have to worry about this much longer," he said more to himself than anyone else.

To the west, I saw bright white thunderheads towering up and up towards the heavens, the underside of the clouds black and threatening. A flicker of lightning went from one cloud to another.

The sheriff approached me, and as he did with the men, placed the noose around my neck, coiled the rope, and gave it to me.

Reverend Maccarty helped me into his carriage. I sat composed, looking at the crowd; it was as if it were a favorite social event. The reverend entered the carriage and put his hand on mine.

I watched out the window as the procession began with the sheriff's men forming a "V" down the road, pushing the crowd off to the sides, yelling for them to make way every minute or two. At one point, a hundred yards after we'd begun, the crowd surged across the road halting our death march.

"Get out of the way!" one man yelled.

"Stand aside! Stand aside!" another shouted.

"Damn your eyes," another yelled, pushing three men to the ground. "Go, you sons of bitches!"

The crowd parted slowly, people struggling for a place where they could see the procession and get a good look at me, knowing they'd probably never see anything like it again in their lifetime.

The procession resumed moving slowly. It took a solemn half hour to cover the mile to the gallows.

Thousands upon thousands of people came to witness our execution, a form of public entertainment. Some I was sure had traveled up to fifty miles, if not farther.

As I got out of the carriage, I saw boys and men hawking two pieces I knew had been printed by *The Massachusetts Spy*: a mourning poem and the dying declaration of Brooks, Buchanan, and Ezra that had been taken a week ago.

When we reached the place of execution, a large, wide, flat area a few hundred yards south of the center of the town, we stood before the ladder, each of us looking up. I saw the thick oak beam over which my noose would be slung. One of the sheriff's men prodded the men up the ladder. I'd determined to die like a lady and had emerged from the carriage with all the grace of a woman of my station, a gentle smile on my lips, my head held high, in anticipation of meeting my Maker. I believed in my heart that I was ready to die. One of the sheriff's men took the rope from the carriage and stood by my side at the foot of the ladder. As I began to ascend, he gently tossed the rope onto the platform where it was picked up by the sheriff.

As soon as I stepped onto the platform, people began yelling.

"Go meet your Maker in Hell, you damn lobsterbacks!" shouted a grizzled patriot waving a torn tricorn hat, standing near the front of the crowd. There was a terrible din around him.

"Huzzah!" yelled the crowd. "Huzzah!"

Someone in the crowd threw a rock that hit Brooks in the head. He dropped to the platform before being hauled to his feet by one of the sheriff's men, blood trickling down the side of his face.

"You bastards! Die and be on your way to Hell!" someone screamed.

Thunder began to rumble as the air went still; not a breath of wind moved about. The crowd quieted at the show of nature. A massive bolt of lightning split the sky, followed a moment later by a terrific boom that seemed to shake the very ground.

I was led to the far right, where I stood waiting. Looking out at the crowd, I saw several people I knew, including Mary, who was crying into a handkerchief, and Martha, grim-faced, with her arms folded. It was my turn to feel the mob's wrath.

"Whore!" screamed dozens in the crowd at the same time, the ferocity strangely stoked by the females on hand.

"Tory wench!" yelled a man at the back of the crowd.

A weathered, elfin woman issued a taunt that captured the moment: "Your father won't save you now!"

I bowed to those I knew before the rope for my noose was thrown over the beam. I turned my head and saw John Avery standing there, watching me, and wearing a smile of satisfaction. I hesitated a moment before bowing to him. His smile faltered as he must have been taken by surprise at my show of dignity.

The sheriff gently tied my hands in front of me.

"I don't doubt that all will be well with me, for I'm dying justly," I said. "I hope to see the Christian friends I leave behind in Heaven, but that none of them go there in the disgraceful manner that I do."

As the sheriff read the death warrant in a booming voice, the baby kicked; I gently wrapped my bound arms around my belly. A wave of black despair coursed through me at the thought that my baby would also die in a few minutes. I turned a mournful gaze upon Ezra.

I shivered as the gusting wind cooled me, and the thunder rumbled again, louder and closer, as a burst of lightning illuminated the ever-blackening afternoon. Another white-hot bolt split the sky as the sheriff bound Ezra, Brooks, and Buchanan's legs and placed black hoods over their heads. He came to me and tied my ankles with rough rope before sliding the coarsely woven hood over my head.

Three bright flashes of light filled my vision as the thunder continued to explode. The rain suddenly fell in a torrent, so hard and fast it drenched me in a few seconds. I lifted my head to the sky, feeling the rain cleanse me. I trembled in anticipation of the moment to come. After a few moments, the rain and wind suddenly stopped. Through the hood, I saw a golden beam of light fill my vision. I felt the warmth on my face as a deep calm and sense of peace came over me. I smiled, waiting for salvation.

EPILOGUE

The sheriff pulled the lever, the platform fell, and the prisoners dropped to their deaths. Their bodies swayed at the end of the ropes.

The crowd dispersed, having seen what they'd come to see. After another ten minutes, one of the sheriff's men climbed a ladder to the oak beam and cut the ropes, causing each body to fall to the ground with a loud thud. Buchanan and Brooks were placed in their coffins; Ezra's father and brother put his body in his coffin. Mary and Dr. Green stood over Bathsheba's body, looking at what was left of the lively, gay, funny, graceful, and intelligent woman they'd known and loved.

Her body was taken to the jail.

Doctor Green, accompanied by two other physicians, removed Bathsheba's once beautiful clothing as Mary stood to his side, watching.

Bathsheba's naked body lay on the table, her head tilted up to the right, the wide burn marks from the rope circling her throat, her cold skin a sallow yellow. Her eyelids were closed, but there were dark circles around the eyes.

Taking a scalpel, Dr. Green began to cut into the body, making an incision from the bottom of the breastbone to the pubic bone. Peeling the skin and muscle back, he cut into the womb and saw a perfectly formed five-month-old male fetus. He gently removed it, feeling the cold skin of the innocent babe, and placed it on a table near the coffin.

Mary cried and ran out of the room into the fresh air.

The doctor then began the task of sewing the incision together, the needle making a popping sound as it passed through the cold flesh.

When Dr. Green came out of the jail, he directed that the bodies of mother and child be placed in the coffin. Reverend Maccarty had arranged for a wagon to transport it.

Earlier, Mary had recognized that, what with the general sentiment of hatred still flaming against Bathsheba and their father, burying her sister in the Brookfield cemetery was not the right thing to do. Someone might vandalize the grave, especially since Bathsheba's murdered husband was buried there, too.

Mary and Dr. Green got into their carriage and, with the wagon trundling ahead of them, made a solemn procession to the Green estate where Bathsheba and her unborn child were buried in a lonely, unmarked grave.

The Spooner children went to live in Roxbury, Massachusetts, with their guardian, Joshua Spooner's nephew, John Jones Spooner. The oldest child, Elizabeth, married at age twenty-two and had two children. She died at the age of fifty-two. Joshua Jr. went to sea in 1789 and was not heard from again although he may have died in London in 1801. The youngest, Bathshua, married twice and had two children by her first marriage. She died at the age of eighty-three, reportedly insane for many years before her death.

Bathsheba's father, Timothy Ruggles, served on active duty in the British Army until 1780 and was granted 10,000 acres of land in Nova Scotia. He settled there in 1782 with his sons John and Richard. He developed an estate as bountiful as the one in Hardwick and died in August 1795. His wife lived with their third son, Timothy Jr., in Hardwick until her death in 1787. After his mother's death, Timothy Jr. followed his father and brothers to Nova Scotia and became a prominent citizen.

Mary Green lived in social prominence until her death at the age of seventy-four. Dr. Green continued to build his medical practice and was elected to the Massachusetts General Court for two terms. His estate, enlarged and improved by his descendants, was gifted to the City of Worcester in 1905 and is now Green Hill Park. Thus, Bathsheba and her unborn child lie somewhere within the park.

Martha Tufts became a widow in 1787 and lived in Brookfield until she died in 1813. She and her family are buried next to Joshua Spooner's grave.

Justice William Cushing was appointed to the U.S. Supreme Court by George Washington to whom he administered the oath of office at Washington's second inauguration. Robert Treat Paine, in addition to being a member of the Continental Congress and signer of the Declaration of Independence, was appointed to the Massachusetts Supreme Court in 1796. Levi Lincoln was a member of the Massachusetts House of Representatives in 1796 and the Senate in 1797. In 1800, he was elected to Congress and served until March 5, 1801, when President Jefferson appointed him Attorney General of the United States. He held the office until March 3, 1805. Jedediah Foster was elected as a delegate to the First Provincial Congress. The Massachusetts House of Representatives elected him to the executive council in 1775. In addition to being a colonel of militia during the Revolution, he was one of a committee of three chosen to draw up the original draft of the Massachusetts constitution, the oldest written constitution still governing in the world.

ACKNOWLEDGEMENTS

My wife, Barbara kept me on course and offered sage advice and excellent critique when needed.

Jack McClintock, Mary Anne Slack, Ruth Lyons, Anne Sroka, and Heather Gablaski all provided invaluable criticisms, comments, and insights.

For those interested in learning more about Bathsheba Spooner and the times in which she lived, I suggest:

Chandler, Peleg. *American Criminal Trials*, Vol. 2. Boston: Timothy H. Carter and Company, 1844.

"The Dying Declaration Of James Buchanan, Ezra Ross, and William Brooks." *Massachusetts Spy*, July 9, 1778. www.brookfieldsresearch.com.

Earle, Alice Morse. *Home Life in Colonial Days*. Great Barrington, Mass.: Berkshire House Publishers, 1993.

Earle, Alice Morse, *Child Life in Colonial Days*. Great Barrington, Mass.: Berkshire House Publishers, 1993.

Fiske, Nathan, A.M. "A Sermon Preached at Brookfield on the day of the interment of Joshua Spooner," March 6, 1778. www.brookfieldsresearch.com.

Green, Samuel Swett. "The Case of Bathsheba Spooner." Worcester, Mass.: American Antiquarian Society, October 22, 1888.

Lawson, John D., ed. *American State Trials: A Collection of the Important and Interesting Criminal Trials Which Have Taken Place in the United States, From the Beginning of Our Government to the Present Day with Notes and Annotations.* St. Louis, Mo.: F. H. Thomas Law Book Co., 1914.

Maccarty, Thaddeus, A.M. "The Guilt of Innocent Blood Put Away: A Sermon Preached at Worcester, July 2, 1778. On the Occasion of the Execution of James Buchanan, William Brooks, Ezra Ross, and Bathshua Spooner, for the Murder of Mr. Joshua Spooner." July 2, 1778. www.brookfieldsresearch.com.

Navas, Deborah. *Murdered by Her Husband.* Amherst, Mass.: University of Massachusetts Press, 1999.

Noone, Andrew W. *Bathsheba Spooner, A Revolutionary Murder Conspiracy.* 2021.

Paige, Lucius R. *History of Hardwick Massachusetts and Genealogical Register.* Boston: Houghton Mifflin Company, 1883.

Raphael, Ray. *The First American Revolution.* The New Press, 2002.

Roy, Dr. Louis. *History of East Brookfield Massachusetts, 1686–1970.* Worcester, Mass.: Heffernan Press, 1970.

Stanton, Elizabeth Cady. "The Fatal Mistake That Stopped the Hanging of Women in Massachusetts." *The World,* 1899.

Temple, J. H.. *History of North Brookfield Massachusetts.* Town of North Brookfield, 1887.

Wilder, Robert. Map of Brookfield 1778. www.brookfieldsresearch.com.